Redemption

Volume Three
Raptis Trilogy

Tracee Raptis

VOLUME THREE: RAPTIS TRILOGY

****

Redemption

**Volume Three
Raptis Trilogy**

Tracee Raptis

Metaterra® Publications

****

Metaterra® Publications
REDEMPTION
VOLUME THREE: RAPTIS TRILOGY
Tracee Raptis
Copyright © 2017, 2016, Tracee Raptis and Angela Browne-Miller.
Copyright © 2017, 2016, Metaterra® Publications.
www.Metaterra.com
Library of Congress Cataloging-in-Publication Data.
Raptis, Tracee
REDEMPTION
VOLUME THREE: RAPTIS TRILOGY
/ Tracee Raptis, Author / Angela Browne-Miller, Afterword /
1. Thriller. 2. Mystery. 3. Crime. 4. Drug Smuggling. 5. Treasure. 6. Scuba Diving.
7. Romance. 8. Psychological. 9. Oceans. 10. Heroines. 11. Adventure.
Title:
REDEMPTION
VOLUME THREE: RAPTIS TRILOGY
ISBN-13: 978-1-937951-38-2

See Amazon.com for Paperback and Kindle Ebook formats of this book.
ISBN information for the other volumes in this Raptis Trilogy
(also on Amazon as paperback and Ebook):
DIVE TOUR • VOLUME ONE: RAPTIS TRILOGY
ISBN-13: 978-1-937951-37-5
TREASURE HUNT • VOLUME TWO: RAPTIS TRILOGY
ISBN-13: 978-1-937951-36-8

Published in the United States of America for U.S. and worldwide distribution.
Metaterra® Publications, www.Metaterra.com
Book interior design by Metaterra® Publications & Angela Browne-Miller.
Afterword and Editing by Angela Browne-Miller.
Book Cover Concept and Design by Alicia Beulow with Tracee Raptis & Angela
Browne-Miller. Interior art – Basic Scuba Diver Gear Diagram by Tracee Raptis.
Book Cover Illustration by Alicia Beulow.
AUTHOR, PUBLISHER, RIGHTS, & PRESS CONTACT: DoctorAngela@mac.com
Ordering information and bulk ordering information available through:
Amazon Paperback and Amazon Kindle. Also contact Info@Metaterra.com.

This is a work of fiction. Names, characters, businesses, places, events, and incidents are either the products of the author's imagination or used in a fictitious manner. Any resemblance to actual persons, living or dead, or actual events, is purely coincidental.

Dedicated to
all those Terri's out there.

You know who you are.

VOLUME THREE: RAPTIS TRILOGY

****

Table of Contents

VOLUME THREE: RAPTIS TRILOGY

****

Prologue

Casually crossing the bright blue sky, wispy spring clouds in their pastel colors were slowly changing, revealing ever new shapes and patterns. Lush green hills dotted with bright orange and red tropical flowers were cascading down into hidden valleys and canyons. Luscious mango, coconut, and papaya trees dripping with fruit were lining the edge of the white sandy beach. There were just enough trade winds to cool the skin's surface perspiration.

"Beautiful!" Terri looked out across the beach and then directly down. The glistening water was so crystal clear she felt she could actually touch the bottom, simply defying the reading of fifty feet on Mitch's depth finder. "Look at that, how crystal clear, and wow this beach! Have you ever?" Terri stood at the bow in awe of Mitch's new boat and the pristine nature all around them. She felt torn between two lovers: the water and the fruit, so ripe for picking.

Looking out to the deeper blue waters, she could sense they were filled with unsuspecting spiny lobsters, and groupers asking to be barbecued as they waited for someone to pull the trigger on a spear gun. Yummy yes, but then there was that white sandy beach just a short swim away with all that ripe, low-hanging fruit dripping down from the trees. Terri knew she could go there and reach up and pick the luscious orange globes off the tree herself. This was heaven on Earth.

"Drop the anchor! This is it!"

Mitch put the Whaler in neutral as Terri dropped the anchor straight down. The very next moment she jumped in, ready to

1

cool off, slipping her fins on while treading water, then her mask. She looked down below and shouted through her snorkel for Mitch to quickly join her.

Terri glimpsed a deep blue channel brimming with life. She took three deep controlled breaths, exhaling completely, then one large inhale. Immediately she bent down like a jackknife, then lifted her legs straight up above her. As she did, the weight of her body effortlessly pushed her downward to investigate the beckoning channel. A large school of amber jacks circled around her as she glided down. She reached out and tried to touch the swirling wall of amber fish around her; they spread out, keeping an exact distance away from her.

It was a virgin reef full of gorgeous, long, soft corals of all colors dancing with the slight current as the sun glistened through, casting long shadows. Looking into a crevice, she spotted two of the largest lobsters she had ever seen. They were staring back, unafraid as they watched her in curiosity, their long antennae twitching back and forth.

Suddenly Terri saw something behind the lobsters, something shiny, bright gold. She quickly tried to reach past the spiny creatures to grab whatever it was, hurriedly as the breath in her lungs had expired. But her arm was two inches too short and she needed a breath. Looking up to the surface for signs of Mitch, she swam up quickly in excitement. "Mitch! Mitch!"

PART ONE

SNEAKING AWAY

VOLUME THREE: RAPTIS TRILOGY

****

<u>1</u>

"Mom, Mom! Wake up!"

Terri didn't want to open her eyes, not now, not in the middle of her favorite dream when she was just about to reach for that piece of gold she had discovered.

"Just ten more minutes, ten!" Terri shouted back. She pulled the covers up over her head, refusing to open her eyes.

"Come on, Mom! We're late!" Kendra was standing over the bed, neatly dressed, her clothes ironed, hair combed, all put together already. She began shaking her sleeping mother awake.

"Nooo...." Terri refused to wake up and leave the dream. She hadn't had this dream in a while. Of several recurring dreams, this one was by far her favorite. Yes, there she was back there with Mitch, down in paradise on a beautiful sunny day, it just couldn't get any better. She could even feel the sun on her back so warmly enveloping her.

"Mom!"

Terri pressed her eyes still more tightly closed, unwilling to participate in any of the morning's events.

"Mom! Now!" Kendra screamed at her, swinging her purse at the bed, then pulling the sheets back. "I'm waiting for you in the car, I can't be late!"

Terri removed the sheet covering her head and looked up at her daughter's pouting face. There she was, that lovely face with those piercing green eyes, the petite girl with that beautiful long dark hair. She loved her daughter so much and always wondered how something so perfect had come out of her. Terri smiled at her daughter's now red, contorted face. *So intense!*

Kendra hated being late, unlike her mother.

"OK honey, on my way." Terri groaned as she gave in, flinging the rest of the covers off herself. "Ough," Terri moaned as she swung her legs over the side of the bed, stiff. "Ugh," she added as she looked down at her feet and wiggled her toes. Then, stumbling to the bathroom, Terri multitasked as quickly as she could.

Terri, now the mom again, was good to go out in public in less than five minutes. *Good enough anyway,* Terri told herself.

Kendra always wished her mom would spend at least an additional ten minutes pulling herself together. She could pull her hair back, or maybe just brush it regularly, perhaps use some lotion? A little make up? *She isn't getting any younger*….

Pulling on jeans and a clean tee shirt, Terri quickly glanced at herself in the mirror and ran her fingers through her home-style bleached locks. She looked around for her hairbrush to no avail. Rushing toward the front door, she stopped at the kitchen and opened the refrigerator, grabbing the first thing she saw. It was a leftover half-eaten spicy pork burrito, held together by torn pieces of aluminum, but Terri was glad she had saved this bit after devouring the first part the day before.

There was a light impatient tap on the horn in the driveway.

"Crap." Terri rushed faster, racing out to the car.

The car door opened with a loud creak and Terri skid into the early model Mercedes diesel, slamming the door behind her while sticking the key in the ignition. When the rearview mirror shifted to a slant with the slam of the car door, she reached up and adjusted it the way she always did.

Right then, she caught a glimpse of herself in the revealing morning sun which cast shadows across her wrinkles, making them appear even worse. She groaned as she noted the deep dry gorges leading to her mouth. "Aagh! When did I grow so old?" She scowled at herself in the rearview mirror, pulling and tugging at the sun-damaged wrinkles around her mouth, trying to straighten them out.

Kendra had been watching all this from the front passenger seat. "Mom, we have to go now. Please, I don't want to be late," Kendra looked at her watch and tapped it with her index finger to make her point. She thought about how her mom had a way of trying to leave early, trying to be on time, but somehow always getting distracted and always arriving late. This made Kendra so anxious. And, strangely, her mom just couldn't explain what this behavior was because she always saw herself as punctual. But Kendra felt there was indeed an explanation for this, and constantly accused her mother of never emotionally leaving the islands where she had lived so long ago now. Her mother still lived in that world of "island time."

"Oh my God, stop it! We're right on time, you've got to learn to relax!" Terri turned the key in the ignition again.

The engine begged her to stop turning the key. Ya-ya ya-yaaa, yaaa. It just would not turn on.

"Huh?" Terri tried again.

Yaa-yaaa—

"—I don't know what's going on here—"

—Aaa...yaaa...aaaa....

And with that last murmur, the engine stopped. The battery was dead.

"What the hell?" Terri was afraid to look over at Kendra.

Kendra was making another face at her mother, this one filled with deep disgust, a venomous look that only a teenager could dish out. "Mother...."

Terri hated it when Kendra started her sentences this way. This was like being called your full given birth name to announce, "You are in trouble now...." Terri cringed at what was coming.

"When was the last time you put gas in this?!!!" Kendra screamed at her mother as she pointed to the gas gauge on empty.

Terri sat there with no defense. "Well, Kendra, this is a diesel, it doesn't really use gas." This car had become a curse.

"I fucking know that!"

The tension between the two was so thick you could cut it with a knife.

"Hey now, don't talk to me like that, young lady!"

Kendra already had the passenger door open. Now she screamed at Terri as she got out and slammed it. "I hate you, I hate you, I hate you! I'm going to be late now!" She cried as she stomped back into the house to call a friend.

Terri's head slumped forward. She half consciously hit the car horn with her forehead with a thump, letting out a long, loud, "Honnk!" She thought this would make Kendra smile. But it didn't.

Tired of it all, of everything, Terri sat there with her head down, motionless, trying to figure out her next move. *Mmm, can't call AAA, I've used up my freebies, they'll charge me.* Terri looked into the small satchel she had thrown around her chest, searching for something, anything. She found credit cards with nothing left on them, business cards from people she didn't know, four one-dollar bills, three quarters and two dimes. "Crap." Terri looked at the small wad of useless stuff in her lap.

Kendra came back out of the house.

A car pulled up to the curb, music blasting loudly enough for all the neighbors to hear, inaudible words screaming out of the speakers, making the loudest "Look at me!" statement possible.

What the hell? Terri turned to see Kendra's friend, Derek, get out and open the passenger door for Kendra. Terri made eye contact with her daughter who cocked her head to the side and flipped her mother off with her middle finger. Then Kendra got into the car.

Derek shut the car door after Kendra got in, avoiding eye contact with Terri.

Terri watched sullenly as Kendra took off down the road with Derek. "Damn kids...no respect." Terri got out of her car and kicked the tire in frustration. Kendra's attitude was getting worse, and no matter how hard Terri tried, no matter what Terri did, Kendra was determined to just be mad at her mother.

Terri wanted to give up but couldn't. This was her daughter after all.

VOLUME THREE: RAPTIS TRILOGY

****

2

"Come on! Take the tour, take a tour with us!" Terri shouted out to the masses of people as they strolled by out on the pier, licking their ice cream cones, reapplying their sunscreen. The scores of people walking by were looking into the many stores that lined the pier, staring into the large glass plate windows filled with knick-knacks, tee shirts, and seashells enticing onlookers to come inside.

"Take a tour with us today, ma'am?" As Terri handed a lady a brochure, she tried to make eye contact with the woman by putting on a happy face with a big smile.

"No, no thank you." The lady responded firmly without looking back at Terri as she kept walking, not skipping a beat.

"How about a one hour boat tour for you and your family, take a tour with us today, sir?"

The man quickly passed by Terri, and then looking the other way, walked still faster. He told his family, "Just ignore that woman, don't make eye contact with her, she's just a saleswoman."

Terri ignored the insult and continued on with the next people, "Looking for a good tour?" Terri reached out with a brochure to a group of young adults walking by.

"No, thank you," the group said in unison.

Well, at least they were polite about it. Terri tried to keep her head up, standing tall, rejection after rejection. *No one wants to take this stupid tour, this stupid fucking tour, it's all so stupid....* Terri tried to keep a smile plastered on her face as she looked down at the polyester tour shirt she was forced to wear. She looked as ridiculous as she felt. *No wonder people cross to the other side of the pier to avoid my sales pitch, I would too if I saw me standing here. But ten bucks a person, Terri, ten bucks a person, you can do this. You can do this blindfolded. And you need every bit of this money, pennies that it is.* Terri kept telling herself this.

Terri stood there trying to smile, hating her job. It just couldn't get any more humiliating. She was a tour guide on a stupid sixteen-passenger tour boat. For her, this was like a silly kiddie ride at Disneyland. She had to sell tour tickets on the pier in between boat rides, twice a day. This was part of her job, *darn it. Seriously, me?*

Then she would give the tour while her even stupider boss got to drive the boat. He drove slower than molasses, and it drove her nuts. *He claims this saves on gas.* Terri insisted to him that it also saved on any possible thrill factor, that the fun just wasn't there. "Outdated and uninteresting," Terri had called it to her boss's face. Day after day, the same old stories: "Oh, look at the harbor seals, we have a wide variety of marine life here...." Terri would ramble to boatload after boatload of tourists as they maneuvered around the small harbor. She often wondered how the tourists would react if she just up and said, "I quit," then dove into the water and swam away.

Halting her efforts to sell the lame tour to uninterested tourists, Terri walked over to the edge of the pier. She stared out at the water. It was calm, a deep dark green, she couldn't see the bottom. Cold and alive with plankton, full of life, she knew all about it from learning how to scuba dive in these waters. *But what different conditions and visibility here, so different from what is there in the Caribbean where it is teaming with so many more fish colonies, so much amazing kelp, tons of exciting rocky outcroppings. So much life!*

Here the visibility was a mere ten to fifteen feet on a good day. Terri's mind wandered as she daydreamed about different underwater scenes. It had already been a couple of years since she had been scuba diving. Now she didn't maintain her own boat and was completely bored with what the offshore dives around there had to offer. She had seen each dull cove numerous times, each one now more and more crowded with people.

Just finding a place to park next to a cove and dragging the equipment down to the water's edge was getting to be more work than Terri cared to do these days. She had spent the past few years navigating the scariest waters of all, teenagers. Mothering Kendra had sucked her dry, bone dry. These days, there was nothing Terri could do, say, or bring home that got any sort of approval.

To the left of her, a man began wildly reeling in a dancing mackerel at the end of his line. It was a twelve-inch fish and he was thrilled with this, his first catch of the day. One mackerel usually meant many. He removed it, baited the hook, and had the line out again, hoping for more mackerel to take home and feed his family. Terri looked at his clothes and equipment. He was smiling, so happy for his catch. He knew what he caught would probably be the family's protein for the day or week.

Terri wasn't big on the fishy taste and oily texture of the mackerel, but she definitely missed the hunt.

"Hey, Terri, how many people have you booked for the next tour?" Jake, the owner, stepped up behind her, jostling her out of her thoughts. This was just one more time Jake had caught her looking down at the water instead of out at the people, instead of selling tours as was her job.

She turned around and saw he had on that ridiculous sailor's hat she hated so much. With his red and white striped shirt and sailor blue pants, he looked like a Raggedy Andy doll. Even his dark brown eyes were beginning to look like black buttons. Terri chuckled to herself at the visual of him dancing like a rag doll.

"And where is your hat?" Jake's round cheeks grew bright red as his face became more animated.

"Don't make me wear the hat, Jake. You can't make me wear that stupid hat."

"Terri!" Jake was fifteen years younger than she was. He was an adopted only child to his elderly parents who were old guard members at the oldest yacht club in town. They had dressed him like a sailor boy from the time he was a little kid. Somehow the style stuck, it just fit his nature.

Jake's parents had bought him a small open-passenger boat when he had completed his captain's license in order to start his own enterprise. Actually, Jake did have more knowledge about this bay and its ecological system than anyone else Terri knew, and he had taught her a lot. She had to give him that. His world was small to Terri though, as he had never traveled anywhere or left the comfort of his own hometown or local bay waters.

"Haven't sold any, Jake, no one's interested in sitting in a big boat today. Seems like everyone's all about those kayak tours." A group of kayakers paddled underneath and away, splashing, having fun. "Hey! Here's a suggestion!" Terri said, pointing to the kayakers. "Maybe we should rent out kayaks and do kayak tours, too!"

Jake stood there, his hands on his hips, fed up with this suggestion. There was room for only one captain on his ship. "Terri, we run a tour boat," he said in a most serious tone.

Terri couldn't help but burst out with a short loud giggle. Then she stopped herself and tried her best, working to look serious as he started in.

In fact, that was her last giggle as an official employee of Captain Edward's Guided Sea Tours. Jake was done with her bad attitude. "All right, Terri, I'm sorry, but you're clearly not at all happy here. We're a happy organization serving happy tourists, making and creating happy days." Jake went on as if he had just memorized all this before coming out and talking to her: "I'm afraid I'm going to have to let you go, I have to find someone with a more positive attitude." His arms were crossed and he tapped his foot as he talked. "Sales have slumped too far and this is our season."

Terri stood there half smiling, enduring his speech.

He stopped talking and looked at her, waiting for her to show an attitude adjustment. He really wanted to see a happier Terri, she did have a way with his clients, she did make them laugh and have fun. She could do this when she wanted to, and do it well. *So why not do it for just eight hours a day, and not even all of that?*

"Are you done?" Terri was trying hard to keep the smirk off her face, but could hardly manage this.

"Yes, Terri. What do you think? Do you think you can put on a smiling face and be happy?" Jake stood there with his forced smile, looking at her as if the smile underneath that ridiculous sailor's hat was going to be contagious.

"Well Sailor Raggedy Andy," Terri really couldn't help herself, "I think you've made me happy now!" She handed him her remaining flyers and removed her snazzy polyester over-shirt with its name plate attached. She wadded it up and passed it to him as well. "Thanks for all the happiness but, it's just way too happy for me. I'll see ya around." She waved as she walked away, smiling.

I'm never going to wear another polyester uniform again! Ever! Terri made her way down to the bar at the end of the pier in an attempt to regain some dignity.

"Hey Terri, what's up?" The lady behind the bar smiled at her.

Relieved, Terri sat down at the long shiny wooden bar. "I was fired today. Can you make me one of those spicy beer drinks you make so well, Doris? A chalada, I think you call it? I could really use one today, and a shot of tequila on the side, your best!" Terri pulled her little satchel out in front of her and was reminded once again of her financial situation. She let out a sigh, "Wait, wait a minute—can you make that a house beer today? Tap, please!" She put her last few dollars on the bar top and winked.

"Anything for you, Terri. Fired, huh?" Doris shook her head, commiserating with her.

<u>3</u>

Terri sat at the dining table, working on a bottle of tequila. Emptying it one shot at a time, it was all there was left in the cupboard. There was a salt shaker next to it as well as a handful of lemons from the neighbor's tree. She had carefully cut them into quarters on a tiny little cutting board with a pocket knife.

"Really, mom? Geez, tequila at this hour?" Kendra looked at her watch, seeing it was four o'clock in the afternoon. "That's disgusting." Her daughter had just come in through the front door with Derek. Now she shot Terri a look of disdain. Kendra, at her young age, prided herself in being straight edge. She didn't even drink caffeine, she was such a definite contrast to her mother.

"Well, I got fired today." Terri tipped her head and took a celebratory shot.

"And this is a surprise? Or should I ask why?" Kendra reached over and took the bottle from in front of her mom. Kendra took this bottle with her as she walked back to her bedroom down the hall.

"Hey! Stop, that's mine!" Terri yelled out to deaf ears. A loud thumping sound blared on, it shot right into Terri's temples. The complicated beat pulsed through the veins in her head. Boom, boomity, boom-boom.

"Turn that down!" Terri shouted out. Half drunk, she was beginning to feel on the edge of despair over what had become her life. There was nothing, not one thing in the world or in her life, she could control right now, especially not her daughter.

She let her head slump to the table and covered her ears with her arms, trying to calm her rising frustration.

The music pulsated through her body until she couldn't take it anymore. She angrily stomped down the hallway, knocked, and quickly opened the door. Poking her head in, she didn't know what they were doing. But both kids were on opposite sides of the room which helped Terri to relax just a little. She was half expecting a different scenario, one that made her cringe now that she was the mom.

After all, her daughter was now turning sixteen and they still had yet to have "the conversation," the "talk"—although Terri knew by now her daughter could probably tell her more about it than Terri herself ever knew.

"Can you turn it down, it's so so loud, I can't think." Terri caught a few words of the graphic lyrics. "Wow, I can't believe you listen to that, this stuff is awful." Terri's ears were clearly offended.

As the young man reached up to turn it down, he looked over at Kendra. Not about to obey anything Terri said, Kendra gave him the signal to turn it louder. He was caught in the middle of the two women. So now, against his better judgment, he followed Kendra's lead and turned it up.

"Derek! Turn it down! Right now!" Terri had her hands on her hips, looking at him sternly. She had known Derek since he was just a small kid.

He obeyed her and turned it down. He was actually half afraid of her.

"This crap is terrible!" Terri shouted over the loud beat.

"It's what we call music, Mom," Kendra announced.

Terri walked over and pressed the eject button. The music abruptly stopped and the CD player's lid slowly opened. Terri grabbed the disc and looked at it. She walked over to Kendra's desk and snapped the CD into two pieces on the edge of the desk as both kids looked on in disbelief.

"Really? I call it garbage." Terri was pissed, she had had her fill of Kendra's mouth for the day and was done. There was only so much disrespect she could tolerate in one day. "It's time for you to go home now, Derek."

"That was Derek's band, mom! His own music! You broke and threw away his CD, mom!"

Terri stared at Kendra with a "Do you think I'm stupid?" look.

"Yeah, it is, we worked hard on that...." Derek was in shock over what had just happened. *How could she do this?*

Terri still had her hands on her hips. "Really? You worked hard on that noise? Maybe you need another opportunity to work harder!" She looked at Derek and pointed her finger to the door. "Go home. You can make another copy."

He stood there frozen like a deer in headlights, watching Kendra for a clue.

Terri walked out the door first. She made her way down the hall and back to the couch where she flopped down and turned the TV on.

"Wow, man, your mom used to be cool." Derek looked at the remains of his CD there in the trash.

"Oh sure, she once had her moments." Kendra snorted. "But they're long gone now, she's a bitter mess, and she drinks way too much now...."

"What's wrong with her?"

"Her usual complaints, being female in today's world, she's too fat and unfit, not only that, she's turned forty."

"Wow, she's forty?"

"Yeah, don't be impressed, that was years ago. She just loves to complain now."

"Yeah, haven't heard her talk about being a big diver and all that in a long time...."

"Yeah, and all that. And she's managed to lose or spend, or spend and lose, who knows, a small fortune in less than ten years. And this guy Rick, he was married to my mom very briefly a long time ago, well, he's taken the rest. Never helped us with a thing but his lawyers took tons of so-called alimony. She tried to fight it and then her own lawyers took tons more. She's just grown bitter." The girl's anger toward her mother over her bad decisions was hard for Kendra to disguise or keep to herself at all. Now Kendra had stopped trying to hide how she felt about her mother. *Why bother hiding the obvious*, Kendra said to herself.

"What? What's with this guy Rick?"

"Never mind him, I don't want to talk about him right now, maybe later. Come on, let's get out of here." Kendra took Derek's hand and led him down the hall to the front door.

"He's leaving now, mom."

Terri sat there on the couch watching television, shaking her head yes, acknowledging she had heard Kendra as the front door opened. Somewhere after that, Terri heard Kendra say, "Bye Mom, I'll be back in a bit," right before the door closed.

Terri sat up. "I hate it when she does that! She didn't even ask if she could leave!" Terri leaned back into the couch with a huff. She looked at her watch to get the time and got distracted admiring the Rolex watch on her wrist. She noticed that half of the gold plate was worn off now and that the bezel turned freely. She still wore it every day, everywhere. Now she brought it up to her lips and kissed it gently. "I'll always remember you, Melvin…." Terri smiled thinking of him. His smiling face, the way he laughed with her, filled Terri's vision. He had passed away so suddenly from an illness the year before. She hadn't talked to him in over a decade. It had been so long, she missed him.

Her old friend, that same old guilt, began to creep in. She went back to Kendra's room and rummaged around for the bottle of tequila Kendra had confiscated from her. Terri was going to turn her attention back to the couch and the television, lull herself back to sleep, back to that dream, that wonderful dream. Maybe Melvin would be in it tonight….

Terri found her bottle of tequila sitting on Kendra's desk, on top of a piece of scratch paper with writing on it. Terri picked up the piece of paper and glanced at the writing, not caring much what it would say. She could make out the words, "St. Todos" written there, and on the next line, "Plane ticket info."

Plane ticket info? To St. Todos? What? Terri was startled. *Why? Who?* She put the paper back down, arranging it the way she found it, and grabbed her bottle.

On the way back down the hall, Terri grabbed her shot glass and went to her office. She sat down at her desk and turned the computer on, clicking on the icon for the computer's search history.

VOLUME THREE: RAPTIS TRILOGY

****

4

Terri woke up on the couch still dressed in her clothes. She had fallen asleep waiting for Kendra to come home.

The front door opened and a fresh-faced Kendra walked in all dressed and put together for the day. She had a smile and two coffees in her hands.

"Nice, Kendra, but you didn't even come home last night? You didn't call? You're only sixteen! You can't do that. Where were you?" Terri was rubbing her eyes, waking up, assessing the situation from the couch.

"Nice back to you, Mom. I mean you were passed out when I came home last night, and you were still passed out this morning when I left the house to go get some groceries and coffee. Here." Kendra handed one of the cups in her hands to her mom.

"Oh. Sorry. Thank you, well, great. You do know you can't spend the night out without telling me, right? I'd be really pissed." Terri did her best to be a mom. Her own mom was gone now, and she didn't have anyone to help her with parenting advice except her dad. He always did the best he could, a pillar of support for both Terri and Kendra. He knew Terri was often in over her head with this being a mother thing. He did what he could which wasn't much, especially as Terri didn't want his help most of the time.

Terri was fortunate Kendra was an inherently responsible young lady. It always surprised Terri how grown up her daughter could be, despite the disrespectful mouth she had.

"Drink it all, mom." Kendra sat down next to Terri and sipped her coffee. She didn't want to fight with her mom.

"St. Todos, huh?" Terri couldn't help herself, it just slipped out without any planning. She had to know.

"And you've been snooping in my room?" Kendra frowned at Terri as she questioned her mother in a tense high pitched tone.

"No, no, I just went to get my bottle, *my* bottle of tequila which you had in *your* room! It was right there on the table, under the tequila, the words, 'St. Todos,' " Terri defended herself.

Kendra let out a deep exasperated sigh.

There was a long stretch of silence as the two looked straight ahead, rather than at each other, simultaneously taking sips of their coffees.

"My dad has contacted me through Facebook." There it was, she'd said it out loud after practicing those words for a week.

The statement dropped between the two of them like a huge lead balloon, a balloon neither of them wanted to be the first to touch. There was a long and uncomfortable silence as they again both took sips of their coffees and stared out at nothing.

Her dad? What dad? Rick? Damn him! Who does he think he is? Terri said to herself, feeling angry that anyone, especially Rick who'd only taken from them and never given a thing, would contact Kendra before talking to Terri about this.

Terri and Kendra still sat there saying nothing.

Terri finally gave in and broke the silence. "I think you just told me Rick has contacted you?" Terri began to twist her neck around from one side to the other, trying to get her neck to pop as the tension was beginning to grow. "How and why in the hell did he find you?"

"I just told you, my Facebook page. He left a note saying he'd love to see me." Kendra knew he'd been so absent and just wanted money from Terri all these years, but she told herself she needed a dad.

It came out slowly and carefully while Terri did her best to hide the fact that she was seething inside, "Did he now?"

"Yes, he did, Mom, he is my dad, after all."

"Yeah right." *Her dad, yeah right, forget that,* Terri said to herself. Terri fidgeted on the couch and took her last sip of coffee before standing up. "Do you remember him?" Terri began to pace the front room floor waiting for Kendra to answer.

"No, no, I don't mom. I do remember the trip you took me on, you know, down to the islands, and we went diving!" Kendra thought maybe the word "diving" would get her mother excited.

"I know, that was so great! Wasn't that great?" Terri went off in her head chasing wonderful memories of the two of them snorkeling at Terri's old haunts, with Terri showing Kendra everything. *Well, almost everything. But Rick wasn't there, thank goodness. And sadly, Mitch wouldn't see us, of course. He wanted nothing to do with us, with me. Ever. Wouldn't even answer my calls.* Terri flinched momentarily as she thought of Mitch. Kendra had been so young, five years old, so cute. *And Mitch would have loved her,* Terri said to herself. *But Kendra and I had fun anyway.* That trip pretty much cemented things, she and Kendra were alone. But they did have each other.

"I remember I felt bad for you when your old friend, Mitch, the one you always talked about, refused to see you." Kendra, being the teenager she was, had to throw in that piece of psychological warfare.

Terri flinched hearing Kendra say Mitch's name now. *There is so much to say about Mitch, but why?* "Yeah, well, who can blame him...." Terri walked to the refrigerator and opened it. She didn't want to talk about Mitch right then, not at all. Too painful. *And the truth would just cause Kendra pain.* "Am I really out of beer?"

Kendra heaved a heavy sigh, exhaling slowly, shaking her head no.

"I was going to mix the beer with this tomato juice, OK? Add a little Tabasco, a celery stick, and yummy!" Terri was busy fumbling through the kitchen cabinets, looking for the Tabasco sauce.

"This is why I didn't want to tell you. Drinking? At seven AM, mom—really, can you please stop this?" Kendra pleaded.

Terri put the tomato juice back in the refrigerator and looked at Kendra. "You're right honey." *We're out of beer, I've got to remember to get more beer later.* "Do you have twenty dollars I can borrow?"

"Like you're going to pay me back." Kendra walked over to the dining table and reached into her purse. She pulled out her wallet and opened it up. She had a little after school job but didn't really make enough to keep loaning her mother money.

"I will pay you back. I will, as soon as—"

Kendra joined in on the chorus: "—the alimony lawsuit is reversed."

Terri stopped talking as Kendra continued.

"The alimony you pay my dad—"

There was more silence as Terri stood there and tried to keep her composure. *Rick, he calls himself her dad now?* Terri hated that bastard. Now that bastard was inviting Kendra to the islands. "We were married less than a year! Somehow after that short marriage, that bastard got half, half of everything I had already before I even met him. And he still does get it, as you know, getting that bogus alimony so many years now. What a corrupt court. Somebody paid somebody to make that weird order."

"I know, Mom, I know, you've told me many times...."

Terri looked around at what things were left of her world. Not much that wasn't already outdated. Everything at one time had been the best of the best, back when she had been on top of the world. Back then, traveling here and there, sparing no expense, her money had afforded her everything she had needed and wanted for herself and her daughter. And the money had seemed endless, endless. Until it did end. She had kept expecting that bogus alimony order to be reversed but it never was. Meanwhile not only Rick but the attorneys involved ate so much of the money. And they still were. Eating her money up. All of them.

Building an unmaintainable lifestyle and making one bad choice after another, which had included Terri's husband, Rick, now the money was almost gone. Worse than that, the credit cards were racked up, and now the house needed a new roof.

Terri couldn't maintain a job in the States to save her life. Her confidence was dwindling down from the size of a redwood tree to a toothpick. Now her attitude worsened the more she fought with her ego. She tried everything to let go of the anger and frustration that had built up inside, but couldn't.

VOLUME THREE: RAPTIS TRILOGY

****

5

"Mom, in less than two weeks it's my birthday." Kendra was getting dressed for school, putting on the final touches of her perfectly matched and ironed outfit. "And in four days, school will be out!" Kendra was unusually chatty this morning. She turned to talk to her mom as she curled her hair meticulously with the long curling iron.

Terri was up early with Kendra. "Yes dear, are you planning on working this summer? Finding a more interesting job?" Terri was looking at the newspaper want ads. "You'll probably find places that want you. But for me, ugh, not a lot out there. Not for me." Terri tapped the table with her pen, scouting the lines, looking for something to circle.

"This summer I'd like to do something different." Kendra was trying to throw out a gentle hint.

"Yeah, here's one, kid! Product ambassador." Terri circled the words with her pen. "I wonder what a product ambassador is? I'm sure whatever it is, I can do that." Terri looked at Kendra.

Kendra's long dark hair was neatly curled and coiffed, her fingernails always manicured and polished. Kendra was such a great contrast to her mother.

"Now, well, that's something different!" Terri smiled at Kendra, trying to connect.

Kendra was standing by the front door, listening.

Terri turned her attention back to her own world, hovering over the newspaper at the table.

Derek's car drove up. Terri had heard it approaching from a half block away, his bass line up at full volume.

"This summer, I want to go see my dad."

Terri looked up from the newspaper. Kendra grabbed the door knob and turned, swinging the front door open. She made her escape, running to Derek's car.

Terri scrambled around the table, barely making it to the front door as it was registering in her head what Kendra had announced.

"Like hell you are!" Terri shouted back as Kendra fastened her seatbelt and the two drove away. Kendra turned to Derek who was focusing on the road with both hands on the wheel.

"Like hell I'm not!" Kendra plopped her purse on her lap, pulling out the plane ticket. She already had it in her hands, it had come yesterday. Her dad had sent it to her.

Kendra was beyond excited. She had never met, or maybe really didn't even remember, she wasn't sure, this man Rick, her dad. That was the fun part of Facebook, he had found her after all these years! Her dad! *Why not meet him? No matter what my mom says he did to us, I have a right to know my dad. And maybe he can make up for all the money he took from us.* It wasn't her fault that her parents didn't get along, she told herself.

Kendra thought to herself that she may have played things up a bit with him, not wanting him to know what a complete loser her mom was now. After all, on his Facebook page he had pictures of a beautiful house on the waterfront with a late-model Range Rover parked outside. It was all so plush, so beautiful. Kendra held the ticket up, smiling at it.

"Look at this, Derek! I'm going to the islands in less than a week! I'll be there for my birthday!"

He didn't look over. He was a safe driver, always eyes in front of him.

"Yeah, I don't know. I got a bad feeling about this, Kendra. I just wish you'd tell your mom. I get the feeling she's gonna blame this one on me...." Derick looked tough and he loved to play the part but inside he was a good, sensitive young man, always wanting to do the right thing.

He loved Kendra and would do anything for her, but he was concerned for her safety. The islands were so far away, and she would have no cell phone. Kendra assumed her dad would have a computer and she could keep in touch that way.

"You? Blame you? Be serious, I'll be gone, she won't even know how to find you." Kendra reached over and gave Derek's leg a playful squeeze.

"Of course your mom knows how to find me. You know she had me write down my contact info for her, years ago."

Kendra rolled her eyes and hid her face in embarrassment. "Oh, my God. I can't believe she did that. Does she do that to everyone behind my back?"

"She just loves you, Kendra."

Kendra was silent.

"We won't even be able to talk for two weeks...." Derek was already missing his best friend and he wanted to change the subject.

"Yeah, whatever." Kendra wondered how resourceful her mom would be when she left. She had to think of a good cover. "Anyway, we're almost at school, only four more days." Now Kendra wanted to change the subject and she did. She loved Derek too, he was her best friend, they did everything together.

They both knew she always had had plans to take off, and as soon as she could. She wanted to go away to school and grow in different ways. She had big dreams for herself.

She let out a cheer as Derek made a left turn into the school parking lot. "We're almost done with this place for the year!"

"Yep!"

She smiled. "Yep, another year done. Are we going to the rally tonight?" Kendra had a knack for changing the subject, but it didn't change in her head. Kendra hadn't figured out yet how she was going to tell her mother what her plans were.

6

Terri stood in her front yard inspecting her work. Over the years, she had spent many hours tending to this yard. She loved her flowers and plants, especially the ones that bore tropical fruits and flowers. She could lose herself in the beauty of these surroundings, tending to them, pulling the weeds, watering.

But now, looking up at her house which she had years ago paid cash for, she was nothing short of completely disappointed. The paint on the eaves showed signs of wear, it was chipping away and in some places pretty much gone. The color of the house's exterior walls was tired and faded after so many years of no maintenance. Terri no longer had the money to pay someone to take care of these things for her.

Of course, she had always thought she could do it all herself, and that she could do a better job. Now Terri told herself, *This is something I could do to fill my time.* She could scrape and paint this house herself. She stepped back and examined the job. *Accomplishing something, anything, would feel good right now. I need this. Perfect*, she said to herself, *I can save money doing this myself and at the same time accomplish something. A win-win. Or at least not a lose more and more here.*

****

Terri went into the house and grabbed a notepad. Opening the pad to an empty, clean page, she wrote the number one down and circled it. Next to it she wrote, "paint eaves." Thinking hard of what to write next, she scribbled the number two and next to it, "buy everything it takes to paint house." But then her

33

momentum froze, knowing she didn't have the cash it would take to do even that.

Terri looked up from her notes, scanning the inside of the house. All she saw were the same tired walls, and the many undone chores. There was the vacuum cleaner standing there, plugged in ready to be pushed around. There were dishes next to the sink, too many to even know how to begin to clean them. Terri put the pen down and walked away, discouraged. She headed back outside where she belonged. *How could there be so much to do while I feel so bored, so done with it all?*

****

Terri bent down and dug into the dirt with her hands, pulling at the weeds and anything else out of place. She dug faster and faster and harder and harder, trying to push her frustration back by doing something she knew she could do, taking on something she knew she could control, by pulling weeds. But no matter how fast and hard she dug, Terri couldn't block her thoughts, they were everywhere.

****

Terri's anxieties had built up over time, setting into deep imbalances that she had a hard time escaping. And any time she gave in to the frustration, the big anger would surface. No matter how she tried to suppress this, she was always dealing with this anger at herself and at her self-imposed circumstances arising out of her own bad choices. Whether she was paying attention to it or trying to stuff it away, this anger and frustration consumed every breath and thought.

She found it easiest to dissipate her anger through sweat and hard work. It was the fearful anxiety-driven dreams she suffered many nights that kept her from sleeping, fueled by troubled memories of intensely haunting experiences. Sweet dreams would begin with wonderful days somewhere but turn into nightmares in which she was killing a man—always the same man, always the same fears.

Again and again, Terri relived the look on the man's face as the life extinguished out of him.

Then came the second part of this repeating dream, disposing of the evidence, of the body. The feeling of fear she would be seen. *Fear fear fear,* she never let herself admit to. It was this anxiety that woke her, the fear of getting caught. She would wake up sweating, panting as if she had just run a hundred miles from nonexistent detectives.

Reality would set in as she would wake up and slowly realize once again it was just a dream. What had really happened was that the big time criminals Terri had long ago discovered down there had killed each other off. They had tried to kill her, what they did to her was horrible, but they got each other instead. Still, the whole thing continued to haunt her, nagged her; she still struggled with this all the time.

7

Now it was broad daylight. Terri was staring at her neatly groomed garden, the only part of her life she could somewhat control. Then she was glancing at her dilapidated house, which she felt she could not do much about. The bitterness floodgates opened. Again and again, she just didn't have the strength to close them. She looked around to try to escape these feelings. *Find weeds to pull, dead leaves to rake, things to cut back.* But there were no weeds left to pull, nothing left to rake, and all the tree branches were already neatly trimmed.

Rick! Her ex-husband—*how can this guy possibly be back in my life again? Really?* No, she couldn't believe it. *It can't be! Not now, not ever! And why in the hell did he bother Kendra, how dare he? Who in the hell does he think he is?*

****

Terri felt sick thinking about it. She had met Rick two days before she was to marry Mitch. Rick was an incredibly beautiful man and Terri was drinking at a bar, all by herself. She had been sitting there, obsessing about the final two days of her life—or at least of her freedom, which she felt was coming to an end because she was about to get married. Not that she didn't love Mitch, she adored him, but she just wasn't ready. And being with Mitch somehow reminded her of the terrible events she, and they, had survived. She kept reliving it all, and never told anyone how bad this was for her. She wouldn't admit this was haunting her.

The Rick thing had just happened, just like that. He had just so oddly appeared in her life. Suddenly there he was at the bar that night, as if he had known she'd be there, and he seemed to know a lot about her. She thought back to the way he kept buying her drinks. Somehow the alcohol hit her far harder than ever before. *What was in that stuff,* Terri still wondered. Had she been drugged or what?

After that first kiss that night, Terri swore she felt something she'd never felt before. And she had foolishly mistaken it for love. That fleeting kiss with Rick, that moment, it had lasted two whole days, right up until the day of the wedding when she didn't show up. She'd been in some kind of altered state those two days, a state of mind that, even all these years later, she didn't understand.

And before she knew it, she'd left Mitch at the altar with all their friends standing by to celebrate their love. She still couldn't figure out what had happened that night, where that Rick had come from, how she could have been so lost to let that happen. *Not even I, the wild Terri, could have been that out of it,* she told herself all these years later.

She had left Mitch a note saying, "I'm sorry." Well, actually, Rick had dictated the note. She had left almost everything behind for Mitch to clean up and put away when she abruptly sailed away with Rick on his sailboat. Yes, she had left almost everything behind except for a few keepsakes, valuables, and some banking information. She and Rick had made it almost all the way clockwise around the Caribbean in seven months before Terri finally insisted they pick a port, buy a house, and settle down. A baby was about to arrive. *A baby.*

They had landed in San Diego, arguing all the way there. Terri had been ready to settle down with the baby, but he hadn't been ready, and in fact never was. It wasn't part of his dream. Before she knew it, Terri was being served with fancy divorce papers—yes, she had married Rick along the way and no sooner than she'd had the baby, he was rejecting her.

Now, all these years later, she was still shocked that he'd managed to win half of her small fortune in the divorce, claiming it was also his after such a short marriage, and then just up and leave on his sailboat. What kind of divorce works like that? Who had worked that out? She could never figure that out. Rick had known people in various places and they had stepped forward for him.

Rick had had a list of all that she owned, of her worth, of the treasures she had, which she already had before she met Rick. None of them were his. Terri couldn't remember when he got this list, but it must have been while they were sailing around the Caribbean. *How else could he have gotten this information,* Terri had been wondering for years.

Then, after all that, six months after the divorce, she had heard from Rick and his attorneys again. He wanted more, even more, and had filed for alimony payments from her, alimony which he then won!

Ever since, all these years, she had been fighting both the totally unfair divorce ruling, and the entirely absurd alimony ruling. But every month, more and more of her dwindling money was being drained by those absurd and long term so-called alimony payments and lawyers' fees for fighting those alimony payments and the divorce ruling. *What a racket.* Now, all these years later, Terri knew she had been swindled big time, even tricked into marrying Rick on some little island somewhere, away from the protection of the United States, so he could bring about his plan to get her money for life.

But yes, things had not always been terrible. Over the years, she and Kendra had enjoyed life. There had been lots of fun and lots of money spent, for years. But even then, during the good times, Terri had been haunted by bad memories, and by Rick too. With these things plaguing her, somehow Terri hadn't managed to settle well into her role as mom. But she knew, she always knew, she had a beautiful daughter, the first real love of her life. Kendra was her life now. Terri knew this. Now, when she thought of Kendra, she felt so badly, and so responsible for her beloved daughter.

At first being a mother had been so fun and new, an adventure. But then, juggling a child, wow, there was so much to learn. There were the simple things during the day, things Terri had never thought of before, like naps, and meals—kids eat three times a day! At least! And kids need structure, lots of structure. The structure thing proved to be the hardest for Terri. And when Kendra had gotten a little older, Terri had found out that kids actually have to go to school every day, or eventually everyone gets into trouble.

She'd been entirely unaware of the seriousness of kindergarten, and so she had never attended the meetings at Kendra's school. She had thought, *How hard can it be, sending your kid to school?* School had never seemed that serious to Terri when she was a kid. But once Kendra was born, Terri was forced to take life more and more seriously. The problem was that all this seriousness about a child, all this structure—it just wasn't just Terri.

Terri had even briefly considered home-schooling Kendra, so that the two of them could travel anywhere on a whim. But Terri decided against home schooling when she discovered there was actually a whole curriculum she would have to follow and be responsible for. Homeschooling was no vacation. So the public school system had to work, because it was the best way to educate her daughter. Plus it was required by law.

When the money started to run out, it was a shock and then an adjustment that Terri just wasn't prepared for. Who was going to take care of the pool and mow the lawns? The first time the electric company turned the power off for lack of payment, Terri thought she could slip someone a twenty to get it turned back on, long enough to wait or earn some more money to keep it on. That's the way she used to do it, down on the islands. But unfortunately, no matter how hard she tried, it didn't work that way in California.

****

So things were very different now. Terri was no longer a rich woman and her life was quite hard. Unprepared for the consequences of the choices she had made, she was unable to cope with the stress, and found it difficult to adjust to a different lifestyle. And she had to work now, to earn money for food and gas, and for repairs on the house. The money she needed just wasn't falling off the trees or coming in the mail anymore.

Terri thought about her old self with some anguish. Could she still earn money diving? Teaching diving maybe? *Probably not.* It had been a long time since Terri had taught diving. Now she felt old and past her prime. Maybe she could manage something—*Maybe, but what?* What could she do anymore? *Who would want to hire me for anything?* There was nothing out there for her. Terri followed her psyche down, down, as it dove to the bottom.

Sure, Terri had proven herself to be a good worker, always throwing herself into any job or project offered. But most managers found Terri bossy and arrogant, always knowing better than her bosses exactly what to do, exactly how to make it better and run it more efficiently. There had been a time in Terri's life when she had everything under control, and quite effortlessly. But even then, back when she was good at all this, and much younger, she could only do it until boredom set in.

And now that old boredom was back, but there were no new opportunities waiting. So she often found herself daydreaming of the good parts of the past or living for the next adrenaline rush. She tried not to imagine what life with Mitch would have been like. She missed Mitch, but he wanted nothing to do with her. These days, Terri kept herself in constant motion, absent-mindedly running away.

What to do next had become a constant question.

8

Terri knocked on Kendra's door as she opened it, asking, "What are you up to, so secretive in your room?" She hadn't seen much of Kendra these past few days, and when she did it was just "Hooray! School's out!" or a quick "Hello, good bye." Terri knew Kendra was upset that she'd put her foot down about the St. Todos thing, but there was absolutely no chance in hell that Terri could let her daughter go down to the islands to be with Rick.

Kendra had seemed to shrug it off as she had instead negotiated Terri's OK for a three week road trip to Oregon with her friends. A friend of Kendra's, Diane, had invited Kendra on her family vacation which would be heading north. Terri was glad Kendra had something to do so she wouldn't be totally bored the whole summer, and was glad to let her go. When Kendra invited her mom to walk into her room, she was finalizing her packing.

"Are you all ready to go? Do I need to call and talk to Diane's parents tonight? You feel you have enough cash?" Kendra looked so grown up. But quick answers of "No, Mom," or "Yes, Mom," were all Terri was able to pull out of the girl.

Kendra was about done packing. Deep in the bottom of her suitcase, she had hidden the mask and fins which she had so meticulously cleaned and packed. Her dad had promised her that everything else she would need would be there waiting for her.

"Don't you think it's going to be colder up in Oregon? Looks like a lot of tank tops and shorts you packed in there." Terri was trying to make some last attempts at conversation with her daughter. There had been so few in the last weeks.

"I'm not going to Alaska, Mom, just Oregon, I'll be fine." Kendra was on edge, holding so much guilt in, she could hardly look at her mom let alone look her in the eyes. Her mom was so clueless, so unaware that her daughter was leaving tomorrow for St. Todos! Kendra thought about how her dad was going to pick her up when she flew in and then take her to the island where he lived, a smaller, private resort island with just a few full-time residents. He had written her that he wanted to get to know her. And Kendra sure wanted to know him. He had taken care of everything, planned her whole trip, even sent her a signed parental permission slip to use at the airport when she was boarding.

Her mom would never be the wiser. Diane was coming tomorrow morning to pick her up, and she would say her folks were busy packing the other car. Then Diane and Kendra were going to swing by and pick up Derek, of course. They would drive to the airport and the two were going to wave goodbye to Kendra as she snuck off to see her dad. No harm done, and she would be back in two weeks. Her friends would pick her up, bring her home. Her mother would never know. It was going to be that easy.

"Well, I'm going to miss you, sweetheart, please be careful and tell Diane's parents I said thank you. Are you sure I shouldn't call and talk to them?"

"No, no, no, talk about what? They're fine.... I'm going to miss you too, Mom!" Kendra really meant it, she was already feeling funny inside. She didn't like lying to her mom, but it was time to take charge of her own life. She was going to be sixteen, after all.

****

The next morning Kendra said goodbye one last time as she placed her bags in Diane's car. Terri threw her a kiss and waved goodbye as the car backed out of the driveway and drove off down the street. Then Terri turned, walked past some new weeds that must have sprouted overnight, and walked into the front room of the house, surveying the interior. OK, so she had it all to herself, and couldn't remember the last time when she had had zero responsibility. Terri sat down on the couch, thinking of what to do.

Two weeks…mmm two weeks. What can I do with these two weeks? No money for a hotel—I could camp! Mmm…the old car won't go that far, and camping is so much work by myself. Terri reached over, turned off the little lamp on the table next to her, and sprawled out on the couch. It was a great time for a leisurely late morning nap.

VOLUME THREE: RAPTIS TRILOGY

****

REDEMPTION

****

PART TWO

TRAPPED

VOLUME THREE: RAPTIS TRILOGY

****

9

Kendra was no stranger to the tropics. She loved the warm tropical weather and was a well seasoned young traveler. She had taken many exotic warm vacations with her mother back before the money ran out. Kendra had loved those times, back when her mom was so alive.

Now Kendra had no problem maneuvering to and through airports on time to meet her dad on the other end at St. Todos. It was one o'clock in the afternoon when the plane touched down. Kendra stepped out of the plane and walked across the runway into the terminal.

She spotted her father right away.

He looked nothing like the picture he had posted on Facebook, nothing like the young and handsome blond sailor. He was old, and he looked even older than her mom with his graying hair receding and a paunch for a stomach. His old skin was a dark leather brown. But when he saw Kendra, he smiled widely with pearly white teeth gleaming. It looked as if he had a full set of teeth except for the one missing there on the top right side. Recognizing her, he opened his arms up for a hug. She looked just like her recent photo.

"Well, well, well…. Well, well, well!" he said to her over and over as he wrapped his slightly sagging leather brown arms around her. He squeezed her tight. "My baby girl, after all these years." He stepped back, his hands still on her shoulders. "Let me look at you." He smiled wide as she blushed. "You grew up to be a beautiful young woman!"

"Thank you, uh—" she stopped, embarrassed, not knowing what to call him.

"Dad. You can call me Dad." He picked up one of her bags and put his other arm around her as they started to walk. "Imagine that, here you are, I have so much to show you in just two weeks."

Kendra picked up her carry on and tried to keep up with his long hurried steps. The wave of hot air hit them as the double doors opened and they walked out into the tropical heat.

"I've been to this island before, this is where my mom spent most of her time way back when, right?"

Her dad, Rick, looked at her. His face squinted as he tried to remember what Terri had done on the island.

"Yes, yes, I guess so. She ran some dive shop here or something like that, I didn't know her then. She doing OK?" Now his voice had a nervous, slightly tense tone.

The unspoken tension along with the tropical heat was beginning to overwhelm Kendra. She was dripping wet, sweating profusely. The tropical summer air stuck to her overheated tired body and accumulated into droplets. Now the light synthetic sleeveless dress she had changed into on the plane stuck to her body, clinging to her in embarrassing places as she walked. She stopped and put her bags down to get her dress adjusted. She was hoping no one was paying attention. She realized what bad judgment she had used in choosing to wear her thong underwear. She answered her father, "Oh yeah, same ole mom, going here, flying there. Who knows where she is these two weeks I'm gone!" Kendra smiled innocently. She knew her mom could barely afford gas for her car this week, and probably had spent the little money she did have on beer, so she wasn't going far.

"Oh good, that's terrific to hear. She must've managed her money well then. I hope she's gotten over some of those hard feelings she's had...."

Kendra thought it best to not comment on the hard feelings part. It was all her mom had left these days, hard feelings. And her mother sure felt she had a right to those hard feelings.

Out in front of the airport, her dad raised his hand, calling for the next taxi which then slowly drifted forward. When it reached them, her dad opened the door for her.

Ah, a taxi. Kendra was exhausted but excited to arrive, and now glad to get into the taxi and sit down again. She relaxed a little. Her dad was friendly enough, sort of affectionate, and kind of well-groomed, even if old. *So far so good.*

"Don't you worry about my mom, I've got her all under control." Kendra sounded positive.

"We're just in time to take the three o'clock ferry over to where I live." It was a ten minute ride to the ferry dock. Once on the ferry, they ate snacks of peanuts and warm bananas for lunch during the crowded fifty-minute ferry ride. After the ferry, they got off and walked over to a small speed boat for another thirty-minute ride.

The snacks switched to sunflower seeds and lukewarm beer. Kendra never drank and even detested beer, but today she was thirsty and in the heat, even lukewarm beer tasted good and did the trick. Soon she and her father were having a grand time, and she was drunk.

The sun was tilting westward. The shadows began to cast long and different shapes across the landscape as they approached the tiny island. Kendra was in awe as they pulled up to the private dock, she could see the large beautiful house. *Wow. Just like the picture!*

"Here it is." Her dad turned the motor off after tying the boat up to the cleat on the private pier. Then he helped her off. He led her up the immaculate concrete walkway which was surrounded by a lush, beautiful landscape leading up to the house. "We take our shoes off and leave them out here, OK?" He slipped his shoes off and wiped his feet before stepping in.

Wow, he's so clean and neat, like me! Not like my mom is these days.

****

The interior of the house was immaculately clean, spotless, almost as if no one lived there. *He must have a maid*, Kendra mused as she noticed only a few breakfast dishes in the sink, unlike her mom's house, which always appeared perpetually unkempt.

Rick led her down the long hallway to a back room. It was decorated like a magazine picture, and it looked perfect and perfectly empty. She couldn't even find a personal picture or a personal anything as she looked around the large room. *Wow, he's so anal retentive, so that must be where I get it from, not my mom, that's for sure!*

"Dad?" Kendra was having a hard time standing up after such a long time in the heat and as she was half drunk, dehydrated, and getting dizzy. The trip there with its two boat rides and no food or water except nuts and beer was taking its toll on her petite frame. "Can I pass out now? I'm so tired."

"Of course dear, make yourself at home. This is the bedroom I have set up for you. You have your own bathroom down the hall, and you saw where the kitchen is."

"And Dad?"

"Yes?"

Kendra stumbled over to him, threw both her arms around him, and squeezed. "You're amazing, thank you."

Rick was a little taken aback by Kendra's hug and compliment, but he hid his surprise.

Kendra made it over to the bed, and plopped her body down onto the soft pillowy surface, yawning and smiling as she did. She kinda liked the way that beer made her feel, but now she couldn't keep her eyes open.

"Get some rest, tomorrow we're gonna have some fun." He backed out of the bedroom, closing the door behind him.

He walked to the kitchen and opened the refrigerator; it was barren except for a few used condiments, eight beers, and less than a quart of milk. The single box of sugary breakfast cereal in the cupboard was half empty.

He poured himself a large bowl of cereal. He then wolfed it down, standing up like an animal over his bowl, milk dripping from his mouth back into the bowl as he chewed. Then he rinsed his bowl and left it in the sink. Then he opened the refrigerator and reached for two beers, one to chug fast and the other to sip while he sat and thought.

VOLUME THREE: RAPTIS TRILOGY

****

<u>10</u>

Kendra was outside, sitting on the dock, dangling her feet in the turquoise water. She had woken up early that morning feeling refreshed. Her dad didn't come out until much later in the day. He was still yawning when he walked out to the backyard to find her.

The short manicured grass was a beautiful dark green. The sound of the private waterfall dropping into the small pond had lulled Kendra into complete serenity. Nothing could bother her, it was all so perfect. Off to the side there was a private gray water recycling area to keep the gardens lush and flowering. *So beautiful, so very first class!* Kendra was thrilled.

She looked up and saw the clear bright sky, the beautiful white house with its lush green grass, and her old-ish but still sort of handsome dad walking down the walkway. She was in paradise. This was going to be her first whole day there, with only twelve days remaining, and she already didn't want to leave.

"Hey, Cupcake."

Kendra smiled at the nickname.

"Let's go out for some breakfast, I've got a whole day planned." Rick came up to Kendra sitting there on the grass, sunning herself. Kendra noticed that he had a five o'clock shadow this morning, and observed he was capable of growing a full thick beard.

"Oh boy! Are we going out on the boat?" She looked out, thinking of some of the small harbor areas they had passed by yesterday on their way there. Cute little restaurants, white sandy beaches with coconut trees, she couldn't wait to jump in.

She was prepared for anything that day. She already had her bathing suit on and was thinking of taking a swim right there in the passage that morning to cool off. She hoped her dad would join her.

"No, not yet, let's go to town, get a bite to eat. I have to meet with a friend and then I'll show you around."

"Meet with a friend? Oh sure." She stood up and followed her dad inside. "Should I leave my bathing suit on? Just in case?" She was really hoping to be in the water as soon as possible that day. She had a tan to work on!

Breakfast with a friend. She imagined answering one million irrelevant questions from another grown-up about her life back home. But that was back home. And that's exactly where she wanted to leave it—this was her vacation! Kendra followed her father into the dark garage. It lit up as the large garage door opened with a touch of a button, revealing an empty garage with a glistening, clean new car.

"Wow, is this your car? Beautiful!" Kendra went over and touched it. It was a late model Range Rover, dark forest green.

"You like that? The real deal, none of those funny California emissions laws here! Pure power." He patted the hood, then held the door open for her to get in. They backed out of the garage and out of the gated entrance, pulling onto a narrow two lane road. They slowly wound around, turn after turn, for what seemed to be an eternity. Each turn that faced the ocean had its own breathtaking view, but after over an hour of this at twenty-five miles per hour, Kendra couldn't help but wonder if it wouldn't have been easier taking the boat.

But she decided to make the best of it. "I love history, Dad, what things can you tell me about this island? Any special landmarks I should see?"

Rick was surprised at her question and clueless about an answer.

"Oh gosh, Cupcake, I haven't been here long enough to learn anything like that about the island. You...hungry?"

"But I thought you...." She trailed off, it wasn't important. But she thought he had said on his Facebook page that he had been down on this island for years. Maybe she had misunderstood.

"What, Cupcake?" He looked at her and smiled.

"Nothing, Dad. Nothing."

****

On the long ride, Kendra started feeling bored to her core and finding that her dad wasn't much of a conversationalist. She brought up many different subjects, *trying to find something* in common with him that they could talk about. Nothing worked and she eventually stopped trying. She would have to have something left to talk about on the long ride back....

They eventually came to a very little town on the waterfront. There was a one pump gas station cafe and then two or three other little storefronts of some kind. Rick pulled into the narrow driveway of the gas station, maneuvering back and forth into position in front of the single pump.

"Sorry, almost out of gas!" He announced out loud as he stopped. He opened the gas tank and put the nozzle in to pump. He stopped, reaching up and patting himself all over, seeming surprised. He leaned to the window of the car and said, "Darn it Cupcake, I must have left my wallet at the house. I'm embarrassed to ask, but did you bring any cash with you?" He opened the door and poked his head in the driver's side, smiling at her, blushing about his blunder.

"Oh sure, Dad, yes, no problem…." Kendra reached back and tugged her purse onto her lap and opened it. "How much do you need?" she asked while looking through her wallet.

"Oh, seventy dollars?" He smiled wider at her with his bright pearly white teeth. He gave her a wink with one eye. "It's a big car, sorry Cupcake."

"Sure Dad, no problem." Kendra counted out four twenty-dollar bills. "I have eighty, I don't have anything smaller than twenties right now."

He reached his hand out across the interior of the car to her.

"I'll pay you back as soon as we get home, OK?"

She handed the money over to his come hither, wiggling fingers.

"Sure Dad, I'm not worried, it's not like you don't have any money to pay me back." She laughed out loud, wondering how rich he must be. She thought to herself how she would never loan her mom eighty dollars, not even for a day.

In four minutes he was done pumping gas. She noticed he only put in twenty-five dollars' worth of gas. She half expected he would give her the remainder of the change back. He never brought it up.

****

Breakfast went pretty much the same way, they had a delicious breakfast. When the check came, again, he acted surprised he forgot one more time he didn't have his wallet and no money to pay. He looked at her and asked again, ever so nicely. If she could, just forty dollars more would round it up to one hundred and twenty dollars, only if she had it, of course. There was plenty at home to pay her back.

Her reaction was paralyzed, she wasn't ready for any of this, she didn't bring a lot of money along. There was no mention of the leftover money from the gas station. She thought about asking, but didn't. "Sure, no problem," she smiled and handed it over. She excused herself to the bathroom where she stood in the stall and counted her remaining cash. *Yikes! Not much.* Only eighty dollars left and it was only her first day!

He said he had a few errands to run with his friend, which he would do after his friend showed up at the cafe, and that she should just sit at the cafe and relax, maybe take a walk around town, that they would be right back. His friend came in, a funny looking guy who looked completely out of place in the tropics. Her dad left her there in the cafe, sitting all alone. She watched through the window as they walked out to the car.

Her dad's friend was dressed in a colorful long sleeve polyester shirt and long slacks. Perspiration continually dripped down the man's always wet forehead. He kept using his handkerchief to blow his red runny nose. Then he would meticulously fold the handkerchief into a square, then wipe his forehead off.

Kendra watched this man, surprised, as he was such a contrast to her dad, who was neat, clean shaven. Well, at least that is what her dad was yesterday morning; this morning they had left the house in a hurry, no time to shave. *Hmmm, he was still dressed in yesterday's clothes....*

The two men left her there, waving goodbye, and drove off.

They had said they would be back in thirty minutes. Three hours later, Kendra was still waiting.

While she waited, she went back and forth between the small grocery/laundromat and the cafe/gas station/post office at least six times. The one other place there that she could have wandered to was just a home rental place, she didn't bother walking into it. But she spent more of the time just sitting and waiting. She drank way too many of those frozen piña coladas that were being offered to her. Offered at a discount, of course. She didn't know they had rum in them, and they were yummy! Somehow she had already spent another thirty dollars just waiting on her dad. If he weren't so wealthy she would have been in a panic.

She was clearly drunk, and stumbling sideways, slurring her words. She had remnants of banana split on her shirt and her hair was not in its usual properly combed style. Instead, it strung down uncharacteristically in her face. She frowned, not knowing what had hit her as her dad walked up. He was alone now and helped her into the car.

"I don't ... I don't ... know what happened." She slurred her words as she tried and tried to sit up. "I thought they were...virgins...virgin coladas, I didn't know...." She kept telling her dad this, over and over until she passed out on the front seat. Halfway home, she begged him to pull over, to stop and let her puke.

She insisted it was the heat and the slow, long winding drive back to the house making her nauseous. It was much later in the afternoon when they pulled into the private entrance and down into the garage attached to the house. Rick had to wake Kendra up and help her into the house.

"Gosh Cupcake, I'm sorry, I didn't even think of what to do for dinner tonight." The thought of getting back in that car for any more long twisting rides made her lightheaded, her stomach began to rock.

"Don't worry about it, I don't feel well." Her body was already feeling hung over from the sugar drop and still feeling nauseous from the roller coaster of a car ride. "I'm going to bed."

"OK, Cupcake, sleep tight, I got a big day planned for us tomorrow!"

She stumbled off and closed the door behind her. The sun was barely setting but her eyes had already sunk.

Rick went into the kitchen and reached into the pantry for that last box of cereal and shook it, his stomach growling. There was just enough cereal along with the last of the milk to make one bowl for himself. He slurped it down with a large serving spoon while leaning over the sink.

Kendra lay in bed. Her head was spinning and she didn't know how to make it stop. When she closed her eyes her head just spun faster. She was hoping tomorrow would be more fun. She looked at her fingernails, she had a chip in the polish on one of them. She resisted the urge to fix it at that moment, she was just too groggy, couldn't sit up, and didn't want to move. Today was not her idea of fun. She was anxious for the real vacation to start, to go diving, work on her tan.

VOLUME THREE: RAPTIS TRILOGY

****

11

Kendra had been gone for a few days now and Terri had yet to leave the house. It was hot and humid outside as these were the summer months. The temperatures were soaring and people of all kinds, tourists and locals alike, were parking their cars right there on the street outside Terri's house. Many people walking by were going to the beach. As they did, they peered in through Terri's barely open window blinds.

Terri hated this lack of privacy. Once she painted the whole front curb of her house red to try and keep people from parking there. The neighbors and parking officials quickly objected, fining Terri the costs of re-painting the curb, much to Terri's loud protests.

Terri had been keeping all the shades drawn for days. She lay inside on the couch, drinking her daily vegetable intake by way of a spicy V-8 mixed with beer. It was a barely tolerable cheap beer. Her cash flow was low, but she knew a trip to the grocery store to restock with something at least somewhat edible was imminent.

Gosh, I thought maybe Kendra would have checked in with me by now. Oh well, no news is always good news. Boy, she sure is her mother's daughter. My kid. Terri was bored and the good stuff on cable TV had been turned off for years now. She had flipped through all of the game shows, disliked most of the talk shows, and couldn't find a decent show to watch.

Terri thought about Kendra. This kid was always busy with her own life and her school activities, and was never one to sit on the couch and pass time by doing empty-minded things like watching thirty-minute TV shows. So Kendra rarely joined her mother in this sort of thing. Usually Terri didn't mind, as she liked her space. But now, with Kendra gone on a trip, there Terri was, alone, stuck with herself. Wallowing in her solitude, Terri found she couldn't move herself away from the comfort of guilt and self-pity. She kept thinking about how different things could have worked out for her. *Ah, yes, if only....*

That Kendra, what a kid. Kendra had the drive to move forward, much like her mom had had in her own younger years. From the time she was little, Kendra had a high curiosity level, one which forced her to have to know things. The kid was constantly hungry for knowledge. And Terri had taught her at a young age to understand and realize what an opportunity was and how to use an opportunity as a chance to grow and learn. *At least I taught her a few things*, Terri consoled herself.

But Terri had somehow let her own bitterness snuff her own drive, stop her own ability to move forward. Her bitterness had made Terri quite cynical about new opportunities, even blind to them, until she couldn't see any for herself anywhere. She was stopped, depressed, sinking.

And Kendra knew this about her mother. She'd watched it happening to Terri. In fact, this was why Kendra purposely didn't tell Terri more about the terrific opportunity her father, appearing on Facebook of all places, had given Kendra: An all-expense paid vacation, and the opportunity to meet and get to know her dad. For Kendra, this sounded like one of the biggest opportunities in her young life.

Terri went to the hall closet. Sliding it open, she reached up onto the highest shelf way toward the back. She pulled out her old Kodak slide projector and blew off the dust. It was worn but still intact. She admired it, it had been top-of-the-line in its time. It had had all the latest features. She heard something rattling loose as she set it down on the table, pointing it at a blank wall.

Next, she pulled out a larger box. It was filled with reels of slides. She pulled out a random slide and put it up to the light, smiling at the view. It was an underwater cavern she and Mitch had discovered one day. The next moment, her mind took her right there....

****

Terri was there underwater with at least two cameras strapped around her neck. All she wanted to do was to get that perfect shot of her dear friend, Stephanie, swimming into this underwater cavern with a beautiful back light.

Terri swam through the underwater arch and into the cavern first. Then she turned around, dropped down to her knees, and got herself situated. Once the silt settled to her satisfaction, Terri waved for Stephanie to swim toward her through the long cavern.

Stephanie sat on her knees on the other side, shaking her head in a soundless, "No."

Terri was busy looking through the lens finder at Stephanie, encouraging Stephanie with her left hand to float through slowly. After a minute of waving "come forward" and getting a "no" with both of them signaling again and again back and forth, Terri watched Stephanie rise to the surface. So Terri rose to the surface on the inside of the cavern and called out to Stephanie over the volcanic arch that separated them.

"Come on Stephanie! There's plenty of room!"

"No Terri, no, I don't want to!" Stephanie shouted back. The conversation reverberated off the volcanic island for all her friends in the boat to hear.

"What—what do you mean?" Terri was confused, as they'd swum through this cave before.

"The shark! The large nurse shark you swam by, he's tucked in the corner, he keeps looking at me, giving me the eye to stay out. I don't want to swim through there!"

"What?" Terri let the air out of her buoyancy compensator and dropped back down to her knees. She looked through the cavern, she didn't see any shark…. Suddenly the large nurse shark swam out of his deep crevice on the left side. Terri had not noticed him before that moment.

He turned, his small black beady eye looking at Terri as he passed by. His tail whipped as he swam in a tight circle. With his very small teeth housed in an even smaller mouth, he wasn't exactly a fatal threat to Terri, but he did feel threatened and trapped. He began to circle wildly in the small cavern, showing his discontent.

His long body seemed longer, his small beady black eyes looked menacing as they eyed Terri. She rose to the surface and inflated her buoyancy compensator. She couldn't swim through there now, that shark was pissed. She didn't know what he could do to her, but she wasn't about to find out. She had to get out of the water by going another way.

"Damn it! I hate that!" Terri shouted. She attached her strobe light to the camera, lifting it up and setting it on a stable rock above. As she began to slowly climb out of her little cavern, the weight of the tank pulled on her back. She held on, hoping she could make it all the way up the rocky slope, coming out of weightlessness. She climbed up and around to the other side of the cove. All that was a lot of work, but she wasn't about to swim back through that crevice. Everyone was laughing at her endeavor. But she didn't care what anyone was saying or calling her, she didn't like the way that shark looked at her. She had seen the look in his eyes.

****

Terri was making herself laugh out loud as she thought about that story and how silly she was. *Finally some laughter.* It had been a while since Terri had laughed, really laughed from deep in her heart. She got up, went to the refrigerator, and pulled out the last beer. Then she put the round cartridge filled with slides on the projector. She dimmed the lights and watched the show.

She even gave it a title, which she spoke aloud now: "This was a long, long time ago. This was your life." Then she announced each slide to herself aloud as she clicked through. As she was watching, Terri laughed, drank, cried, eventually becoming a sobbing mess, wondering what had become of her life.

She got up, turned it all off, including the lights, and went to go lay in bed.

With the shutters tightly closed, it was dark in her room. Whatever time it was, she was done, ready for bed before the end of the afternoon. Life wasn't exactly over, she just didn't know how to live it now.

VOLUME THREE: RAPTIS TRILOGY

****

12

Kendra woke up in her luxurious bedroom. She lay there, looking around at the carefully placed objects d'art, wondering who had decorated the place. She thought about her vacation trip so far. They had never ventured out the day before or the other days preceding, and now she was literally going stir crazy.

She could never find the right time to ask her father when he was going to pay her back the money he owed her. Now she was beginning to wonder whether he had forgotten he borrowed it. Maybe he was going to surprise her with a large wad of cash when it was time for her to leave. She remembered when her mom used to do that. *Used to....*

Her dad's friend, Joe, came over early in the afternoon every day. He would bring some kind of prepared food and drinks to share with them. Fried chicken, sometimes half a casserole, and that was all they had to eat. They never had any food in the refrigerator, so they didn't cook at the house. When she asked her dad why, he just answered, "Why bother, Joe is taking care of us."

Joe would bring bags of junk food, potato chips and cheap pretzels, for them to snack on until the next day when he would come back with more. During the day while Joe was there, Joe and her dad would just sit around fanning themselves as they asked Kendra questions about her mom, Terri, and what "good old Terri" was up to.

They could see Kendra was growing more and more restless. "Not a good day for the beach," they would tell her every day as they looked out into the passage during the morning hours.

Kendra never saw what they were looking at to determine this. Sure, it was beautiful up there at the house, but it was not exactly the tropical sandy beach she had been looking forward to lying on. At least there was that garden of serenity she had discovered at the house on her first day there. But now she realized it was just a well maintained garden with a hardscape down to the wooden pier. Her expectations of visiting her rich father on the islands for fun let alone real serenity were now blown.

Not that it wasn't inviting to a teenager to just lie around and lounge in the shade. But most of the time, she was forced, out of politeness, to sit at a table under an umbrella. She pretty much had to do this all day every day, sit there and drink water, laughing when it was what she was expected to be doing. *Sure, it was alright to do a bit of laughing with these two good old guys about some kind of good old days they remembered, but a bit of this was enough.* Kendra was now so bored with it that she dreaded walking out of her room in the morning.

She then realized that she couldn't take one more day of this.

****

Joe showed up early, very early that morning. He wanted to know if Rick had learned anything new and to figure out what their next steps would be.

"This isn't what you said it would be, Rick," Joe complained. "That little bitch, she turns out to be just as big a liar as her mom."

Rick bit his lip. He just couldn't get any information out of the girl. And now they were out of money and the food supply at Joe and Peg's place was getting low. The casseroles were going to have to become more and more creative, stretching the last of the groceries they had bought with Kendra's money, that money she had "loaned" Rick.

"You've been led on." Joe lifted his cloth hanky up to his nose and blew hard. He folded it into a square and wiped the sweat off his brow

"Once again. I'm asking you—why would she lie about stuff like that? All those pictures, all the stories on Facebook. That wasn't, it couldn't have been, all made up."

"You know, it could all just be bullshit, a teenage fantasy world to show off to her friends." Joe held out papers for Rick to see. "Peg ran every credit report on Terri, checked out everything she possibly could. If she does have any money, she's hiding it and very well. She's got a list of creditors longer than this." Joe spread his two hands far apart, suggesting they couldn't get any wider. "They're all trying to get at her." He wiped his dripping nose on his sleeve. "We've spent the last of our money getting that little bitch down here. How much cash do you think she has left in that purse?"

"I don't know, she doesn't leave it out of her sight for very long. It was hard enough lifting the wallet out to look at it the other day, and no time, couldn't count it. I grabbed a twenty."

"Well, at least little Kendra's got good credit, just young and no job! I couldn't find anything else on her."

Rick stroked his chin, his eyebrow cocked to the side. "How're we going to get her to talk? I don't want to rough my own daughter up."

"We've got four more days before she finds out that all you got her was just a one-way ticket, that the separate return ticket was forged. We're gonna have to do something." Joe grinned at the thought of slapping that innocent teenage smirk off her face, demanding answers. Truth was, he was really too much of a coward and inherently gentle inside. He just talked big and liked to think he was a tough guy.

"Shut up Joe, I'm thinking. We have to be outta here in less than those four days. I don't want him to catch on that we're here. I hope anybody we don't know about doesn't swing by and find us here."

"Relax, Rick. Don't worry about the fat man coming by. He's too lazy and frankly pretty weird from what I understand. He would never make the thirty minute boat drive over here to check on his own property. And if he does, I'll have Peg make sure to keep him busy while we tidy up and get out. But still, now we've got to make this thing we're doing happen, and fast."

****

Joe was right about fast.

Peg and Joe had been together for years, childhood friends from Long Island. They were never married but considered themselves married in every way. They were drifting grifters, bonding with Rick years ago, latching on to what money he had had. Always promising a bigger than average return, Peg and Joe had been wrong so many times. And Rick had watched his money dwindle, slowly at first, then faster and faster the bigger the schemes got.

Peg with her smile and stunning natural good looks had administrative ways and always managed to work her way into a job somewhere. Joe never had that kind of luck. He admired Peg and treated her like the queen he knew she was. He kept using his skills and wit to find the next golden goose to pluck. And now they were plucking Rick for Terri's money, plucking right through Terri's little Kendra. Rick was broke, he didn't have anything else but this now.

Joe and Peg, and now also Rick, were in a mess up to their necks now. Peg was working at a small real estate office on the island. She managed, bought, and sold the large mansion getaways springing up through the island. It was every rich man's folly or write off, his large dream vacation home—or hideout.

Using stolen information, Joe and Peg had borrowed into the equity on many of the homes they managed, continuing their lavish lifestyle, borrowing from one to pay back another. Rick had gotten involved, deeply involved. The three of them, plus whatever girlfriend Rick could find at the time, would go sailing or vacationing somewhere different each week. They'd rent or just borrow themselves a boat and then sell boat rides to tourists. Rick always wowed their customers with good times and great stories while they bought him drinks, lent him money, did things for him.

Joe, Peg, and their "friend" Rick had managed to live this life of rock stars for quite a while, that is until they finally stole the wrong identity. What had appeared to be a harmless rich wife with more money than God, someone who would never take a moment to notice some of the money disappearing, turned out to be the wife of a vicious drug lord.

It was quite a situation. The rich wife had insisted her vicious drug lord husband take the house on the secluded island, even though he detested the sun and the color it would leave on her porcelain skin. But it did prove to be secluded—too secluded. She used that house to rendezvous with another man, another

VOLUME THREE: RAPTIS TRILOGY

****

drug lord, and when her husband found out, he was too humiliated. Now that she had been quietly missing for over a year and presumed dead, he was in a hurry to sell. Break all ties to the deceit, and to her, the deceiver.

But Joe, Peg, and Rick had borrowed well over a half million dollars on that house. And at the moment, they had no other house to borrow against to pay it back, and nothing they could take without anyone else noticing. Now the hammer was coming down on them hard, and the grift quickly unraveling. They needed a half million dollars and right away. This is where Terri came into the picture, into their picture anyway: Rick had Joe and Peg convinced that his ex-wife, yes Terri, could get them out of trouble. He told them she was worth millions.

Their plan had unfolded as they used the information they lifted out of Kendra's wallet to look into Terri. But alas, Terri was broke. Worse than that, Terri owed everyone money.

So now the wicked dilemma was getting worse. They had Kendra, Rick's sixteen year old daughter, and they had no means or money to send her on her way, to get her back home.

****

Kendra stretched her torso and stepped out of the house onto the back patio. It was another stunning morning. She had her mask and fins in her hands. She was determined to make her own adventure that day, with or without her dad. She was going to swim around that point to the left, and that was that. After all, this was *her* vacation. The water looked to be deep out there around the corner, so maybe there would be something interesting for her to see. Certainly, just about anything would be more interesting than this place had become, because here no one wanted to do anything but sit around!

Kendra could hear her dad up early with that friend of his, Joe. She grimaced as she heard Joe sniff and blow his nose. She knew the next thing he'd do was fold his handkerchief in a square and wipe his brow. *Ugh.* She was having a hard time standing just the sight of Joe.

Kendra went around the house, following their voices, which she found were coming from inside the garage. "Dad? Dad?" She knocked lightly while turning the knob, helping herself in.

The two men looked up, like little boys caught secretly doing something bad, when the door opened and she walked in.

"What are you guys doing in here?"

"Nothing, Cupcake, nothing." Her dad quickly walked over and shuffled her back out through the door.

"Going for a swim with me?" Kendra asked hopefully.

Joe stayed behind in the garage as the father and daughter walked away. The paranoia started to grow in Joe's head as he wondered how long Kendra had been standing on the other side of the door. *What exactly did she hear?*

"No, no, I'm sorry Cupcake, can't go swimming right now. Daddy has too much work to do today!"

Daddy? Now he's my "Daddy?" No thanks, just "Dad" is fine, and maybe just "Rick" is good enough, Kendra thought to herself.

"What kind of work is it you do? You don't even have an office here. No internet or computer?" Kendra's hands were on her hips as she spoke. She doubted her dad even had a job as he still had not paid her back the money he owed her. She also thought the homemade sweet sixteen birthday card he fashioned for her out of an older tourist magazine cover was, let's face it, downright lame. She had graciously pretended she liked it, but this whole thing was getting ridiculous, even if it was a free vacation.

"I'm a businessman, Cupcake. I go out and do my business. So now Joe and I have to go into town. I'm afraid I'm gonna have to ask you to stay here this time, I don't know how long we'll be." He turned and walked away.

She stood there silently with her mask and fins in hand as he headed back through the door to his stupid sniffling friend in the garage. She heard the automatic garage door open and the car back out.

She finally said it out loud. She had wanted to say it for a while now: "Fuck you!"

But Rick and Joe didn't hear Kendra as they were driving off.

13

Kendra looked out across to the passage. The water seemed calm, really inviting. The light turquoise color over the bright white sandy bottom below called her name. She shielded her eyes like a visor and nervously made a plan by herself. Her plan was simple—snorkel down the shoreline. It was hard to tell exactly how deep it got out there. The sandy bottom would be boring, but maybe she would see some live seashells, maybe a conch or two walking around. It would be fun.

She looked out to the left point. *What's around that corner?* She could see the dark blue water line, it appeared there was a deep drop-off of some kind.

Once down at the water, Kendra removed her sandals and placed them neatly on the edge of the low pier. She sat down on the edge of the pier and put her fins on. She stepped into the water looking outward.

There was no one for as far as she could see, she was all alone in paradise. She rubbed the liquid dots of anti-fog around the inside of her diving mask lens. She hated the practice of everyone spitting in their masks to keep them from fogging up. That was completely unnecessary and well worth the five dollars it cost to buy anti-fog. She was glad she had brought it.

She was ready to get wet. Her mom's face suddenly flashed in her memory. She was getting ready to break her mom's rule by going out by herself. *What she won't know won't hurt her.* This was Kendra's summer of independence.

She splashed water up on to herself, relieving her of the heat setting in overhead. She adjusted the mask on her face and dropped forward into the water. The coolness brought instant relief to her lightly tanned skin.

She floated face down. The water was five feet deep and the sun's rays sparkled and danced on the white sand below. Bright blue damselfish darted out from the pier's pilings. They looked for something new to peck at as they investigated the hairs floating upward on her arms.

She swam out to the left. The water was like a gentle bathtub. She quickly became mesmerized by the underwater scene below. There was so much to see, such beauty. She saw two live conch walking slowly through the sea grass, a long path through the sand behind them. She spotted a small yellow seahorse hanging on to a blade of the sea grass with his tail, his body at an angle with the current. She watched him let go and float with the current. She was finally able to enjoy a bit of this vacation.

She was too busy watching the scene down below to look up. The scenery began to move by faster and faster as she floated along looking for live seashells. She wasn't paying attention at all to where she was. All of the sudden she began to notice a big difference in the underwater landscape. The water became a dark blue green. It seemed that, within but a moment, she had watched the bottom drop out from beneath her.

****

It was a sudden and deep drop off, like an underwater gorge, dropping below some seventy-five feet. She could see large mysterious looking volcanic outcroppings. A large grouper sat in a crevice, staring at her as she floated by. A large barracuda swam by, spooking her. She lifted her head to see where she was. She was surprised to find herself drifting away in the strong current, drifting out to the center of the passage.

The large white house she had left that morning was now a small white dot in the distance. She turned around three hundred-sixty degrees, looking at her options as she kept floating further away. There was a small deserted island on the other side of the passage, out there on one side of her, pretty far off though. But the island she had just floated from was now far behind. She couldn't see any houses or any roads on either island. She could see a small patch of white sand further up the island that she had come from. She realized that the current had taken her all the way around the corner, and had swept her all the way around the left point.

"Oh no! Oh no!" Kendra shouted to herself, into her snorkel. She had her head up out of the water, with her eyes opened wide. She tread water anxiously as she was drifting on so quickly, trying not to panic. She put her head back down and tried to see the bottom. But now the sea had given way to darkness, she couldn't see the bottom. She talked to herself out loud to keep from panicking. There was something about the dark she hated.

Don't swim against the current, don't swim against it, she reminded herself. *Diagonal, diagonal, relax, relax, you'll get there. You'll get there!* She remembered her mother's words from a diving lesson long ago. She focused on her breath and the efficiency of her kick, trying not to think about the darkness below her there on the bottom, and blocking out any thoughts of what might be swimming down there. She could make out shapes moving deep below, but they weren't clear. *Don't panic.*

Her mind drifted as she struggled with the current, her arms growing heavy. It was hard for her not to think of how stupid she was. Her mom was going to be so pissed off, so pissed that she was out swimming all alone. *But mom won't know.* No one was watching or knowing where she was, no one knew her itinerary. She was all alone. *Watching … watching—oh my God! What if there is a shark watching me!* She started kicking with a splashing panic toward the shore line, giving it all she had. *Shut your eyes, don't look down, don't look down!*

With her body now awash in an adrenaline rush, fight or flight took over. She couldn't stop, the terror consumed her. Gasping for her breath, her eyes were shut as she kicked hard toward the shore. She prayed hard, promising over and over that she would be a good girl, a very good girl, if she could just get to the shore alive.

A small surface wave where the currents mixed pushed her up and into a large volcanic rock jutting up from the shoreline. She didn't see it coming with her eyes closed, kicking in a panic. Her mask was pushed upward and her arms scraped on the rough edge of the rock. She held on, trying to catch her breath.

Kendra finally opened her eyes to see where she was. On the other side of the large rock was more of that comforting, calm, bright turquoise water. She could see the bottom, white sand again. As soon as she regained her strength, she repositioned her mask and headed for the light blue water, swimming like an athlete diagonally through the current. Being able to see the bottom again gave her the confidence she needed to reach the shore.

****

"I made it!" She cried out as she reached the white beach. She plopped down on the white coral sand, exhausted, so tired she didn't care that there wasn't a beach towel between her skin and the earth. The immediate heat felt good, rewarding, as she had been starting to get chilled in the deeper water.

She looked back at the length of her journey. The point which had been far off to her left when she had started out was now far off to the right. She couldn't see her dad's white house but knew it was a long swim, now a swim against the current, to get "home." She was stranded on the sandy beach.

"Now what am I going to do?" Kendra looked around at her surroundings, wondering what to do as her great thirst began to set in. The afternoon heat from the sun, now straight up above, was at its most intense. She had no immediate cover, nor shoes to wear to walk for help through any of the underbrush she was going to have to go through. There were coconut trees for some shade, a not too distant walk, but after that, well there was no path through the underbrush. And she didn't have any clothing on to protect her skin.

She sat there stuck, lost, looking out to the passage. She was exhausted. She laid back and closed her eyes, the heat lulling her into a deep sleep.

VOLUME THREE: RAPTIS TRILOGY
****

14

"Kendra! Kendra!" The men were shouting out as they walked around the opposite sides of the house.

"Come on, Cupcake! We've got some dinner for you!" They had searched every room of the house twice looking for her. The men had been gone almost all day, for over six hours. They were both mentally drained, and now, one more incident to deal with.

The gated entrance to the drive was closed, it would have been open if she had left that way on foot. Everything else was just as they had left it. Could the man they'd been talking to just an hour ago have been that swift?

They had lost track of the time at the office with Peg. She had been busy emailing, calling, doing what she could to convince the owner of the house it was not the right time to sell. There were other options she could offer him, she told him over and over.

The next phone call, she tried to tell him how important keeping that house would be, as an investment. He should wait one more year, the return would be so much greater, she insisted. But this was all to no avail, their time was up. They had now pushed the limit of his small patience, he was done.

He wanted the house sold immediately at any price, he didn't care. He only cared about distancing himself from the past, and quickly. He was insisting the house be sold right away and all profits deposited in his Swiss bank account upon completion of the sale.

****

Of course the owner hadn't explained that the house had come to him for nothing. It had been compensation for a large drug deal that was hijacked. With no way to prove who was behind that highjacking, splitting the loss was a gracious olive branch from the other drug lord. He thought the other drug lord was being quite gracious with this offer.

Actually, including the house in the settlement had been his wife's idea. Unfortunately for him, he had never questioned how she knew the house existed. At her insistence, he had taken the other drug lord's olive branch for what it seemed, a good offer, a good compromise.

This is how he had let his competition have control of three distant islands and the activities out there that he had been eyeing. Neither of these two drug lords had wanted a war with each other, nor had either of them wanted any more unnecessary eyes watching them or paying attention to any of their other activities.

It turned out that his beautiful wife, who he thought reveled in his eccentricities, had played both sides quite smoothly. She had manipulated him as well as his competition. He had been taken. Horrified once he found out, he did away with her rather than let his competition have her. He then turned much more of his attention to his "doll collection," as he had decided to call it. These were other women, women he had collected and stored, women who all obeyed his demands even more now. Now his eccentricities and compulsions grew bigger and grander, and took him over.

****

Rick and Joe searched every room for Kendra, calling out her name. Then they came to her room. They saw that her personal belongings were still in her room, that her stuff was untouched and neatly stacked, just the way she had left it, all organized as was her style. An alarm started ringing in their heads and Rick began to panic. His heart strings were being tugged on just a bit now, which surprised Rick and worried Joe a little. Rick caring about this kid, this kid he called his daughter now, wasn't part of the plan.

"He's got her, he came to this house, saw her and took her!" Rick insisted, "He took my Kendra!"

Joe looked around for other possibilities, he wasn't convinced. Everything appeared untouched, there were no signs of struggle anywhere. Joe looked over at Rick, who was giving him a paranoid suspicious look, then he pulled his hanky out and blew his red nose again. He folded that hanky neatly into a little square and wiped the sweat off his brow. "Hey, don't look at me, I've been with you the whole time. I didn't do this."

"Yeah, yeah."

Joe's nose started to drip again. "I hate these damn fucking tropics, I'm allergic to everything." Joe opened the hanky back up and blew, starting his ritual all over again. There were no signs of Kendra, no signs of trouble. *If she did walk away, how far could she go?*

They had just driven back from the town. Going twenty-five miles per hour on that long and slow winding road, they would have seen her. There was nothing for miles and miles the other way down the road, nothing except for two other large homes with long private driveways, and they were miles away. She would still be walking or turning back.

They walked out into the backyard calling out her name, sitting down to rest. The late afternoon trade winds blew the words back toward the house as they yelled. The sun was beginning to tip westward toward the sea, it would be setting in two hours. They called out and then listened, they heard nothing but the gentle lap of water against the wooden pier.

They were looking out, scanning the water when Rick noticed the sandals. There they were, women's sandals lined up next to each other on the side of the pier. They were flat and tan colored so at first glance, they blended in. Rick looked out to the sea and across the passage, scanning the waters for any sign of Kendra. A look of concern came over his face, concern and fear at the thought of Kendra swimming out to the left or to the right. Either direction was dangerous. The surface currents in the passage during a tidal exchange could prove deadly.

"Joe! Get the keys and then get in the boat. We're going to go look for her." Rick was already climbing in, getting ready.

"Gas Rick, we need gas." Getting angry, Joe stood on the dock, unwilling to participate. "Check the gauge. Remember? We couldn't afford much gas to get you to St. Todos and back. I don't think we have much left." Joe wasn't a big fan of the small speedboat, or of anything moving on the water for that matter. He preferred the shore.

"Dammit Joe, don't be a pussy, we have to look! She's got to be out there somewhere! I just know it!"

Joe couldn't move fast enough for Rick as he watched the angle of the sun growing closer to the sea. "We don't have much time."

The engine started and Joe was right, there was less than a quarter tank of gas. That wasn't much gas for a search and rescue. They would have just enough gas to explore one way, or the other, but not both. That was the hardest decision. Go to the left? Or go to the right? Which way did she go?

Rick watched the water's surface, thinking, trying to guess Kendra's direction. He was looking for currents, as he was a sailor, or at least he used to be. He looked up to the small slice of moon hanging in the distant sky, ready to take over for the night. Currents, what are the currents doing? He studied the ripples of the moving water. "The current would be moving hard to the left," Rick concluded confidently.

Joe pulled his hanky out and blew.

****

Rick had been an expert sailor in his younger years. His parents had died in a car accident leaving him an orphan at age thirteen. He had turned his hurt and pain, as had many others, to the mother sea. She was the true mother of us all. He had cried away his tears in the sea's salty enveloping arms, which made the saltwater coming out of his own eyes make more sense. All the pain became just part of it all.

Rick's parents had had enough of a life insurance policy to make Rick interesting to adoptive parents: he came with his own small trust fund. He had always lived by the ocean, and had insisted on staying near the sea back then and for as much of his life as possible. His new parents had easily gone along with this.

Rick never learned to work, all he did was learn to sail. It was his passion. Everything he had went into sailing. He had had mentors, good ones. He had crewed on other boats and raced. By eighteen he was able to leave the foster care system. He bought his very own sailboat, determined to take charge of his own life and of what remained of his trust fund. That's exactly what he did.

He had sailed around each sea, taking his time, falling in love with the different cultures and people, sometimes with women, never attaching to anyone or anything except the ocean. He had followed boat racing circuits and made extra money crewing as his cash flow began to dwindle.

Rick had planned to be on St. Todos that fateful spring night, fateful for Terri anyway. There he had found the famous and wealthy Terri he had heard about; that night she was just the sad drunken girl at the end of the bar. *Ripe for the picking*, he had told himself. He knew that was the night to make his move. He had made it his mission to do what it would take to make her get involved with him.

It wasn't long before he was able to slip a little something into her drink. She was quite distracted, vulnerable, depressed, and already drinking. He was intrigued by her attitude, and her look. He had asked her what she was doing there all alone.

"I don't know, I'm making a mess of things. Maybe it's too late to fix. Maybe I'm throwing it all to the wind, watching which way it blows," she had said almost desperately. She confessed she was about to marry her best friend in the whole world and for some reason she was still unhappy inside, even though she knew she loved him. She was so nervous and so confused. Terrified.

Rick had listened closely, and watched carefully. There was something in her desperation and confusion he recognized. He could read her like a book. He would close in on his prey with care. Then would come "magical" kiss and then the "shocking" dare to live. And with this, Terri would be reeled in, that was that.

Terri wasn't herself that night, and she knew it. But she was feeling so lost that not being herself felt normal. He helped her to his boat. She passed out there.

****

When she awoke, they were already out at sea. Things were magical for a while, spellbinding even. At least for Terri. Rick's motives were not obvious to her, she had no idea what he wanted. She had no idea what all he knew about her.

The months immediately after this night became a string of one incredible day after another as they sailed clockwise around the Caribbean. The fun never stopped until the belly started to bulge too much and Terri's constant uncomfortableness set in.

She couldn't sit on the bow any longer, couldn't be looking out at a sunrise or a sunset without thinking of the future, and the baby. But Rick had never signed up for any of that. He was confused with the unplanned early pregnancy. He had never even given that kind of responsibility any thought. He always did whatever pleased him whenever it pleased him. He never thought about wanting kids, let alone having one.

VOLUME THREE: RAPTIS TRILOGY

****

15

The boat sped out to the center then veered to the left. Rick was behind the wheel.

Joe held on real tight for his life, looking through the binoculars up the shoreline. "This is pretty far down Rick, you don't think she'd swim this far, do you?" Joe sniffed and wiped his nose. The binoculars were hard to look through as the boat bounced and Joe was getting queasy.

Rick instinctively looked at his watch, worrying about the gas and the amount of sunlight left, trying not to pay attention to Joe's whining.

They made it out to the left point. There Rick maneuvered to the middle of the channel and put the boat in neutral, letting the current speak to him.

Joe sniffed and watched as Rick was deep in thought.

The currents were swift. The boat whirled in a small eddy. They began moving through the passage with the engine in neutral. The currents took them further around the point.

"There she is! There she is!" Joe was pointing past Rick's face toward the shore. He could see what he thought was Kendra there at the shoreline. She had seen a boat from afar and was standing up waving. They were relieved to see her as they raced over.

Rick put the boat in neutral and commanded Joe to take the wheel, jumping in and wading over to her. Her skin was sunburnt red. She was shivering from the exposure and dehydrated. She started crying when he waded up to her.

"I just wanted to go diving, I just wanted to do something," she cried.

Rick removed his smelly shirt and made her put it on despite her objections, it was icky dirty. He needed to get her out of the sun. He hoisted her into the boat and climbed in, racing back to the house.

He made her eat aspirin and drink a lot of water. She hurt all over, her skin burned and ached, including her scalp, which was red and inflamed. Rick did his best with a freshly squeezed aloe concoction he made to bring her relief. He had her rub it all over, including on her head.

They gave her a stiff drink to help with the pain. She felt sick and wanted to go lay on the soft bed. There she could lay flat and relax with the fan spinning above. It took her awhile to fall asleep as she cried silently for her mommy....

"We cannot risk leaving her here one more day alone, Joe, it's too dangerous." Rick wasn't sure what to do. He was fighting his natural instincts that were telling him to run or sail far away, to leave this side show called Joe and Peg. But he had to stay there, he had to now for Kendra, his *daughter of all things*.

"She appears to be a danger to herself." Joe sniffed as he tried to think. "You don't think it's a bigger risk bringing her into town with us? We don't know if we're being watched."

"I think it's less risk...." Rick felt a new weight on his shoulders, one relating to having his daughter there, and this was hard on him, this was too much. He had never had to be a dad before.

Rick had followed Joe and Peg for so long now that he had lost his own voice, he was always outvoted. What was he supposed to do with this strange protective feeling now? He was the one responsible for the idea of using his daughter to squeeze more money out of his ex-wife, he had come up with this in their desperation, in Joe's and Peg's desperation. Now Rick looked over at Joe who would have no problem placing Kendra on a street corner and walking away. Rick bit his lip, wondering if that would be best, thinking maybe Kendra might be safer that way – safer all alone than with the three of them.

It had all started out so harmless. In the beginning of their work together, it had even seemed magical with Joe and Peg. Rick remembered the tingle he felt when the first large chunk of money had appeared with little or no effort. With a flick of the pen, a signature here, a signature there, more houses were leveraged, and or swapped and sold. No one would ever notice, at least not for a very long time and by then they would be long gone. Rick had grown addicted to the ease of stealing from the über rich and had gone all in on Joe and Peg's grifts.

****

The sun was up and Kendra still lay in bed. The fresh aloe had helped sooth the pain last night, but today was a different day. She lay on her back in pain, then she painfully rolled to her stomach with her face leaning off the bed so it wouldn't touch the sheets. She knew she had to stay out of the sun with this dangerous sunburn, not just for today but for the remainder of her trip.

She was awake when her dad knocked on the door. Frustrated, she made him knock twice before letting him in.

"Good morning, Cupcake," he walked in with a glass of water and more fresh aloe, it was all they had in the house.

"Morning." Kendra was sullen, looking out the window and so wanting to be out in the morning sun. Her bright red back faced her dad.

"I know you've got to be exhausted, Cupcake, but today we've got to go into town."

She turned around quickly, her bright red skin stinging as she moved. "Ouch!" She looked right at him. She wanted to cross her arms but couldn't because her skin hurt too much.

"What do you mean, we need to go to town? Really?! Again?!" she shouted, letting it all out. "What kind of vacation did you plan for me anyway?" Her anger was beginning to well up past the point of containment, she couldn't control it. "Look at me. I'm in pain! And what the hell is going on with you and your slimy friend?" She held her finger up below her nose and made a mocking sniff, sniff, sniff sound. "Joe!" She shouted Joe's name out at Rick.

Rick stood there in silence. Hearing Kendra go off took him back sixteen years. This was like being married to her mother, all over again. He reacted. "OK, so here's the way it is, Miss Perfect. You're going to get dressed, do what it is you do, and then you're coming with us. We're going into town, we leave in fifteen minutes." Rick wasn't going to take no for an answer, he couldn't. Now he was seeing red and it wasn't her back. He had nothing left to lose, his world was closing in by the minute.

****

As Rick slammed the door shut, Kendra shouted back at him. "Miss Perfect!? I should have stayed home with my mother!"

She emerged from the bedroom forty minutes later, and slowly. She had painfully changed her clothes four times trying to figure out what fabric and design was going to hurt the least when she bent her arms and legs.

"It's about damn time!" Joe blurted out when he saw her. He had absolutely no patience or compassion left for her, none whatsoever. *This fuckin' kid….*

Rick was mad in all directions. Mad at Kendra for her attitude, and equally growing more and more angry with Joe, his "business" partner. Rick saw no end to all this, no way out of this mess. And now, every time Joe sniffed, Rick wanted to punch Joe's red dripping nose to make it stop.

"You can ride in the front, Cupcake." Rick opened the door for her. As he did, he was staring Joe down, while Joe was trying to cut in front of Kendra.

"Thank you," she murmured. She didn't want to speak to Rick. Carefully, slowly climbing in, she tried not to bend her knees or elbows. Rick handed her an aloe leaf wrapped in cellophane. He had cut the leaf in half and wrapped it in a napkin so she could soothe her burns as they rode in the car. "Here, just keep smoothing this on while we're driving."

She took it from him. "Thank you," she half murmured. She didn't want to look at him, or have him call her Cupcake anymore. And the more she thought about it, the more she was done calling him "Dad." All she wanted to do now was go home.

VOLUME THREE: RAPTIS TRILOGY

****

16

"Hello, sweetheart," the woman said while she smacked at her chewing gum. "I've heard so much about you." Peg walked over to give Kendra a semi-fake hug. She couldn't help but notice the painful sunburn, and she awkwardly put her arms out but didn't want to touch. "Your dad has been so happy to get to know you."

Kendra stood there. *So this was Joe's other half? Wow, she was actually shorter than little old Joe. And that obnoxious gum chewing, she probably started that to drown out the sound of Joe's constant sniffing. Or maybe Joe started sniffing to drown out that smacking sound. A perfect match.*

Kendra carefully lifted and extended her once neatly groomed hand to ward the lady away from her. Her French manicure was half worn off now. She had a broken nail, bright red skin, and a coral scraped elbow.

"Nice to meet you," was all Kendra could muster while she made it known she did not feel like participating in a hug.

Peg shook Kendra's hand lightly instead.

Kendra looked around at the small but nicely furnished office. Pictures of beautiful mansions graced the wall. Fresh flowers, a few books, and a computer! *Yes! A computer!* "Dad, I want to go home. I see the computer, will you change my flight?" She looked at the others as they stared at her. "I'm sorry Dad—or Rick, I'll just call you Rick—but this just wasn't what I expected."

It wasn't what the other three expected either. The three looked at each other.

This conversation wasn't in their plans. They didn't have a real return ticket, nor did they have the cash or means to get her one.

Now Joe couldn't take it anymore. He started to panic as Peg stood there, snapping and gnawing at the ball of gum in her mouth. Joe leaned in toward Kendra, threatening, "You're not going anywhere until we get what we need!"

Kendra looked at Joe in shock. And she looked at the other two as well. They looked as shocked as Kendra: Joe's outburst was not in any plan either.

Joe moved right up to Kendra, a few inches away from her. "You're going to sit down, shut up, and empty that purse," Joe demanded, grabbing Kendra's purse from her. He then poured its contents out onto the desk.

"Joe! Be nice!" Peg's instinct was to defend the young girl.

"Shut up, Peg, shut up," Joe demanded, again wiping his nose then blowing, then quickly folding the hanky and wiping his brow.

"Look Joe—" Rick stepped forward to put in his two cents.

"And don't you ever, ever tell me to get in the back seat again!" Joe was screaming now, "especially not behind this little snot-nosed brat!" Joe began going through Kendra's belongings, grabbing her wallet and opening it. He pulled out the last of the cash and counted it. "We're gonna need this."

Kendra was in shock, stunned. She scrambled on the desk for her return plane ticket. She had seen it fall out of her purse. "I just want to go home." She got this out before she started to cry.

Peg walked over to Kendra, smacking her gum. Peg tried to put an arm around her, but Kendra pulled away.

"I said you're not going anywhere," Joe scowled and pointed his finger at her.

Rick sat down and looked the other way. He couldn't look at Kendra now, not the way Joe was speaking to her. He wasn't ready to her tell Kendra everything, but he did say, "You don't have a return ticket."

"Yes I do." Kendra searched the desk again, but then she saw that Joe had the ticket in his hand.

"This is a fake, a forgery." He waved it at her. "You see, we only had enough money to get you here."

Kendra stood there listening, confused about everything she was hearing.

"We need a half million dollars transferred to us, and you are going to get it for us." Joe got to the point.

"Me?" Kendra pointed to herself in disbelief.

"Yes, you'll get it from your mother," Joe insisted while he tried to resist the urge to sniff. All eyes were on him.

"My mother? She doesn't have anything."

"Well, you made a point of telling us otherwise. Everything we look at, she comes up broke. Where and how is she hiding her money?"

Now Kendra burst out laughing. The joke was on them—*What the hell*?! "My mother's broke!" she shouted out, still laughing at the trio. "She doesn't have anything! I just didn't want you to think she was such a loser. She can't even hold a job!!!"

Kendra continued laughing as the three looked at each other. All their suspicions were now confirmed. *Now what?*

Joe's face turned red.

"We'll be back, we have to talk." Joe looked at Peg and Rick, giving them the "let's go" look and pointing his head toward the door. He then looked at Kendra and ordered, "You stay here."

"What if someone comes?" Kendra stopped laughing.

"Lock the door and don't answer it, we'll be right back."

"I'm starving! When are we going to eat?"

"I said, we'll be back." Joe wasn't sure what they were going to do as they took the last of her money and left her standing there.

Peg turned the key from the outside, locking her in.

As soon as they turned the corner, Kendra sat down at the computer and turned it on. She glanced out the window to see and hear the three of them walking away to the car, arguing, shouting.

Rick had a very angry look on his face. "I know Terri still has that money clip, that one medallion. It's worth a small fortune, no way she would have sold it, it's somewhere. She always said she would never sell it. No matter what." Rick was convinced they had to lure Terri to the island, and get her to bring the medallion with her.

****

The computer in the office was an older model. Kendra had to wait impatiently for it to fire on so she could get to the internet. It felt like it took forever. All the while, she continued looking over her shoulder, watching.

She found the internet program and double clicked. *Shit.* No immediate response. She was about to double click again with impatience when she heard the ancient *oh-ee-oh* of a dial-up service. Rolling her eyes, she waited until she could finally use her computer skills to bypass everything and get to her email account.

There. Quick. New message. She started typing the first thing that came into her head, she had so much to say: "Help! Don't tell my mom but I'm being held hostage for money, a half million dollars. I don't know where I am, I don't have any money. I need help to get out of here!"

There was a loud knock on the door.

Kendra turned around and saw through the window a very large framed man. He had sunglasses covering his eyes as he stood at the door. She raised her finger up to suggest she would be a minute and tried to continue: "I don't know exactly where I am being kept. I need help. I don't have any money." But in her rush she deleted that part that by mistake, and started writing more. She lost track of exactly what she had written.

The man impatiently banged on the door. She turned around and looked at him again, giving him the eye, she was busy.

"Just a minute!" she shouted. Unnerved, she quickly typed more so she could press send, taking no time to gather her thoughts: "I need help to get out of here! I am kidnapped! Right now I am locked in at Luxury Home Rentals and Sales, on

Route 16, on Grand Key, but they are taking me out of here soon. Help!"

She began to type her name when the man at the door, irritated at her apparent indifference, began to pound on the door quite hard. Kendra's shoulders raised up in anxiety as she tried to quickly finish her email. She pressed the "send to all" but didn't notice she forgot to remove her mother's email address from the list.

She gave a quick sigh of relief and got up, walking to the door. She told the man through the door that she was locked in, that she couldn't open the door. "I'm sorry, but the owners aren't here—"

Now the man began to throw his body against the door to break it open....

17

Terri woke up early, restless. She hadn't been very productive since Kendra had left on vacation, not at all productive. Now, Terri told herself, with one day left until Kendra's return, she sure had a mess to clean up. The whole house looked like an uncared for dorm room.

Dirty dishes were piled up next to the sink. Sweatshirt after sweatshirt was draped on the chairs and the couch. The trash cans were filled with used ice cream wrappers and cheap processed food boxes. The recycle bin was full with empty beer bottles carefully stacked and balanced six inches above the rim. Terri herself had gone on vacation to that exotic place called "the couch." She had sailed away on an ocean of self pity, and now it was time to come back to reality.

She surveyed the mess and began cleaning it up. An annuity check would be arriving that day and she would have money to grocery shop. Terri's dad had had the good sense to insist she take a portion of her remaining money and put it into an annuity type account. This assured her some kind of income every month to barely cover the most necessary bills, and some food and supplies, and this income proved invaluable.

Today was the day she would go grocery shopping and put some much needed diesel fuel into her old car. With half of the dishes washed and drying on the rack, she decided to reward herself with some computer time. She had been hoping each day that she might hear something, anything, from Kendra.

She was over the moon when she saw Kendra's name in the inbox. She clicked the icon and hoped for a fun picture of her on vacation in Oregon and read: "Help! Don't tell my mom but I'm being held hostage for money, a half million dollars. I don't know where I am, I don't have any money. I need help to get out of here! I am kidnapped! Right now I am locked in at Luxury Home Rentals and Sales, on Route 16, on Grand Key, but they are taking me out of here soon. Help!"

"Don't tell my mom?" Terri laughed as she repeated that line out loud. *Boy, these email hackers, what a hoot, "Don't tell my mom" indeed! They must have read all of Kendra's other e-mails, realizing Kendra didn't and hasn't been telling her mom anything for a long time! Grand Key? Where's that? Africa somewhere?*

Terri's mind spun on all of the scenarios of email hijacking she had heard about. "Who believes this stuff? And the dumb ass didn't even realize he sent the help note to her mom! Stupid hijackers, I wonder if Kendra knows." She was disappointed that was all there was, and no Kendra.

She looked through the rest of her mail, it was all junk, so she closed the program. She then played three games of solitaire before turning the computer off. *Shit, time to get back to cleaning.* She was sure everyone received the email that day, and everyone had had the same basic reaction—"Oops, poor girl had her email account hijacked."

****

Kendra's grandfather read that email and briefly considered calling Terri to make sure everything was OK. He never really knew what to expect from his daughter, but Kendra? She was never any trouble. His golf schedule took priority and he knew he would hear from Terri the next Sunday, like every other Sunday at eight o'clock in the morning.

Derek also received the email. He called Diane to see if she had received it as well. Could it possibly be real? Or was it just another stolen email account? Kendra was going to be flying home in one day. So all was probably OK. But the words "don't tell my mom" were particularly unsettling as Kendra had made both Derek and Diane take that oath several times already.

VOLUME THREE: RAPTIS TRILOGY

****

18

"Kendra? Kendra!" They had returned and found the front door broken open, the computer on, and Kendra gone.

"She did it again!" Joe knew it, he knew he couldn't trust her. He sniffed, then blew his nose hard. Then the folded hanky thing.

Peg's body sprung into an adrenaline rush, one she couldn't stop. Her anxiety had taken over and now she fretted out loud. "How far could that girl go? We took all of her money, she is severely burnt. She must have slipped right by us somehow."

Peg turned to the computer and began checking its history while frantically snapping at her gum. She couldn't get the computer to operate any faster. "She's been on email." Peg's fake acrylic fingernails clicked away on the keyboard.

"Damn it, now what!" Joe went over to the front door and stepped out, looking both ways. The trade winds hit his nose, and he sneezed.

Rick stepped out to Joe's side.

"We'll find her, stay cool…." Rick nodded at a passerby across the street. This was a small island and everyone knew everyone. Rick pulled Joe back inside. "You're starting to draw too much attention, you and all your fucking sniffing and blowing. It's getting on my nerves!"

Back inside, Rick told them, "Peg, you stay here in case she comes back. Joe you go to the left, look in every store and around every building. I'll go to the right. Don't spook her if you find her." Rick lifted a finger and pointed it at Joe. "I don't want any more trouble. Go." Rick took command.

Within half an hour the two men were back, not much further to look. It was a small street with few businesses. They realized that if she had taken off by foot and left town, it would actually be easier to search for her by car. They had a quarter tank of gas left. *Now which way to look?*

****

The large man had dragged Kendra out the door, then picked Kendra up kicking and screaming, then carried her down to the boat he had tied up to the small public dock across the street. All the people had turned their heads away, ignoring Kendra's pleas for help. They all knew of this man and did not want to be involved. They would keep their mouths shut.

This man tied Kendra to the boat. Then he took the boat straight to St. Todos where he knew his boss would be waiting at a private house out on the east end, an estate complete with its own private dock. A small private runway was not too far from the boss' house out there on the far end of the island, and that was enough for the boss to come and go from as he pleased, especially now.

Kendra did her best with her long fingernails to scrape them across any of the skin of the large man that she could reach. His grip and demeanor were quite painful. He brought her in, bound and gagged, carrying her over his shoulder to his boss, whose name was "Sir." "Careful, Sir," he said as he wiped at the scratch marks on his shoulder.

The unusual looking short pudgy man called "Sir" nodded back at him, looking her up and down. "Bannister, she is exquisite; I wasn't expecting such a beauty."

The large man, Bannister, pushed Kendra forward, offering her for further inspection.

Kendra froze.

The odd little man, Sir, turned her all the way around. "Yes, yes, yes, perfect," he hissed in a low tone, delighted at what he saw. "Her skin so naturally white, but it's burnt so bad. We must take care not to let it peel...." He tapped the fingers of both his hands together as he thought.

Kendra's head swirled as reality was setting in. Her bad vacation with her dishonest weird dad just got worse. And now, who was this ugly short fat man here, this so-called "Sir," and why was she bound and gagged before him? Trying not to panic, she looked around the room for any escape route, any way out. Bannister, who the short squat man had just called by name, was the size of a small interior wall as he stood over Kendra at her side. How was she ever going to get past this guy?

"Bring her to me, closer. Sit her down here, on my lap."

Kendra resisted the urge to vomit.

The pudgy man who Kendra was trying to think of as "Sir" patted his knee. Try as she did, Kendra couldn't help but name him "Pudgy" in her mind. She told herself to be careful not to call him Pudgy by mistake, it could infuriate him.

Bannister complied with Sir's order and brought Kendra closer.

Now Kendra struggled, trying to resist this Sir who in turn grew impatient with her and pointed to the chair next to him. "Let's make a phone call, then we will teach her some manners.... Gag her to start, Bannister."

******

The phone rang and the word "Private" appeared in the caller ID box. The three looked at each other, then Peg picked it up.

"Hello?" There was a short silence before she heard the familiar voice on the other end.

"She is quite beautiful, isn't she?"

Peg looked over at the men and whispered, "He has her!"

Peg pressed the speaker phone button and Rick exploded. "Let her go! She has nothing to do with any of this!"

"You give me one reason why I should let her go…." The man stroked Kendra's long brown hair and snapped his fingers. His assistant came to his side. "And I'll give you several why I won't." He put the phone on his shoulder as he gave Bannister orders. "Now, go get more of that fresh aloe, so I can watch you rub it on her back and shoulders. I want to see that beautiful porcelain skin underneath."

Her mouth was gagged now, she couldn't yell. She shot him a look as she sat with her hands tied in back of her. Her hands had been tied in front of her until the men had found it necessary to tie them back when she had started picking up glass objects and throwing them down, shattering them, demanding to be let go. They had gagged her to shut her up.

The man put the phone back up to his ear.

"She is so feisty this one, and naturally beautiful. With some taming, so to speak, she will be worth far more than that house to me. But I digress, let's talk about the house."

"Damn you!" Rick shouted into the phone. "I said she's just a kid, let her go!" Rick was getting louder and louder and growing more and more out of control.

The short squatty man laughed at Rick's efforts.

"Heh, was that Daddy? What kind of a father figure are you anyway? Poor thing hasn't eaten properly in days." With his hand never leaving the soft strands of Kendra's hair, he began to stroke her head and locks again.

She looked at his other pudgy hand as it was holding the receiver to his ear. Then she noticed the glistening nail polish on his neatly manicured fingernails. *Yikes! So what kinda guy does that?*

Even in that muted light, this man, who Bannister referred to as "Sir" for some reason Kendra could not understand, never removed his dark wraparound sunglasses. He was dressed in slacks and long sleeves, fighting away perspiration with his silk handkerchief.

Her eyes moved down to his overly stuffed belly. His shirt was tucked into his pants with an expensive leather belt wrapped around his middle and holding it all together, creating a distinct division of his top and bottom half. She cringed as Sir continued stroking her hair. She tried to lean away but couldn't.

"Here's the deal, I think you learned your lesson. Never con a con. I'm afraid I'm going to have to add an additional quarter million dollars if you ever want to think about getting this young lady back. Mmm, I could probably get more money than that for her." Sir ran his index finger up and down her arm.

Kendra's eyes widened further as she listened.

"Or maybe, just maybe, I'll keep her for myself." Sir was smiling at her. She couldn't see his eyes through the dark glasses but she could feel them staring at her. She tried to shout through her gag but only muffled high pitched sounds escaped. She stomped her feet, even though they were tied together at the ankles.

"I love feisty," Sir insisted.

Kendra stopped fighting. She didn't want Sir to love anything more about her.

19

The house was clean, mostly straightened up, and Terri had a half spring in her step. It had been almost two weeks and Kendra was coming home today. Terri folded the newspaper open to the want ads and carefully placed it on the table. Terri wanted Kendra to think she had been busy looking for work while Kendra was away.

****

Diane picked up Derek, they were anxious to see Kendra at the airport. But a new unspoken tension was growing, bouncing between the two of them as they thought about the email. That email message was so absurd, it had to be fake, a joke or a scam. They were excited to soon hear the stories about Kendra's trip and were glad that whatever all this was, it was soon going to be all over.

They arrived at the airport early. They parked the car and walked into the terminal where they ate expensive lousy hamburgers. They pretended they were going somewhere exotic as they looked out the windows, watching the airplanes coming and going on the tarmac.

The loudspeaker announced Kendra's flight had arrived and would be at gate number nine momentarily. They lined up near the big glass door the passengers would walk through. There they were, waiting, standing with the others who were waiting for their friends and loved ones.

The large glass doors slid open and the passengers began to pour through, each one rushing to be first. Diane and Derek worked their way through to the front of the crowd, anxious to catch a glimpse of Kendra. Passengers dwindled down to the last few, and Diane and Derek stood there in silence, waiting, waiting…. One more person … *No, no, she's not Kendra.*

The flight crew began to come out, their suitcases rolling behind them.

"Excuse me, excuse me, miss?" Diane stopped a neatly dressed flight attendant as she walked by. "We're waiting for our friend, Kendra, to get off, are there many people left in there?"

"No honey, everyone is off the plane now, only the flight crew left. A new crew is coming in now while they clean the cabin and get ready for the next destination. Any chance she missed her flight?"

The two looked at each other. "Maybe, maybe she missed her flight." They were both stunned and scared as they stood there feeling helpless, refusing to believe the nice lady. They watched the door as the flight crew walked away. Derek had a sick feeling in his stomach as they waited longer and longer. Now they both knew Kendra wasn't going to come through that door.

How were they going to tell her mom? What were they going to say and which one of them was actually going to say it? Derek didn't want to be in the same room with Terri when she found out.

****

Terri sat on the couch listening, trying to wrap her mind around what Diane and Derek were trying to tell her about Kendra's vacation to Oregon. Terri was shifting gears rapidly, waking up to a whole new level of parenting.

"So...what you're trying to tell me is that there was no trip to Oregon with your family." Terri looked into Diane's eyes.

Diane sat there on the hot seat. She tried to look away but couldn't. Looking away was hard to do with Terri's eyes focused so sharply on hers.

Terri's breath grew deeper, slower, as she forced herself to inhale slowly, trying to contain her anger.

"Yes ma'am, Kendra told me to say that, I'm sorry!"

Derek looked at Diane, knowing he was next.

"And you knew about this the whole time?" She was looking at Derek now, reaching into his eyes with hers. Terri's face was bright red now as she did her best to hold her emotions back.

"Yes ma'am, I'm sorry, I'm really sorry." Derek looked down at his shoes as he tapped his toes on the ground in fear.

"Kendra was sent a round trip ticket," Diane offered. "She should have been on that plane."

"She was really excited to see her father, Rick, she said. He told her he wanted to see her and had it all under control, the tickets, the trip, the vacation."

Rick??? Terri's head was spinning, she hadn't spoken with Rick in years. *What the hell is he doing acting like a father suddenly?* The only communication she had had was the occasional letter from his attorney regarding more spousal support. "That son of a bitch," her voice began to escalate further as she stood up and began to pace the front room floor. "Damn him."

The kids didn't know what to do, they both really wanted to leave but were afraid to without Terri's permission.

"Let me see that itinerary." Terri tried not to yell at the kids.

Derek handed it over and she examined it.

"Take me to that Facebook deal! To that page of his! Come!"

The kids followed behind as Terri went into her office and pointed to the chair. She said "Sit," and she looked at Derek.

She was trying her best not to take it out on the kids, but found it difficult knowing that they were both in cahoots with Kendra. Or had been. At least now they had come to her and explained, instead of trying to hide all this from her. But now they really had no choice, did they?

She told herself she had to lighten it up, to make them feel good for showing their bravery and talking to her. She had to have their help if needed.

****

Derek stroked at the keyboard and was quickly on Kendra's Facebook page. Terri saw the picture of the house posted right there with the title "vacation time" under it. Looking at all that surrounded that house, she tried to figure out which island the house sat on. But she couldn't pinpoint it. She was growing more frustrated.

She couldn't see or read any conversations between Kendra and her father, and Diane and Derek swore they didn't know any passwords. They searched for the Facebook page for Rick, Kendra had shown it to Derek. Trying every name combination they could think of, they couldn't bring up his page.

Terri was dumbfounded. Kendra was such a good girl, so responsible, so everything Terri herself wasn't. How in the world could this have happened behind her back?

"I guess I've been living in the dark, kids." Terri was looking at both of them as she spoke.

Derek and Diane looked at each other. They had grown up with Kendra. And they had known all about Kendra's struggles and dreams, centered on overcoming obstacles in life, and on academia and life opportunities. Kendra was sure career focused, unlike her mother.

"You kids get out of here. Thank you for having the courage to stop by." She held her arm up and pointed to the door.

"What are you going to do?"

"I'm going to go get my daughter back."

VOLUME THREE: RAPTIS TRILOGY

****

PART THREE

ESCAPE INTO TERROR

VOLUME THREE: RAPTIS TRILOGY

****

<u>20</u>

This was an intensely disturbing experience for Kendra, being so perfectly polished and made up at the whim of a clearly very disturbed stranger who was holding her captive. Sure, she was used to being leered at and propositioned by men much older than she was, but this guy was like something out of a gangster movie. *Or maybe a mental institution*, she told herself. She cringed and felt nauseated as he stroked her hair and spoke of her beauty.

But Sir found her attempts at leaning away from his reach to be playful, alluring.

Kendra had so far been unwilling to accept the offers for food, water, and rest from this weird Sir and his big manservant, assistant or whatever, Bannister. She had refused everything. She wanted to set her own rules, not trade what they wanted for what she needed. She was furious. Soon they ignored her angry whining noises and withheld everything, leaving the room and letting her sit, bound and gagged, to stew. Finally, after hours and hours of this, her stomach began to growl and churn. She began feeling very lightheaded and real sick to her stomach. Eventually, she wore down; she was so sick, thirsty, hungry, and tired. She very much wanted to lie down and sleep. She got very quiet and still.

However, it was another couple hours before the two men finally returned to check on her. She noticed the pudgy Sir now wore a complete change of clothes, but was still in his sunglasses.

Bannister pulled the gag down out of her mouth.

Sir was smiling at her as he spoke to Bannister, "This shrew is going to take some taming I'm afraid. I'm sure you will help me with this."

Bannister nodded his head yes.

Kendra thought it best to keep her opinion to herself. Her mouth was parched and she had had to pee really badly for at least the last hour, it was torturous. She realized she had to find another way to deal with all this. Had to.

"Please Sir, I'll behave, I promise." She pleaded to her captors, "I'm so hot with this sunburn, and very uncomfortable. I have to use the toilet, I really do. Please, Sir." She looked this creepy Sir in the eye. But she could only see her pathetic reflection in his dark glasses staring back at her.

Sir snapped his fingers, calling Bannister to his side. He looked at Kendra. "My man, Bannister here, by the way, that's not his real name."

She looked at the very large Bannister while the little Sir spoke. *What a strange, awful, evil pair*, Kendra said to herself. *They're real sick men. I have to get out of here, and soon. How?*

Bannister smiled at her, his arms were crossed.

"It's a nickname I gave him myself when I bought him out of a prison. I needed someone with the balance of greed and loyalty, someone who would be eternally grateful."

Kendra saw the way Sir smiled at Bannister, she could tell that Sir was very proud, as if Bannister was a son. "But I also needed someone who would carry out my wishes, sometimes, many times, brutal wishes." He tapped his fingertips together as he explained.

Kendra cringed inside. *Brutal? Why is he saying this?*

"Bannister here earned his nickname because his family abandoned him, banned from a family who insisted he was banned from heaven." Sir spoke as if he were reading a goodnight fairytale to a young girl in bed, his voice light to keep her attention but firm as he was trying to teach her something. "This is what the prison guards told me."

Kendra had no choice but to listen. She looked over at Bannister, wondering what he did to end up in prison.

Sir answered the question in her head as he continued. "Bannister killed his father, for money. The poor man was a priest."

The two men chuckled in unison.

Kendra looked at Sir in disbelief. *How can you trust anybody who would kill his own father,* she wondered silently.

"Now will you behave?" Sir looked at her.

Kendra tried not to stare at Bannister now, and simply nodded a yes.

Bannister began to untie the knots that bound her ankles so she could walk.

"Take her to the bathroom, Bannister, don't close the door. Watch her," the awful pudgy Sir said and smiled.

As Bannister reached for her arm, wrapping his large fingers around her biceps, Kendra couldn't help but grimace and wince from the pain of her sunburn. She tried to hold it in and not complain, but her face said it all. She was truly in physical pain.

"Gently Bannister!" Sir shouted, "Don't harm her skin, it is beginning to blister!"

Bannister quickly loosened his grip and led the way.

****

Once there, Kendra ran to the toilet and relieved herself. She didn't have a choice but to drip dry. Her hands were still bound behind her back, she wasn't about to mention her dilemma to Bannister standing at the doorway. Her cotton underwear was half soaked with urine. She wasn't able to take it all the way down and back in time, not with her hands tied behind her back. Her underwear was uncomfortably rolled in a bunch at the top of her thighs. Then her sunburn stung as she struggled to pull her underwear back up further. She kept all that information to herself.

She looked around the bathroom for any escape route. There was a window, a tall and narrow window next to the sink. She had no idea what was on the other side but she decided that somehow she had to earn their trust enough to get her hands unbound. Had to.

****

She walked out of the room and up to Bannister, standing beside him when she was done. She looked up at him for her next move. Bannister led her to the dining room where he had apparently earlier set the table with opulent china and ornate silverware. Fresh fruit and a banquet of cooked fish and vegetables were neatly arranged there.

Sir walked in. "Will you behave if Bannister binds your hands in front of you so you can eat?"

Kendra nodded and let out a mild, "Yes, Sir."

He motioned to her to sit down at the table. "Sit." She sat and waited as Bannister pulled a seat out and motioned for Sir to sit down as if he were a king. Then Bannister pushed the pudgy man's chair in and handed him his napkin.

Bannister untied Kendra's hands, and then retied her hands in front of her.

King Sir then announced, "eat" as he pointed to Kendra's plate, then began to stuff his face with his fingers.

Kendra saw the animal side of this pudgy dictator. He barely chewed his food before swallowing it. The napkin splayed around his neck and the mess he was making made him look like a lion eating. She waited for the roar.

She was hungry and started with the fruit. She ate the small piece of beef that was served on her plate, it was delicious. When she went for a second portion, she was denied. She noticed she didn't get any of the pasta or potato the fat little Sir had on his plate, even though she asked for some with the utmost politeness.

"I'm sorry dear, we still have some taming to do. It usually takes a little adjusting." Sir lifted the steak bone up to his mouth and gnawed at the gristle.

Kendra couldn't watch, she was afraid that the look of repulsion in her eyes would be too obvious.

After dinner, Kendra was led back to the office and ordered to sit down in the oversized chair. She was exhausted and wanted to lie down and shut her eyes. She was handed a book and forced to read out loud to Sir as he sat and listened. Bannister brought him a cigar from the humidor, first clipping the end before handing it to him. Then Bannister lit it for Sir who began puffing out a large cloud of white gray smoke toward Kendra. The smoke rose to the ceiling and swirled in the current of the fan above. Kendra felt like vomiting but resisted.

****

At the end of each chapter, she thought about asking if she could go to bed, but she didn't ask. Sir just sat there and watched her while he sipped on a glass of amber colored liquor. She could never tell where exactly his eyes were landing on her; she decided to stop obsessing about this as there was little she could do but let it go on.

Then Bannister kept her up all night, even after his master waddled off. When she asked for some water, Bannister went to get it but never returned to bring her the water she asked to drink and desperately needed.

She was half delirious in the morning, being still awake from the night before, and thirsty and hungry. Her stomach was growling loudly and she felt filthy from head to toe.

Bannister led her to the bathroom and then to the dining room where he told her to sit down. She complied, shortly after Sir came in to join her. Now he was clean shaven. His clothes were fresh and crisp as they always were. She had noticed that anytime this sweaty fat man would perspire through his clothes, he would disappear and come back with a clean fresh shirt on. Now he sniffed the air and looked her up and down, snapping his fingers.

Bannister was at Sir's side within moments.

"I can smell her in this room, do something about this. Go draw her a milk bath, cold, not hot, I don't want that smooth skin of hers to blister unevenly."

Bannister turned to Kendra, reaching for her arm.

She looked at the man in confusion.

Sir told Kendra, "The milk bath will be soothing on your skin, I don't want to blemish that porcelain skin underneath, mmm, so beautiful. ... Bannister, afterwards, bring her to me so I can comb her hair."

Kendra stood up and let Bannister lead the way. Her skin was feeling better but it definitely still hurt. Sir seemed so oddly overly concerned about her skin.

Kendra watched as Bannister carefully prepared the water, first mixing a box of powdered milk with warm water to dissolve the white substance, then topping this with cold running water. He turned his head away a little as he told her to disrobe and get in. She could smell herself too as she watched him to see if he was looking at her. She slipped her dress off, then her small cotton panties.

She stepped in. The bath felt luxurious as she dipped her body down under the milky white water. Bannister stepped outside the door, half closing it as she bathed. She took her time, not anxious to go back out. She tried to rest a bit.

Finally Bannister announced bath time was over. She was handed a towel and instructed to pat dry, not wipe. It seemed to Kendra that Bannister had been told to watch her, but not to totally watch her. He watched her from the doorway, not staring straight at her but keeping an eye on what she was doing. He put a set of clean white linen clothes on the counter for her to put on.

Then she was brought back to Sir. Sir first brushed her hair, then used a comb. He used his fat fingers to separate and braid her hair, pulling it upward and tight like a doll's would be. When finished, he wiped a soothing lotion on her face and neck skin.

She closed her eyes and felt herself relax for a short moment as he touched her face, opening her eyes only to see him still

VOLUME THREE: RAPTIS TRILOGY

****

looking at her from behind those dark glasses, all the while with that creepy smile. She tried not to shudder.

She did her best to sit still and gain his trust while secretly detesting him.

21

Terri checked her bank accounts. They were down to the usual minimum, waiting for that next little annuity check to arrive. She had already cashed in all the extra bonus change jars she had been saving. She had spent most all of it while Kendra was away. There was but a little change left here and there. Terri walked around the house looking at everything she owned, wondering what to let go of next. She needed the cash and right away.

She picked through her guitars to see if there was one she could part with. She loved to play the guitar and had treated herself to just about every guitar she had ever wanted over the years. That was before her fortune dwindled. Once her money started disappearing, Terri sold some of her much loved guitars, one by one, here and there, each time to pay for the next much needed item she had to have.

Raising a daughter alone was something Terri had never thought of doing. She wanted her daughter to be raised having it all. And sure enough, Terri and Kendra did have it all, at least for a while.

But then it got bad, real bad. Terri was told she had to get a job of some kind if she wanted any discretionary income, any money to spend, and anything to help pay some of the mounting bills she owed. The maintenance of her boats and cars and house mounted to more than she could sustain. She started letting go of these things, slowly. And then with a bad attitude, she started refusing to pay the remainder of the bills, the ones she deemed unfair. Her credit score tanked. She was now down to her final precious assets. No one seriously wanted her old car, and her house was too much a wreck to sell for a profit.

****

Now Terri picked out the two nicest guitars she had and headed down to the "Pawn This" pawn shop where they had come to know her by name over the last couple years.

"Hey there. What are we letting go of today, Terri? Haven't seen you in a while." Willie behind the counter had become a friendly acquaintance. Willie himself had been born and raised in the Hawaiian islands. He and Terri loved to argue about which sea was best. He would always take the time to hear the story attached to each item Terri brought in; there was always a reason to buy and always a reason to sell.

"Two of my finest today, Willie. I've been holding these babies out." Terri hoisted one guitar up onto the counter and opened its case for him to see it. "I need cash, right away."

"Car take a crap on ya again, or something else broken?" He looked into the case and started inspecting.

"No. I wish. I mean I wish it were that simple. I've got to put together some money to go get my daughter."

"Kendra?"

"Yep, she's taken off to the Caribbean, to go visit her dad."

"And that's a bad thing?" He didn't even look at her, he was busy looking at the guitar, picking it up and strumming it. "Nice."

"Yes, it's a bad thing Joe. She didn't come home when she was supposed to. I'm going to go get her." She put the other guitar up on the counter and opened that case.

Again he carefully lifted it out, inspecting it. "Clean Terri, real nice. What were you thinking?"

She didn't hesitate with her answer. "Five hundred each, Willie, that's fair, they're worth twice that much, easily."

"Five hundred each! Terri! Come on!" He came back at her. "I'm running a business here! You know I can't make any money sitting on these, waiting for the right guy to come in and pay the right price." He shut the cases to make his point.

"Four hundred each, shit, that's stealing them from me." She opened the first case back up so he could see it again.

"Terri, I'd love to help you but the best I can do is five hundred for the both of them, two hundred and fifty each. Firm." He crossed his arms.

Terri knew this would be his final offer. She was desperate for cash. "Damn it, Willie! These babies are worth over a thousand each brand new!" She was becoming visibly frustrated.

Willie had seen this before. He closed the open case and clasped the metal clasps shut.

"Sorry Terri, that's a take it or leave it offer, I just don't need any more guitars no matter how much they're worth." He pointed up and behind him to the long row of other guitars he had to sell there, all hanging from the rack.

Terri pursed her lips and was silent.

Willie didn't say a word.

"All right, damn it! If that's the best you can do, I'll take it."

Willie smiled and reached for his paperwork.

****

Five hundred dollars was a drop in the bucket compared to what she would need to get to St. Todos and back, what with hotel, food, a car. Terri was trying to come up with a figure in her head. Frustrated, she sat down at her desk and went to her rolodex. She called her mortgage broker to see if there was, by chance, any more money she could pull out of the house.

"Sorry Terri, there is not one bank that will refinance your house any more. You have a delicate balance of debt to income ratio now, no one will touch it or even look at it until you can find yourself a steady job."

"Mr. Lopez, you know I'm good for it, I really, really, need some cash now!" Terri insisted.

"I'm sorry Terri, I wish I could tell you otherwise."

"Fine." Terri hung up loudly. She didn't like what she'd heard. Her frustration was mounting with each passing hour. *Five hundred dollars.* She had to try harder! She glanced quickly at the Rolex on her wrist, the one Melvin, her old boss, had presented her so many years ago. This was a gift from someone she greatly admired, even loved. She smiled as she touched it, knowing she could never sell it. *Never. Or?* But it was in such bad shape, not working at all, so she really couldn't sell it anyway.

She went into the closet in back of her room where, way up on the top shelf, she had long ago hidden a box. She slowly slid out and dusted off this box of memories. She thought about what should be in it. But gone was the ring she had planned to put on Mitch's finger the day of their wedding, the one that had matched his for hers. She had pawned it a few years back to put a new transmission in her Mercedes.

Gone was the wedding ring that creep, Rick, had once put on her finger in a hurry, back when he had pressured her to marry him. That was before they knew she was pregnant. She had hawked that ring two years ago for a new roof. There were some miscellaneous pictures and a brochure left over from the dive shop she had worked in, back on St. Todos. She paused and read that old brochure one more time, reliving those days for a moment.

She reached to the bottom and pulled out a little leather box. She opened it. In it was the gold medallion she had found in the money clip while she was out diving with Mitch that day years ago. This was so long ago now, but every once in a while she managed to relive that day in a dream. This was the dream she loved the most.

Oh Mitch, I am so SO SOOOO sorry.... She had tried so many times to call Mitch over the years, even back while out sailing with Rick, starting when she found out she was pregnant. And Mitch had never ever answered, nor had he ever returned her calls. Mitch wanted nothing to do with her ever again, that was clear.

As Terri spun the medallion in her hand, good and bad memories flooded her thoughts. So many traumatic memories rushed in. Russell's dead body. The look on David's face when the bang stick pushed into him. *Killing him.* She took a long gulp. *And Mitch.* Mitch saving her life again, that one more time. *Oh Mitch. Mitch!*

She closed her fingers, clasping the medallion tight in her hand. Her mind drifted again to Mitch. *I should call him, I should let him know I am coming*, she thought. Again she reminded herself that she had called Mitch before, many times. And each time he had not answered, except for when he made a mistake, thought she was someone else, then hung up as soon as he realized it was her.

She knew she had no right to talk to him. She felt so guilty. She had stomped on his heart and then kicked it. What could she say? An "I'm sorry" just never seemed like enough. And it wasn't.

She opened her hand and looked at the medallion. Mitch had told her, even warned her, of its value. He had said to be careful with it, very careful. She never once had it appraised. She didn't want to be tempted by its value. She would never sell it, it was her symbol of victory. No matter what or who she had lost in her lifetime, that medallion was one that she earned.

She shook her head "no," talking herself out of selling this medallion. She put it back in the small leather box and then placed that leather box in the shoebox to be hidden back up in her closet. She grabbed her car keys and the yellow pages.

22

"I'm sorry ma'am, the best I can do cash is five thousand dollars." The skinny man with way too much hair gel on had just spent over half an hour inspecting her car, and she was expecting so much more.

"This is robbery!" Terri insisted as she stroked the hood of her beloved Mercedes. It was the first status symbol she had purchased after her divorce from Rick. "The guy down the street offered me six thousand, how about six thousand?"

"Look lady—" The salesman hadn't liked her last ploy for more money from him and he didn't much like this one either. "I think you should take your car back down to the other guy." His gold front tooth wet with sticky saliva took over his face as she stared him down. There was no other guy and he knew it.

"Five thousand dollars?"

"My best and final cash offer...." He smiled wider, the hook was set. It was just a matter of reeling her in to sign the pink slip away.

"OK...sold...." *Five thousand, that and five hundred dollars, crap.* Now she wished she hadn't sold her two guitars, five hundred dollars had seemed like a spit in the bucket compared to what she needed.

He left her for what seemed like an hour and came back with a cashier's check.

"Hey! I thought you said cash!"

"This is like cash."

"But it's not."

"I had to have my business partner sign it off, the bank will take it just like cash."

She looked at it, not knowing if she could trust this guy.

"Haven't you ever used a cashier's check before?" The salesman gave her that look, she hated it, that look that said "What rock have you been living under?"

She folded the check and shoved it into her front pocket next to the $500 cash she had taken earlier for two guitars. She walked to the bank, looking over her shoulder all the way.

She cashed the check. Once that was done, she decided to just walk the rest of the way home. She didn't realize how far from home she really was, and she had too little patience to stand and wait for a bus. She knew she could get there faster by walking. But she didn't get there faster, and the bus had passed by her an hour ago.... So it was a long slog home.

******

Once home, Terri pulled out her suitcase, her oldest friend. Next she went to the computer to check her emails and to buy a plane ticket. Her email inbox glared the sender's name at her, *Rick Shelding.* She twisted her neck and hesitated, taking a deep breath before she opened and read: "Terri, I'm sorry, I did not intend for this to happen. Kendra has been kidnapped. They want the medallion, the one that was in the money clip, in exchange for Kendra. It's the only way we'll get her back alive. Email me back and let me know when you can get here, hurry! Please! – Rick"

Kidnapped. Kidnapped?!?!? "Kendra kidnapped?! The only way *we'll* get her back?! We? We?! We?!!" Terri kept shouting these words from Rick over and over. "Rick, you mother fucker!" She jumped up, screaming at the top of her lungs, slamming her fist down on the keyboard and knocking it off the desk where it then dangled helplessly from its wire.

She threw herself back down on the chair and cried. "I'm going to kill you Rick, I'm going to kill you when I find you. Kendra has been kidnapped? Bull! No one except Mitch AND YOU know I have that medallion!"

She stood up and began to kick the base of the couch, over and over, harder and harder, trying her best to release the fierce anger erupting inside her. That worked, at least until her foot couldn't take the pain any more.

Terri went to the kitchen and grabbed the bottle of tequila, then sat back at the computer.

Plane ticket, plane ticket … I need a plane ticket. She wiped her face and tried to wrap her mind around what Rick was telling her. She took a long swig of the tequila and grimaced as it sat on her tongue. She swallowed. She hit the reply button and typed:

"Rick, I'm going to kill you."

She hit the backspace to delete and started over. She didn't know what was going to happen but thought best not to put her feelings in writing.

"Rick, you fucker. You lure *my* daughter down to you behind my back and now she's kidnapped? You tell her you're her father? Like hell you are! What kind of father are you? What happened? I'm getting a ticket and coming down as fast as I can. Have you called the police? Who's looking for her? What in the hell have you done!"

Terri pressed the send button as her mind raced around in circles of *What to do, what to do next, what to do about this, what to do.* She grabbed her bottle and took another long swig, setting it down with a bang on the desk. She brought up airline flights and started to search, finding a flight that would leave in eight hours. She could make it to the airport, easily—

"Holy shit! That price will suck up more than half of my money!" There was nothing else she could do but buy it, because with this short notice she wouldn't find anything cheaper. She went through the motions of buying the ticket, carefully punching in the numbers of her bank card, and pressed buy. She watched the round graphic spin on the screen as it digested all her information, then the next sign appeared. "Declined." Her card wouldn't authorize the payment.

"Uggggggghhhh!" She screamed out, reaching for the phone and dialing the eight hundred number of the bank. She knew it by heart, constantly having to check the balance of her account. The automated lady told her she only had fifty dollars and thirty seven cents. It wasn't even aware of her pending deposit yet! She impatiently pressed the number zero to talk to a human.

"I'm sorry ma'am, but your deposit will not be available until tomorrow."

"But I deposited a cashier's check. He told me it was just like cash!" Terri was trying not to scream into the phone but was totally exasperated.

"Yes ma'am, similar to cash, and it's our policy to hold check deposits made after three o'clock in the afternoon. The total funds will be available tomorrow morning."

"Oh my God, I don't understand this!" She put her head on the desk top, she wanted to scream.

"Ma'am, I'm sorry but there is nothing I can do about it, the funds will be available first thing tomorrow morning."

"Fine, fine." Terri hung up, realizing she couldn't even buy a ticket now *until tomorrow morning*!!! She picked up the bottle of tequila and took a longer swig, it was going down quicker, smoother now. Then another. Then another, like the so-called "good" old days. She couldn't see that the same alcohol that was "soothing" her now, had set her up for so many of her problems in her life. Then between a few swallows, she almost realized this, almost.

Turning her attention back to the computer, she was ready now to write Rick another email. She was so scared for Kendra, and now her fears were heightening knowing she couldn't even buy a ticket to the island *until tomorrow morning*. Time mattered and what could she do? She was stuck, it was the worst feeling in the world for her.

There was no new mail in the inbox, it had been thirty minutes since she wrote Rick, *Why hasn't he replied?* Now she was really pissed and started typing.

"All right, you slimy asshole, what's going on down there and how did Kendra get kidnapped? Who has her and who's getting her back? I want answers NOW!"

She pressed the send button. She felt helpless and that was all she could do. She took another long swig and stood up to go to the bathroom, stumbling into the edge of the door. She popped herself on the forehead as she tripped into the sharp edge of the door.

"Ouch! Damn it! I'm so SOO pissed off!" Terri screamed in her frustration. She began her night time routine early. She wanted to pass out, go to sleep right away, so that tomorrow would hurry up and arrive. She finished off the bottle of tequila while she stared at the phone.

She was resisting the temptation, the urge, the need to call Mitch. She wanted to hear Mitch's voice. She wanted to know he was there, she was hoping he was there. She wanted him to know what was happening. She needed him to know. Finally she picked the phone up and dialed, it rang, it went to a recording.

"Hi, this is Mitch, leave a message."

She froze and hung up, wondering if he was on the other end waiting to hear who was calling. *His voice, there it was.* She dialed again and heard the same message, this time she couldn't take it and felt the overwhelming need to talk to him, even if it was just talking to a taped recording.

"Mitch, Mitch it's me, Terri. Wow, it's been so long.... Uh, my, its ... uh, daughter, Kendra.... Oh damn, it's Kendra...." Terri gulped, trying to hold back tears. She knew she was drunk and rambling, not knowing what to say, and she really didn't want Mitch to hear this. She didn't want to say the wrong thing. She swallowed hard in attempt to pull herself together. "I didn't know ... didn't know if this phone number still worked.... I...." Feeling totally stupid for not planning that out better, she was mortified and hung up. She hoped it would sound to Mitch like she had been disconnected not drunk.

She grabbed the bottle of tequila, tipping it upside down toward her mouth. Two drops landed on her tongue. It was empty. She turned back to her computer and checked the email inbox, still nothing from Rick. She shot him another reply.

"WHERE ARE YOU!!! I NEED TO KNOW NOW WHERE KENDRA IS!!!"

She pressed send. Fighting the urge to cry, now Terri stood up and paced. She knew she needed strength, strength to deal with finding Kendra, strength to deal with Rick, and strength to reach out to Mitch again.

Mitch, who probably still hates me, and should. He NEVER wanted to talk to me again. But should he, would he, help Kendra? What I did is NOT her fault. He should know. Should he? He never wanted to know, so should he?

Terri stumbled through the front room and saw herself in the mirror. She was repulsed by what she saw, she was drunk again, and a shell of what she once was. Could she find herself enough to save Kendra now?

Terri set the alarm clock for five in the morning and climbed into bed. She lay there staring up at the ceiling, thinking of Kendra and praying that Kendra would be OK and know her mommy was coming to get her. *Mommy, yes.* Now Terri felt like a mommy again.

She lay there anxiously, almost counting the minutes as the hours passed. She fought away her feelings of helplessness by forming a plan for the next morning. She was all packed, she already knew which flight she wanted to be on as soon as her money was cleared. She needed to rest now, she had to find some energy for what was coming, somehow.

VOLUME THREE: RAPTIS TRILOGY

****

REDEMPTION

****

23

Kendra was scared that she would never be left alone for a minute. Still, she kept a stiff upper lip and did whatever was asked of her. So far the creepy pudgy man seemed to be a voyeur of sorts, stroking her, combing her, primping her like a doll on display for his viewing. Her insides cringed when she felt his touch, his hands were powder white and nail beds almost a pink polished color. She wondered what color his eyes were. His sunglasses never came off.

She had seen enough out through the windows to know that if she could just get through the bathroom window without alerting Bannister, she could possibly make a run for it. Every now and then she thought she could hear the sound of screeching wheels close by. Kendra told herself, *There must be a road of some kind nearby. A road with a tight turn. There has to be.*

Kendra could overhear certain bits and pieces of a telephone conversation Sir was having with someone she assumed was her dad. She even thought she heard Sir say his name, Rick. But Kendra didn't have much faith in her dad or the other two he hung out with to get her out of this situation. Kendra just knew that somehow Rick, Joe, and Peg had gotten her into this mess, all of this. But they were not going to be much help getting her out. At one point, Kendra also thought she heard the words, "that kid's mother," and wondered if they were talking about her own mother. They had to be. *But why? She doesn't have any money and can't get any.*

****

Kendra was asked to read again. Her skin was itchy and blistering in patches as her serious sunburn was healing. Every time she scratched at it, Sir would insist she take another bath to sooth it and rub lotion on it so it wouldn't peel unevenly.

Each bath, and every order she complied with without complaint, her hands were tied in front with a simple knot. And Bannister trusted her alone more and more each time she had a bath. The last time she took a bath, Bannister even allowed her to use the bathroom with the door closed. She thanked him for the privacy. Bannister never talked directly to her but she felt she was slowly gaining a small amount of his trust, trust she was carefully building.

****

Kendra noticed Sir's mouth start to gape open as if he were ready to drift off into a nap. She never could tell for sure with those dark lenses on. She began to rub at her arms relentlessly, rubbing her arm on the side of the chair and scratching at her thighs. It didn't take too long before the pudgy hand rose and he snapped his fingers.

Bannister didn't come to his side immediately. Sir shouted through the house. "Bannister!"

The large man practically ran into the room. "I'm sorry, Sir, I was preparing your dinner."

"Draw her a milk bath so she can soak that skin off, room temperature, while I nap."

"Yes, Sir."

Now Kendra was polite but devoid of emotion like a poker player. Obediently, she stood up and walked with Bannister down the hall, rubbing at her arms and legs as she walked, but not complaining.

"Mmm, milk bath, feels so good, I'm so itchy all over," she confided to Bannister while they walked up to the door. "I'll get it, if you need to get back to dinner," she said so matter-of-factly that Bannister grunted and continued walking to the kitchen down to the right, across the hallway.

Now was Kendra's chance, it was too perfect. She was so nervous her hands shook as she worked quickly, trying not to make a sound, making every move count, starting the moment Bannister turned his back. Kendra turned the bathtub water on and poured the powdered milk in, splashing it around so he could hear. Then she turned the water flow down so it wouldn't overflow the tub while she was escaping. She closed the door just to the point where it was touching—not latched, but so Bannister couldn't easily see in. She could hear him chopping in the kitchen.

Kendra opened the window as slowly as she could, being careful not to make any screeching sound. She tugged on the screen lightly, it came toward her, and she set it aside. She hoisted herself up onto the counter and leaned over to the ledge, perching her foot on the seal then reaching to the side and steadying herself.

Hardly breathing, paying intensely close attention to each step she was taking, Kendra watched the door for any signs of Bannister as she easily slipped out and dropped down to the ground without a sound. Surrounded by lush green gardens, she hurried down the side where she could see across the property, mostly dense vegetation. She pushed it aside and wacked away at the flying insects buzzing around her head.

Once out of earshot, Kendra ran and came to a road sooner than she imagined. The road looked well-traveled and had the solid yellow stripe down the center, indicating a somewhat major roadway. She didn't know which way to go. She turned back and faced the house. Deciding its driveway would come out to her left, she turned to the right and began to run.

<u>24</u>

The alarm went off with a loud buzz. Terri slammed the button off and sprung out of bed. She ate three aspirin to kill the ache in her head and hastily made a large pot of coffee. Turning the computer on, she impatiently watched it start up. She pecked her way on the keyboard to the inbox of her emails. There it was. *RE: Rick Shelding*.

"Terri do not call the police, we will all get killed. I know who has Kendra, he wants the medallion in exchange. I'm afraid of phone calls being traced, email me back, fly into St. Todos, I'll meet you there. When are you coming??? Hurry!! –Rick"

She looked over at the empty tequila bottle, the dull ache in her head had yet to subside. *Stay strong, you have a long day*, she reminded herself. The temptation wasn't too hard to resist, the bottle was empty. She peeled at the bottle's label while her thoughts drifted. Then she resolutely pushed the empty bottle away from her sight and picked up her coffee.

She told herself that the price of a last minute ticket to the Caribbean was highway robbery. And this was going to use up almost half of her money. She would still have to find Kendra and bring her home with her. Terri knew she had to be smart about every penny she had. She picked up the phone and the yellow pages. She was going to call each airline and let them do the work finding her the quickest cheapest flight.

During an hour of frustration and much confusion, she labored over which flight to take. She chose the one connecting in New York, of all places. It would save her a whopping seven hundred dollars. The down side was, it would take five hours longer than the other flights. She decided the reward of saving five hundred dollars would be worth the risk. Not long after she had committed her few dollars to this flight, she chastised herself for this decision, but it was too late. *Kendra!!!* Terri said to herself, calling Kendra's name in her mind, wishing somehow her daughter could hear her.

Terri wouldn't arrive until eight o'clock the next morning St. Todos time. It was hard for her to relax about this, but there was nothing she could do now. She had six long hours before her flight left. Packed and ready to go, she sent a blazing email to Rick. Then she called Derek: she had sold her car and needed a ride to the airport. Derek and Diane owed her one, big time.

She sat on the edge of her bed and looked at her closet door. The leather box sat on the top shelf in the back. It housed her most prized possession, the gold medallion. Mitch had the second medallion. Terri wondered, *Whatever did he do with his?*

Terri had let that medallion of hers sit in there, in that box in that closet for a long time, even as she had been struggling to make ends meet. She had always refused to sell it. And now, after Kendra's brief encounter with that damn Rick Shelding, that disgustingly wicked con man had managed to go after the last of Terri's prized possessions. And worse now for Terri, *after Kendra!*

Karma Terri, payback's a bitch. You shouldn't have been so selfish with your life, now life's leveler, karma, is completing her job. You'll be OK, you'll be OK—fuck! How am I going to be OK unless Kendra is OK?

Terri knew that if she took the medallion out now, it would never go back in. And this was her last piece of security. Terri let out a heavy sigh, one she had been holding back for a long time, as she reached for the small box.

If Kendra had indeed been kidnapped as Rick said, then she didn't have a choice. She pulled the small leather box out and placed it deep in her front pocket.

<u>25</u>

The distant lull of the water running in the bath tub had relaxed Bannister as he chopped away at the vegetables for dinner. But now the trickle sounded different. He put his large knife down and stepped into the hall. Water was flowing onto the white marble floor from under the bathroom door into the hallway. He opened the door and looked to see if Kendra was alright. He saw the window screen leaning against the cabinet door, the window was wide open. Kendra was gone.

His large frame tilted off balance and he slipped on the wet floor as he leaned over the tub to shut the water off. Trying to catch himself, he hit his elbow funny bone while falling down onto the hard surface. He landed with a loud grunt. He was surprised and in pain. His large girth landed with such force.

This little girl, Kendra, had escaped while he let his guard down for five minutes, while his boss was sleeping. How was he going to explain? He stood up and looked out the narrow window, he could see the vegetation disturbed.

He could hear footsteps coming down the marble hallway. He turned to see the pure white skin of his boss's face turning pink with fluster. The boss gaped at the mess, wondering what had happened.

Bannister stood there, right by the open window, with a look of total humiliation. He had the screen to the window in his hand.

There was always a fine line to be respected, the line not to cross, the line where punishing Bannister could result in reprisal. Sir had found that the best psychology for a violent man like this was to show love and compassion, as hard as it was. He knew Bannister was punishing himself inside and would be further motivated to find her, fast. Bannister would then be rewarded tremendously. This strange co-dependent system was already in place, had been played many times in other situations, and worked well for the two of them.

"We need to find her, Bannister, she can't be far." Sir turned and waddled quickly down the hall while giving instructions, never looking to see if Bannister was following. He knew Bannister was following. "Look all around the perimeter, she's probably hiding here. Nowhere else she can go. No way to get anywhere."

Sir had perspired through his long sleeved silk shirt. It was taking everything he had not to explode, not to be screaming with angry emotion. His brow was beading with beads of perspiration from holding his anger back. He patted his forehead with his silk hankie.

Sir was angry and disappointed with his porcelain doll, mad that she was running away from him just when he thought he was making progress with her. *What a shame, her disobedience.* He had wanted to keep this doll for his private collection at his home in Canada. He saw now that he would have to find the appropriate motivation to get her to behave, just as he once had done for Bannister.

Sir could feel a stream of salty sweat run down the inside of his arm as he walked as briskly as he could. He hated the tropical heat, his body couldn't tolerate it. He had been born albino to his dark family in Brazil. They had covered him head to toe at all times, never letting the sun touch his beautiful porcelain skin, telling him how special he was, a gift.

Growing into a young man with all that special treatment made him believe his family's tales about his special powers and wisdoms. So he had begun to use his albino appearance to gain power in more and more devious and deviant ways. People in his country were superstitious about his pure white color with its odd features. He was a barely a young man when he had already learned that the poor and uneducated were easily manipulated into supporting his wrong doings. He was able to begin early in building a drug and weapon processing and smuggling empire across the Americas. Most of his family members were in South America, yet they spread all the way up to Canada. Canada is where Sir had found relief from the heat and where he now lived most of the time. By the time Sir's family had turned against him, he had so much power it made no difference to him, except that he would then take revenge against them.

Being albino and very sensitive to heat and light for a range of reasons, Sir at all times insisted on being neatly clothed in full from head to toe, covering his delicate white skin. So now, Sir went to his room and gave himself a complete shower and changed into clean crisp clothes again.

****

From the bathroom window, Bannister had seen the path Kendra had made through the vegetation. Now Bannister followed that path for a short way, however he knew the property well and rapidly realized she would have made it to the road already. Bannister went back into the house and informed his boss about what he had seen.

Bannister already had the car parked out in front of the house by the time Sir was done cleaning and changing as he knew the man's obsessive routine. Sir got into the passenger seat and ordered him, "Go find her."

They reached the top of the driveway and couldn't decide which way to go, right or left. Kendra was nowhere in sight.

<u>26</u>

Kendra had never hitchhiked a day in her life. But she had heard all the tales, over and over again, of her mother's glory days. Her mother had talked about hitchhiking around everywhere in the islands. Kendra was scared now but so very desperate to get out of there as quickly as she could. She heard a car approaching, so she crossed the road and put her thumb out for the driver to see.

A tan, early model jeep without doors or a back tailgate came around the corner. Kendra tried to smile and stuck her arm out further. The car came to a quick stop and idled. She ran to the passenger side, surprised and relived it was actually that easy. *Almost too easy.* The man looked at her and cocked his head with a smile.

"Hop in young lady, late night out with the boyfriend?" She climbed in and he delicately maneuvered the stick shift into first gear. He stepped on the gas and let go of the clutch. The powerful engine surged forward.

She sunk down in the seat, trying to hide, bouncing with the stiff suspension as they drove off. She hoped no one was watching. The shift into second and third were more graceful and he patted the dashboard when he reached forth gear. They were cruising. "She may be old and slightly worn, but she's been good to me." He laughed to himself and put Kendra at ease the further away they drove. "Where are you going? I didn't even ask."

He looked at her unusual clothing, wondering what her story was. She was so young to be wearing this white-ish gauze outfit. It looked quite expensive but much better suited for some old lady, somewhere at a spa or garden party.

"I got separated from my family…."

"Oh, I get it," he chuckled out loud. "I was sixteen once. You snuck out with your new boyfriend and ended up on the other end of the island." His laugh was contagious, she liked this guy. "Classic, so classic," he assured her.

"Yeah," she blushed, "what are ya gonna do?" She threw her hands up in the air.

****

Kendra had written the P.O. box down, the one from her mom's rolodex, although she didn't have the paper with her. But the box number was easy to memorize. Still, she had no idea where Mitch might live, and didn't even know whether it was his box number or someone else's. She had never even met Mitch, but didn't know what else to do. But she knew from her mother that Mitch was a good person. He would be her only chance off this island. If she could find him.

"I really don't know where I'm going, to tell you the truth. I'll go anywhere but where I was…."

"Mmm. OK, young lady."

"My name is Kendra." She cautiously opened up, not knowing how much to explain. Her instincts told her to relax, so she tried to relax while she could. "I don't know where I'm going, well—I need to find someone."

As the jeep maneuvered around the curves, she held onto the seat with both hands, checking the secureness of her seatbelt. There were no doors, this driver was going too fast, but this was the safest she had felt in weeks.

"I think my family thinks I'm missing, I have to find my mom's friend, Mitch. My mom used to live here."

"Mitch?"

"Yeah, that's his name. I'm embarrassed I don't know his last name, he's an accountant I think."

"Your mom lived here, huh? Well good thing I picked you up, you just don't know these days. The world has changed."

The road came to a fork, one road going down into a town and another weaving further up the mountainside. He continued up the hill, she didn't know why or where he was going, and she didn't ask. She just wanted to go somewhere, somewhere else.

Now the surroundings were lush. There were large ferns, trees of different colors, and blooming beautiful tropical flowers so perfect they looked as if they were plastic. The view opened up on a turn and she could see for the first time the town below.

"Whoa, look at that view!" Kendra was more relaxed now and very tired. She briefly forgot her troubles and her recent escape.

"We're almost there," her new friend announced.

She saw a large home on the hill, and rounding the corner, there was another. The homes were surrounded by luxurious grounds with gated entries, *much like the place that was supposed to be Rick's*, she reminded herself. "Look at those homes! Where are we going?"

The jeep slowed down and stopped in front of one of the gated entrances. The place was very neatly groomed, full of papaya trees. There was a large mango tree in the center of the grounds, and it was dripping with elongated ripe orange fruit.

"We're here, this is it." The man pointed to the private drive.

Kendra was still confused.

"This is Mitch's house." He pointed to the large house.

"You know Mitch?"

He nodded his head yes.

"Oh yes, we go back years, decades. We do business together, I see him all the time."

"Oh, maybe you knew my mom! She used to live here, a long time ago!"

"Maybe Kendra, I've seen lots of people come and go over the years. You think you'll never forget them, but eventually you do...."

He was so philosophical, she liked that.

"My mom's name is Terri, she used to work at a dive shop here."

The man was silent for the longest time as he stared at her. It made her very self conscious. Maybe she shouldn't have mentioned her mom's name.

"Well yes, as a matter of fact, I do know your mom," he finally replied, slowly. "So, your mom is Terri, from the dive shop. Does your mom know you're here?"

The way he said this made Kendra a little nervous. A sinking feeling began to fill her stomach, maybe she did say too much. She had thought she could trust this guy, but then again, she had thought she could trust Rick.

The man reached into his glove compartment and picked up the receiver on his radio. He turned up the volume as it crackled on.

"Mitch, Mitch. Roy, over."

In less than a minute a voice crackled back at him.

"Yes Roy, Mitch, over."

"You have company at the gate, over." Roy looked at Kendra and winked.

"Coming down, over."

Kendra was silent, she was going to meet Mitch. She had heard so many stories about him from her mother, she felt like she already knew him. But right now, as Terri had told Kendra many times, Mitch didn't like her mother. Not for years. Kendra remembered this just as she saw the four wheeled cart coming down the driveway toward them. She panicked.

Mitch was behind the wheel. The large gate opened inward. Mitch set the brake and turned the small cart off. He jumped out and walked over to them.

Roy was standing there with a big smile on his face. Mitch walked up and smiled too.

Kendra didn't know what to say as Mitch stood in front of her smiling. "Hi Mitch, I know we've never met before but…" she extended her right hand to him, "my name is Kendra."

Kendra???? Mitch was emotionless, he had known the minute he laid eyes on this girl exactly who she was. He watched her carefully as she spoke.

She couldn't read what he was thinking. "I know this is totally out of the blue, but I really need your help." Her eyes began to well up. "I'm in danger."

Mitch looked at Roy. Mitch said nothing about that strange message he had just received from Terri, about how she was worried about her daughter; Mitch couldn't help but think of this now.

"I found her on the south end of the island, hitchhiking, all alone." Roy looked at Kendra in a fatherly scolding way. "Just like her mom...." Roy dropped the bomb.

Just like my mom!? Kendra recoiled at the thought. *Not me!*

****

Mitch had been observing this girl, Kendra. He had known there was something special about her, something he felt curious about, something he recognized in her, the minute he laid eyes on her. But what was this, he wondered. She was beautiful like her mom, even scraped and sunburned the way Terri often was. Something was different though, something different from Terri, familiar yes, but different. He couldn't put a finger on it.

"Uh, sorry Mitch, didn't mean to, you know." Roy wasn't sure if he had done the right thing. At first he had thought this was funny, and what a coincidence! *Terri's kid!* But now Roy could see Mitch's deep shock, it was obvious, almost painful. For a moment, Roy studied Kendra's and Mitch's faces, eyeing them curiously.

Mitch had his hands on his hips. He pointed to the golf cart. "Come on, get in," Mitch told Kendra.

"Thank you Roy, thank you for all your help." She extended her hand before she walked to the cart. Roy shook it with both hands. She reached up with her other arm and gave him a quick hug. "Thank you for saving my life, I mean it," she whispered in Roy's ear.

He eyes widened a little. *This girl and Mitch were meant to meet, for sure.* "You be careful out there now," he said as she walked over and sat in Mitch's cart.

"Thanks, Roy," Mitch said as he shook Roy's hand good bye. Then he sat down in the cart next to Kendra. He couldn't take his eyes off her, something about her, so familiar, that smile. The large gate closed behind them as Mitch drove the cart up the driveway to his house.

"This is a surprise visit, is your mom on the island with you?"

Kendra suddenly felt shy, feeling out of place in the outfit the creepy pudgy guy had made her wear. Her hair was still neatly braided, but she kept pushing back the loose wisps that insisted on falling into her eyes. She didn't want to say the wrong thing and was grateful this Mitch had let her in the gate without question.

"Thank you Mitch, I don't mean to be any trouble. No, my mother is not here, she doesn't even know I'm here…." Kendra braced for the response, the explosion. But there wasn't one, just silence.

She took a deep breath and continued. "My mom's going to be real mad. I did a really really stupid thing, Mitch. I'm too embarrassed to even tell you exactly what happened. I came down by myself, and got in serious trouble. I was lied to and came down here believing the lie…." Kendra didn't want to mention her father, afraid that would make Mitch turn around and drive her back to the gate. So she said it had been an internet romance. "And now I don't have a way home."

He noticed she wasn't even carrying a purse, no bags, luggage. He was impressed with the mature delivery of her message. Her pant legs were dirty as if she had been through vegetation somewhere, and her sandals were way too impractical for walking. Her outfit was older, outdated, weird.

He could tell something was definitely up. *But what?* He saw that Kendra's hands were shaking slightly, and that she could hardly look at him. She was trying to keep her hands folded on her lap, looking down at them. He could sense the realness of her shame. *And fear … and despair.*

She kept looking over her shoulder toward the road, worried about being followed, although she never saw another car on the road.

"Let's get you up to the house, you can get cleaned up there. Then you can call your mom. You have to. She's probably very worried, incredibly worried." *This explains that cryptic phone call that I got from Terri yesterday. Guess I should have answered her,* Mitch told himself. *Damn woman, now look at this beautiful kid of hers.*

Kendra looked at him with more fear on her face. She shook her head a little.

"If she doesn't know where you are, you need to call her." Mitch was insistent. He hadn't wanted to talk to Terri for years, and now here he was telling her kid she had to talk to her, fancy that. He parked the cart and led her into his large kitchen. It was immaculate, everything was in its place. He pointed to the phone on the wall and opened the cupboard, pulling out two glasses.

"What would you like to drink?" He opened the refrigerator and pointed to a large selection of chilled beverages.

"Can I bother you for a large glass of ice water? I'm so parched for just water, thank you!"

He filled the glass with ice cubes and filtered water. She drank it in one gulp like she hadn't had a drink in a week. He filled it again. She tried to gulp it more slowly, barely. He poured her another one after that.

"Time to call your mother. I'll leave you alone, give you some privacy." He pointed to the phone again and left the room.

Kendra knew it was a couple of days after she was supposed to have gotten home, and wondered if her mother had noticed yet. Then she wondered whether her mother had contacted either Diane or Derek or both. She took a deep breath, picked up the phone, and dialed. It rang six times before the recorded message came on. "I'm sorry, we're not home right now, leave a message."

She was half relieved to find that her mother didn't pick up the phone. She left a message: "Hi Mom, I'm sorry, I really screwed up, I know you're going to hate me forever for this, and, and you were right. ... I'm sorry, I should have listened to you. I'm on St. Todos island, at your old friend Mitch's house, I don't have a way home. ... I'll try you later. ... Please don't hate me forever for this." *Oh Mom, sorry I'm with Mitch, oh no....*

She hung up and sat down. All this time she had been so strong and now she couldn't hold it back. She started to sob and cry. In fact, she couldn't stop.

Mitch walked into the room, put his hand on her shoulder, and handed her a box of Kleenex. "She wasn't home, huh?"

"No. ... I'll try again later, maybe she doesn't even realize I'm not back or back late. I was so bad to leave behind her back!"

She couldn't stop crying. "What if something has happened to her!"

Mitch patted her on the shoulder. "I'm sure she's just fine," he assured her.

Kendra wasn't so sure. Those guys were bad people, and they wanted money from Terri, money she didn't have. But Kendra chose not to tell Mitch this, *he wouldn't believe this, why try.*

"Come on, I'll show you to a room, you can take a bath, get cleaned up. Maybe take a nap. You'll feel better and we'll try calling again later."

Mitch's voice was paternally calming, and Kendra relaxed some. She finally felt safe.

****

She was very ready to shower off the filth of the past days, to wash away that creepy pudgy guy's touch. She couldn't wait to unwind that ridiculously tight braid and brush her own hair. She sprinkled delicious scented bath salts in the water and soaked in the tub. She looked around at the luxurious surroundings while rubbing off the dead peeling skin with a soft wash cloth. This itself was an endless job, as her sunburn was so bad. She was appalled at the color of her nails. The pudgy man had insisted on painting them and wondered if Mitch had any acetone to remove the stuff.

Mitch had put out an array of clothes for her to try on, to see if something was comfortable for her to wear. He didn't have much to offer but thought anything would be better than the outfit she had arrived wearing. *What God awful thing has happened to this girl*, he wondered.

Eventually Kendra reappeared clean and wearing a pair of his old shorts rolled way up and one of his polo shirts. The clothes were a bit over sized, but she felt much better. "Perfect, thank you!" She was so happy to be out of those awful clothes and didn't care at all that Mitch's clothes bagged on her. She smiled gratefully as Mitch showed her the rest of his home. It was large enough for a family but it seemed just right for Mitch. He was obviously very proud of each room as he had designed and built them all himself.

After the short tour, and promising she could spend as much time as she pleased in his library, he insisted she try calling home once more. But all she got was the recording again. She tried hard not to appear disappointed, but she really missed her mother and couldn't wait to get home.

She hung up without leaving another message.

****

They went back to his library and talked late into the evening. He made Kendra dinner, serving his fish specialty and different local vegetables, steamed with rice. Kendra was very hungry and ate and ate. They laughed as Mitch told Kendra his stories and as Kendra began to share hers.

She ended the evening with a small amount of information about where she had been. She was really embarrassed about her stupidity and naivety, and about her father who she assumed Mitch hated. She didn't want to mention him but finally did. Instinctively she felt as though she could trust Mitch with her feelings.

"Mitch, my dad, Rick, well...."

"Rick."

Kendra gulped. "Yes, Rick, he contacted me on Facebook and said he was my dad. I believed him and did what he said to do. Then really bad things happened. How could I have trusted him, why? Because I wanted a dad so much? I mean, I guess he's really my dad, but what kind of dad would do this? I don't know what to believe now." It just came out of her mouth. "Yep, he said he would give me an all expense paid vacation to paradise, and my mom refused to let me go. So I went behind her back." She looked down in disgrace. "Mitch, that's what happened."

"Wow." *Rick. Rick taking advantage of Kendra. Just like Rick.*

"I guess I must have ditched my creepy dad pretty well, cuz he hasn't found me! Or maybe he doesn't care. I can't believe I was that stupid." She tried not to cry. "I don't know what I'd do without you or where I would have gone! Thank you! Thank you so much."

"I still don't understand why this guy who says he's your dad, Rick, didn't have a round trip ticket for you."

Now Kendra stopped talking a moment and just looked at Mitch in silence, not wanting to ruin anything about that night with her new friend. And, that Sir and his sidekick, Bannister, had humiliated her so very much, she didn't want to talk about them or about how she'd escaped them. She thought she'd better stop saying so much.

She did touch briefly on the medallion, saying that it seemed Rick had needed it to get out of debt. But Kendra was evasive about all this, not wanting to tell Mitch the whole truth, if she even knew this whole truth, which she was wondering about now.

The medallion!?!? Mitch decided to hide his great alarm hearing this. Mitch then offered and arranged to put Kendra on a flight home first thing the next morning.

Kendra was telling herself that Mitch was so nice. How could her mom have screwed up things with Mitch for someone like Rick? *What losers Rick and his friends are. Mitch would've been a much better dad.*

"This was all so dangerous. You don't know who's down here, a lot of driftwood—people floating around here one day, gone the next. And criminals of all kinds. Even pirates. You have to be so careful these days."

Here comes the lecture. I probably deserve it though.

"Promise me you'll never do anything like that again? OK?"

That was it? That was the whole lecture?

"Oh yes, Mitch, I've learned my lesson. A huge lesson." Tears came to her eyes again as her face blushed with shame. She felt like she was still lying to her new friend, leaving out the part about the scary pudgy man and his huge assistant, Bannister. She never wanted to see them again.

Mitch then led her into his office and removed a large oil painting from the wall. Behind it was a secret part of the wall that slid away when he tapped it with morse code or something, and behind that was a wall safe. He reached for the knob and started turning it back and forth until he grabbed the handle and clicked it open. He reached in and pulled out a small leather box and a small stack of papers.

"OK, now I am telling you something you do not repeat. ... Here is the big deal about the medallions," he went on to explain as he opened the small box and held his gold piece out for her to see. "I have one too."

"Yes, this is like my mother's...."

167

"We had quite a time, your mother and I. I thought we were both going to die because of these gold pieces." Mitch flipped the medallion up in the air and then caught it backhanded.

Kendra had heard the story before, many times from her mother, but somehow it was different coming from Mitch.

"Mom said you saved her life." Kendra wanted Mitch to know in case her mom had never been gracious enough to tell him herself.

"I guess you could say that, then she saved my life. What a time we had." He put the medallion back into its small box and showed her the papers. "These medallions were designed by a king, for his son. There were three medallions, history says. We know there were at least two because we, your mom and I, have them. They were brought out here to buy some islands for the king. But they were lost at sea."

"Cool!" Kendra examined all the research Mitch had done on the pieces.

"Owning one of them is something, as they are extremely valuable. Owning two makes them even more valuable, and of course, wow if anyone ever had possession of all three—well, who knows what that could mean. A historian would probably say these are priceless."

Mitch pointed to the timeline on one of the pages. "The story goes, the loss of these medallions caused the fall of that king and his empire. The events that followed two failed attempts across the Atlantic—the loss of the medallions and the resulting failure to purchase those highly strategic islands—left them vulnerable. That king, he lost everything. These medallions should be in a museum, I guess."

"Wow, so you have one, and my mom has the other. Who has the third?"

"Well Kendra, that is the billion dollar question. No one knows who exactly has what...I know what Terri and I have, but the third medallion?" He shrugged his shoulders. "Nobody has ever come forward publicly to say he, or she, owns it."

"Did you and my mom let people know? The public?"

"No, I felt it was too dangerous to tell anyone. A few people here and there were told. I had to show them, as I researched the value and story. But all signed confidentiality statements for me." Mitch smiled a moment, then frowned. *Why did Terri ever tell Rick for God sake!* Mitch cringed inside.

"What, is there more to the story?"

"So Rick knows about Terri's, and wants it. Geez, mmph, now people, everyone will know about the medallions, if they don't know already." Mitch's mouth was terse thinking about it, he grit his teeth. Terri's medallion was not his problem, he could only imagine what she was doing with hers. But now maybe people would figure out that he had the other one. *Not a good idea, not fun, not safe. Terri, your decisions in life are still harming me. And looks like harming this kid too, your daughter for God sake!*

"Kendra, you can never tell anyone any of this, OK? You see how your mother telling Rick, if that's what she did, or Rick finding out somehow else, put you in danger all these years later."

"Yes, I do, and I will never tell." Kendra wondered if now would be a good time to tell Mitch about Sir and Bannister. She decided not to. She was this close to getting home, and would tell her mom to put that medallion in a safe deposit box. Mitch's was locked up, and her mother's should be too. Then she and her mother would be safe again, and so would her mother's medallion, back in San Diego, Kendra told herself.

"Enough said. Are you hungry for some ice cream?" Mitch reached into the freezer.

27

The connecting flights seemed to Terri to go on forever. Two stops, and hours and hours of waiting. She couldn't arrive soon enough. *Kendra!* The whole flight, on both flights, Terri resisted the temptation of her favorite flight drink, a bloody Mary with a beer. She needed to keep a clear head.

With each of the two stopovers, she managed to step outside the terminal and breathe fresh air. The air was growing denser with hot sticky humidity at each stop. With a final layover in Puerto Rico, she was almost there.

She walked up to the large window and looked out at the tarmac lined with tall coconut palms, their fronds waving in the breeze. Below, the locals moved at a slower pace which was somehow the way it all worked down there. Everything was slower, much more relaxed, except Terri. She couldn't stop pacing, her heart couldn't stop pounding. She was tired from the flight and hadn't had enough rest. She couldn't stop thinking about her dear little Kendra being in trouble, being held hostage, and her horrible ex-husband, Rick, and about how much she wanted to hurt Rick for harming her daughter. He wasn't a father by any stretch of the word.

A part of Terri was feeling as if she was coming home, but she knew that this wasn't her home any more. She would now be a stranger in a familiar land. A pit grew in her stomach as she started to think about who she still would know on the island. The list was small.

Things are going to be different now, very different, as so much time has passed. She was much older and her beloved boss, Melvin, was gone now, and that was hard to think about. There would be no one at the dive shop who she would know, no one who would know her. There would be no reason to go into the shop now except for the nostalgia.

Who am I going to call? What am I going to do? Rick said he'd be at the airport to meet her, but he had proved less than reliable in most situations.

She had left that stupid message on Mitch's machine. Mitch had never returned her call, and she hadn't expected him to. Nor could she blame him, she had stomped on his heart so badly, she reminded herself. And she couldn't stop kicking herself for making one bad move after another. *Leaving Mitch at the altar!* He was right to never speak to her again. She had tried to reach him so many times, especially after Kendra was born, but he never answered or returned her call. He clearly wanted nothing to do with her. She had even taken Kendra down there, and tried to find him, but he had made himself entirely unavailable.

She reached down into her pocket, tapping the medallion as she thought of Mitch. Her heart began to race with anxiety— she was walking around with the medallion! Mitch would be so mad at her if he ever found this out, and he would call her totally irresponsible for carrying the piece around in her pocket. *Crap, Mitch.* He was right to think the worst of her.

Mitch was the one who had done the research on their two gold medallions. He had done that research, "to protect us" he had always said. They had shared the two pieces, one for her, one for him, but they were supposed to be for both of them together. Mitch had said that together they were worth so much more than apart, *the medallions that is.*

They had found the second matching medallion in the treasure they salvaged together. Mitch had researched the story of the curious medallions, dating them back to a king, and had told Terri there was a third one out there somewhere, no one knew where.

She never really understood the true value of the gold medallions. Mitch told her they were invaluable. He told her she had to keep hers in a safe deposit box, or a wall safe. But Terri's safe deposit box was a shoe box carefully tucked up in her closet. Now here she was, almost to her destination, twirling her medallion in her pocket without protecting it, and without a plan. *I need a plan.*

****

Rick was trapped on Grand Key with Peg and Joe. The three of them ticked away the minutes which became hours. They were trapped in the small office with hardly anything to eat or drink, waiting for Terri's messages about when she was coming.

Their resources were down to non-existent and the three couldn't stop arguing about what to do next. They hadn't heard anything more from Kendra's kidnapper in the last twenty-four hours and Rick was worried they would never see Kendra again.

Rick had begged Terri to bring the medallion to save Kendra, but she hadn't said she would. They knew she would be arriving first thing in the morning. Someone had to go to St. Todos to meet her. They had less than a quarter tank of gas in the boat, which was out there tied up to the small public dock. That was just enough gas to get to St. Todos, but not enough to get back. And as if this wasn't bad enough, they had left the Land Rover parked a mile away, right where it had run out of gas. They were hoping no one would say anything or complain about the Land Rover just sitting there, but they didn't have any other choices.

Rick sat slumped over in his chair with his hands up covering his ears. The sound of Peg's gum chewing had taken its toll on his nervous system. He wanted to lash out at Peg and make the snapping noise stop. That obnoxious unending sound, coupled with Joe's constant sniffling and the loud blowing of his nose, was too much. Rick felt that the walls were closing in around him.

Joe was too much for Peg. She started announcing "oh gross" every time Joe sniffed and blew his nose followed by his neat compulsive folding of the hankie and wiping his forehead. Peg knew there were only so many ways to fold that hankie without Joe eventually wiping the awful snot on his forehead.

"Why don't you quit it, Joe!" she would exclaim. "You do that then you want me to kiss that forehead?"

Joe would stand there with his bright red nose, watching Peg shooting him a look and proceed with a long monologue of how much he detested the Caribbean and its airborne allergens. He would tell her he had done it all for her, so she should shut the fuck up, end of story.

Rick was stuck with this disgusting duo until the end. And the end, well, Rick couldn't shake the feeling that it was already game over. He couldn't see a way out. *Who knows what that guy did with Kendra, she could be long gone by now, sold to some other drug lord, or made another mistress in his own collection. And when Terri did arrive, how would they guarantee their safety and Kendra's....*

****

They all stared at the phone, waiting for it to ring. When it did, it could be Terri, or it could be the man they only knew to refer to as Sir. They wondered if Sir was holding Kendra at the house right there on Grand Key, but there was no way to find out. Every time the three tried to discuss a plan of some sort, all hell would break loose with their three different plans, none very good, none they could put into effect, ending in silence.

Rick wanted to go to St. Todos alone to get Terri. Joe and Peg disagreed, deciding they couldn't trust Rick. They wanted to go with him, but at the same time Joe wanted to stay behind and avoid the boat ride. Peg didn't trust Joe. *What was he really saying? What might he do here all alone?* Peg was having nothing to do with leaving Joe behind, nor with letting Rick go get Terri by himself. She insisted they all stick together.

The one thing they could all agree on was that Terri had to get to Grand Key quickly, and that the fastest way was for them to go pick her up in the boat. Terri would have the cash to fill the boat's gas tank and feed them. Then they could buy gas to get them back to the office where they needed to wait for their further instructions.

A familiar green Land Rover drove up to the front of the office, all three quickly recognized it. It was the one they had "borrowed" and driven themselves around in. They were all silent as they watched, with the rhythm of Peg's gum chewing picking up speed in the silence. Snap, snap, snap. An extremely large, angry looking man was standing at the door. Peg and Joe automatically looked over at Rick, expecting Rick to get up and answer it.

Rick went over and unlatched the lock on the inside of the door. Bannister pushed his way in, pushing the door with his left arm. He was holding a short, fat wooden bat in his right hand. Rick stepped backward into Joe's chair, falling down onto Joe. Rick was unable to take his eyes off the giant man in the middle of the small room. The three looked at the imposing and terrifying large framed man holding that bat.

Bannister started to tap the bat into his left palm as he began to speak coldy. "My boss requires your presence." His voice was surprisingly articulate for such a barbaric looking brute, his arms larger in diameter than Rick's legs.

"Where is Kendra? Do you have her? I want to see her!" Rick sat upright now. Joe cowardly grabbed at Rick, trying to use him as a shield from the angry looking Neanderthal. Rick pushed Joe away from him and stood up. The room was so small and the man so huge that Rick immediately found himself looking into the large man's chest. The large man reached out and grabbed Rick's neck, wrapping his large fingers around it. Rick reached up and tried to pull those fingers away, but they wouldn't budge.

"I'd rather not kill you, at least not now," the man said.

Rick tried to relax instead of struggle. Rick knew that if the man had wanted to, he could have squeezed and snapped Rick's neck right then and there, but he hadn't. Rick relaxed his muscles and the man began to loosen his grip. Rick was finally able to get a word out.

"Sorry, I'm sorry, I'm concerned for my daughter, we're doing everything we can."

Bannister wasn't impressed by this. He wanted to choke the life out of Rick as well as Rick's precious daughter for humiliating him like she did. But Bannister knew he couldn't. The boss wanted to keep Kendra as his own private pet. And the boss had told Bannister that he needed Kendra's pitiful dad alive, for now. Bannister released his grip, almost pushing Rick away. Bannister's brute strength was undeniable, he could kill them all without breaking into a sweat.

Bannister stood there and tapped the short bat into his palm again, making sure they all understood that Bannister always got what he wanted, no matter what. "You three are coming with me."

"But," Rick started, stopping as soon as the brute looked at him. He didn't want that man wrapping those big fingers around his neck again. But Rick was supposed to meet Terri tomorrow morning at the airport on St. Todos. Their boat was tied up out front, how was he supposed to get the medallion?

Peg tried the only thing she knew how to do, be a girl.

"Come on Rick, let this man show us the way," she said as she looked up at Bannister and fluttered her painted bright blue eye lids at him, then winked. Standing up next to him, she appeared eager to obey his every command.

Bannister pushed Peg forward. She stumbled on the edges of her embellished sandals, catching herself on the arm of a chair. "Hey! That's no way to treat a lady." She looked at him, offended. She chewed away at her cud, checking her long acrylic manicured nails for a scratch.

"Lady? What lady," Bannister grunted as he grabbed her arm and led her toward the door.

Joe remained seated, afraid to budge and defend his Peg. She looked back at him, waiting for him to help with the situation. He blew his nose and stood up, looking down at the floor as he walked the three steps toward the door, standing next to her.

Bannister motioned them into the Land Rover, all in the back. He closed and locked the door, locking them in. They looked at each other, all remembering too late that this jeep had that lock-in function. They were scared. Bannister drove them all away, out of the small town, up the slow windy road.

VOLUME THREE: RAPTIS TRILOGY

****

<u>28</u>

"Now boarding flight 181 for St. Todos."

The loud speaker woke Terri out of her daydream. She was so exhausted and so worried about Kendra that she couldn't think. And with every passing minute, she was growing more confused, scared for Kendra, and afraid about what she was going to have to do. Swallowing hard, Terri moved toward the gate, feeling a greater sense of doom with each step, a sense she just couldn't shake. She had no idea what she was getting herself into.

Plan the dive, dive the plan, she kept telling herself over and over, trying to boost her confidence, only to be followed in her head by, *I need a plan, I need a plan.* She stepped onto the plane and found a seat.

****

The small plane landed abruptly on the short runway. Terri was sitting up in her seat, ready to rush off the stuffy plane before it came to a stop. Just the sight of the island below as they were landing ignited her spirit. She stepped out onto the tarmac at this newly redesigned airport. She didn't recognize anything, it was all new. *It's all different.* And so was she.

She walked inside and looked at everyone, watching for Rick. Her stomach began to growl, she was so hungry. She walked right past two men who were watching her, acting unaware of them. She had noticed them, as they were so neatly dressed in their light colored slacks and crisp overly ironed shirts. They didn't look like typical average tourists, or even like local businessmen. They stuck out, and were very noticeable to Terri who nervously hid her nervousness from them. She just walked on.

Terri sat down in the middle of the terminal. The sticky, humid heat of the tropical summer was already slowing her down. The board lit up, her luggage had arrived. She walked over and retrieved her bag. Sitting down, she waited for Rick to arrive. It was late and she was growing intensely impatient.

This bastard's a no-show, I knew it. He's an idiot. Now what? Guess I should go clean up a bit. Terri gathered all of her belongings and headed to the women's bathroom.

****

"Thank you Mitch, really, thank you so much." A tear formed in Kendra's eye as she realized that this was it, it was time to say goodbye. She had grown unusually fond of Mitch over the last short twenty-four hours. She had been up most of the night before, just lying in bed and wondering who her mother would be, what their life would be like, if her mother had remained with him.

But then she had chuckled to herself, realizing that if her mom had chosen Mitch, then she, Kendra, would have never been born. *So moot point. Mom lived life her way, always her way. Whatever her mom's reasons were, it was her life to live.*

Kendra was really missing her mom.

Mitch too felt that a fondness had developed between himself and Kendra. He found himself feeling rather fatherly toward her. Or maybe uncle-like. There was clearly some kind of connection with this wonderful young lady. He couldn't help but feel a bit envious of Terri, having and raising such a bright, adventurous daughter. But Mitch had also quickly grown somewhat fearful of getting too attached to Kendra. Yes, she was so easy to have around, but yes, she was Terri's daughter.

Still, Kendra needed his help, and he felt it was OK to help her out—more than OK, a must to help her. But he couldn't let himself be invested any further than that. That road would lead him back to Terri. He wasn't going to take that road.

"You're welcome, Kendra, I'm happy to help." He reached and pulled his wallet out of his back pocket, taking out a small stack of twenty dollar bills. He handed them to her. "Here, take this, you're going to need to eat and whatever to get home."

She was stunned at his generosity and so relieved she began to cry. This was something she had envisioned her dad doing. Instead, her dad had ripped her off, lied to her, endangered her, risked her life for money.

"Thank you forever and ever, Mitch, thank you!" She tearfully reached and gave Mitch a quick peck on the cheek and a warm hug. "I hate goodbyes," she said, not able to look him in the eyes, as she felt she was going to cry again.

"Me too. Now go have a good flight. Email me or call me when you get home, please, so I am sure you got there safely."

"I'll be OK, but don't worry I will call or email, yes." Kendra smiled and gave a short wave of her hand. "I hope to meet you again someday, really. And again thank you!"

Mitch nodded, thinking to himself this would have to be when she was older and without Terri.

She closed the car door, smiling at him, trying not to cry.

He smiled back, surprised at the upwelling emotions he was feeling inside. Now he had to cut the tie and let go. As he watched Kendra walk into the airport, he wanted to go run after her, race into the airport and hug this strange kid, Kendra, just to say goodbye again, just to see her off the right way, even though Kendra had asked for a quiet and not too emotional send off. But he knew he had to let go. This was Terri's kid. *Terri of all people.*

****

Kendra stepped into the terminal, looking for the ticket counter. She was quite able to travel on her own, she had learned from her mother while a child. The place was surprisingly uncrowded. She took the opportunity to use the bathroom to tidy up. Her skin was peeling off in sheets. She couldn't control this no matter how much lotion she rubbed on it.

She walked toward the bathroom area, stopping briefly to examine the blue placards, determining which door to walk into.

At that moment, Terri stepped out of the ladies' room, and stepped right into Kendra. "Kendra!!!" she shouted in disbelief.

"Mom!" Kendra was equally shocked. There was her mother, right in front of her! She broke down sobbing, apologizing in gasps and tears, as she reached out to her mother, grabbing her with both hands, hugging her hard.

"How did you— " They both said it at the same time, looking at each other with surprise, stunned. They both started crying and laughing at the same time.

"Mom, Mom! I am so so sorry." Kendra hugged Terri again, not wanting to let go, she was so dumbfounded to find her mother there.

Terri saw the two neatly dressed men she had noticed earlier walking toward them. Something about their posturing sent up a red flag in Terri's mind. Kendra had her back to them and never noticed them until they were right beside them. Each of the men reached and put a hand on Kendra and Terri's opposite shoulders, squeezing, to make a point.

"Kendra, we've been looking everywhere for you," the one man said calmly in a thick accent.

Kendra swung around in disbelief, *Who were these men?* She didn't recognize them. The man grabbed her arm and the other grabbed Terri's.

"Our car is parked out front," the other man announced as he began to pull on Terri's arm.

"Hey!" Terri shouted, trying to pull away. "Let us go! I'm going to scream!" She felt something hard press into her side.

"Let's not draw a crowd," the man said, pushing on the gun barrel even harder to make a point. "These people don't want to witness a public execution, you think?" He sneered at her.

"Mom!" Kendra was shocked and terrified. She didn't recognize these two men, didn't know how they fit into all this she had been through. Were they connected to Rick? In the comfort of Mitch's home, she had temporarily let herself forget about Rick's troubles. "Mom, do as they say."

Terri looked at Kendra, surprised, cocking her head, a rebellious, questioning look.

"Mom, please! Do what they want." Kendra pleaded again as Terri continued to struggle.

"Don't worry, sweetheart." Terri looked back at Kendra as the man with the gun pushed her to the door, the other man pushing Kendra right behind them. Terri couldn't make eye contact with anyone watching, no one wanted to watch, no one wanted to be a witness. No one cared two women were being taken away. She was desperate to recognize anyone, any familiar face. She looked down the row of taxi cab drivers, hoping to see an old friend. *No one!*

They opened the back passenger doors and ordered the ladies into the back seat. They drove away from the airport.

Kendra had her head between her knees. Terri reached out, putting her hand on Kendra's back and patting, trying her desperate best to comfort her daughter. Terri scanned the landscape, finally feeling some familiarity. *Some things here haven't changed,* she told herself.

<u>29</u>

Mitch had stopped in town after dropping Kendra off. He had a quick business meeting with Roy, and they were starting the day over coffee. Roy was still laughing about how small the world was.

"How strange was that? Me picking up Terri's daughter! Hitchhiking!" Roy was curious, he wanted to hear all about it from Mitch. The last time he had seen Mitch was when he had dropped Kendra off at Mitch's house.

"Over the years, I've come to learn how strange life is, Roy." Mitch was in a philosophical mood as he took a long sip of coffee. "Yes, it was strange, it sure did surprise me when, of all things, this girl appeared and ended up at my house!"

"I know! I about shit when she said she wanted to find a guy named Mitch."

The two laughed out loud together.

"Tell me about it, was she a good kid? She sure is beautiful."

"Yes, a good kid. And beautiful. Roy, you can sure see a lot of her mom in her, so feisty," he laughed a little sadly. "But she also had a real different side, something different from Terri. She'd gotten caught up in some kind of mess with her dad, she finally told me last night. Said she couldn't live with herself without telling me the truth. She had wanted a vacation away from her mom, had wanted get to know her dad, she said." Mitch took another sip of his coffee. Something about all this, whatever it was, he didn't know, but it caught his attention again. He just wasn't entirely convinced that that was the whole story.

"What did you do? Did you call Terri?"

"Me? Call Terri? Hell no. I had Kendra call home though, three times, no one answered. She didn't seem surprised. She left a message. I just left from the airport, just now. I got her a ticket back home and dropped her off. She was really grateful, and we had fun!"

Roy listened to his friend as he rambled on.

"She was a nice kid, surprisingly well read for her age. We talked for hours last night, we could have talked all night, but I could see she was exhausted and had been through something quite extreme, whatever it was. Something pretty strange I think. But she's a good kid. Hope she'll be OK."

Mitch had a smile on his face as he was thinking about Kendra. He couldn't stop talking about her. "I gave her two books to take home, stuff from my collection. Turns out she has an interest in engineering, and she loves math!"

"Sounds like you really made a connection. You two have more in common than you and Terri ever did!"

"She'll flip through the pages on the flight and find a few surprises. I stuck a few crisp one hundred dollar bills in each book for her to find." Mitch smiled and took a sip.

"You gave her money?" Roy was surprised but not that surprised. Mitch was forever generous with his money, helping every wounded bird he found, including Roy himself. Mitch had given Roy the opportunity years ago to run the new marina Mitch had bought. It was at a time when no one else would hire Roy. He was a very grateful, very loyal friend.

"Just a little bit of money, Roy, not much…. OK, I'm out of here, things to do!" Mitch had finished his coffee and was standing up, putting cash on the table.

Roy stayed and finished the breakfast he had ordered, once it finally arrived. When he was done with breakfast, he walked down the block to his jeep, pausing to look out at the harbor and take some deep breaths before getting back to work.

****

Terri could see the town approaching. She was looking out the window, looking for someone, anyone that might see her and remember her. Her face was pressed against the glass, steaming the window with her breath. She searched for a face she recognized. She studied each face that she could see.

There he was! Unbelievable! She hadn't seen him in so long she hardly recognized him, but she was sure of it. Shorter, gray hair, a mustache, but she was sure it was Roy, her old friend Roy! He was standing on the sidewalk, stretching, looking out.

Unable to lower the window, she threw herself against it and banged with everything she had, hoping to get Roy's attention from across the street. Kendra looked out the window and saw Mitch's friend, Roy, the one who had picked her up hitchhiking. He was looking right at them, standing next to his jeep. He squinted in disbelief, shading his eyes, looking back at the car as it passed by slowly in traffic.

"Shut up back there!" the driver shouted at the two just as they got Roy's attention.

Roy didn't know what to think. Mitch had just left. But he'd said he had just given Kendra money and put her on a plane home. *And now here she is, and with Terri?* He was sure that it was Terri, it had been years but he would recognize that face in a flash. *What the—?* Roy thought best to check in with Mitch on the CB radio, to tell him what he saw.

"Mitch, Roy, over."

"This is Mitch, over."

Roy started his jeep and pulled out onto the street as he talked, he didn't want to lose sight of the car carrying Kendra and Terri.

"You did say you dropped Kendra off, correct? Over."

"Yes, before I saw you this morning, over."

"I'm following Kendra and her mother right now, I don't recognize the car or driver, over."

"I'm sorry, didn't get that, over."

"Kendra and Terri are in the back seat of a car up ahead. Over."

There was a long silence as emotions began to well up in Mitch's head. Did Kendra play him like her mother used to? Her mother. *Terri? In town?* Mitch tried to keep calm. He had to look into this, as it made no sense that Kendra was not already on her flight out.

"License plate number, over."

"B672UH, over."

"Do me a favor, follow them, see where's she's going, what she's up to. But stay hidden. Over."

"Will do, over." Roy followed the sedan across the island to the east side. Kendra looked back and could see her friend, Roy, following. She smiled knowing someone was watching them, someone cared!

But the two men driving also noticed Roy following them.

When they reached a long lonely stretch of road, they slowed down and pulled over to the side, stopping. "You two don't get out or you're dead," one of the men told them.

Roy pulled up and parked behind them, watching as the two men got out of the car. He wasn't sure what he was going to do or say, but wanted to know if Terri and Kendra were OK.

Terri and Kendra were watching out the back window as Roy stepped out of the car to talk to them. The air conditioner was running and the men had turned the radio up. Terri and Kendra couldn't hear a thing from inside. The two men and Roy were all smiling at first as they appeared to be chatting away. The driver reached out as if to shake Roy's hand, Roy extended his.

Then it all happened so quickly.

Instead of shaking Roy's hand, the man grabbed it and twisted it behind his back. Roy was in a hold, he couldn't fight back. Terri and Kendra banged at the window, watching as Roy became helpless. The other man walked up to Roy while he was in an arm lock from behind. He grabbed Roy's head with both hands. First he kicked Roy in the groin with his knee, to which Roy doubled over in pain. Before Roy knew what was next, the man twisted his head fast and hard to the right, snapping the vertebrae column in his neck.

Roy's mouth dropped and his eyes shot wide open in pain as the men let him crumble to the ground, his knees hitting the pavement with all of his weight before landing face down. Kendra could see his chest was laboring for a breath, while his tongue hung out of the side of his mouth, drooling blood. He had no control over any bodily functions. He soiled his pants then stopped breathing as his eyes stuck wide open with a permanent look of surprise.

Kendra and Terri exploded inside the back seat, banging on the windows, screaming for Roy after watching him killed right there in front of them. The men lifted Roy's limp body into Roy's jeep, and buckled the seat belt around his torso. Then they put the jeep in neutral, and pushed it off the road and into a rock. It was a quick attempt to suggest a one car accident.

The men returned to the car and looked at the women now cowering in the backseat. They were sniffing back their tears, wiping their faces with their hands. Kendra was so traumatized she could not think clearly or stay quiet. "You killed him! You killed him!" she cried over and over.

"Shut up!" the men demanded as they put the car in gear and sped away from the scene. "We're almost there!"

Terri tried her best to keep strong, both for herself and for Kendra. She had to stay alert and aware. She could not give in to fear or panic. She put her arm around Kendra and tried to console her the best she could. Terri's stomach growled and her body was feeling extremely hypoglycemic. She had to work hard on her mental game now, she had to talk herself through this. *Stay calm, conserve energy, don't panic.*

Twenty minutes later they were at a gate in front of the house where Kendra had been held hostage a few days earlier. The men opened the gate with a code and drove the sedan down the steep driveway.

Kendra cringed at the thought of seeing Sir, *Pudgy.* And now here was her mom. *What was he going to do?* She wasn't sure if she could live through anymore of his humiliation, let alone this terror. And she wondered if her mom could.

No one was there to greet them. The men parked the car. They forced the women out of the back seat and down to the small private dock on the water. They stood in silence looking out, watching.

VOLUME THREE: RAPTIS TRILOGY

****

<u>30</u>

Mitch was at his desk when Clift, his good friend and the chief of police, called.

"Mitch, I'm sorry to bother you but it's Roy. You're gonna to want to come over and see dis. Go east on route 27, meet me dere. Hurry."

"Right away." Mitch was numb, he didn't like the way Clift sounded. He knew it wasn't good, and had a feeling it was something very bad.

By the time Mitch and Clift arrived the other officers had already touched everything and moved everything, including Roy's body, out of the jeep.

"Looks like an accident, mon," one of the attending officers said, giving his official opinion as he was writing his report.

"Roy didn't have accidents." Mitch couldn't believe what he was seeing. His best friend, Roy, was dead on the ground, strange pebble marks embedded on his face, nothing else on his body except the small rocks and scrapes on both knees, and on his neck a strange red mark.

Clift came up from behind and put his hand on Mitch's back.

"What happened? This isn't right." Mitch knelt down and was holding Roy's hand, talking to him as if he was going to speak back. He was having a hard time holding the tears back, trying to be strong. Mitch knew the last he heard from Roy, he was following a car with Kendra and Terri in it. This didn't look right. *What had happened?*

Mitch stood up, he had questions about the scene for the other officers.

"Where exactly did you find the car?" The officers stood there, lulling around in the heat, looking at him. One officer pointed to the side of the road.

"He crashed against the rock there, we backed his jeep out."

Mitch walked over, looked at the rock, and walked slowly back to the front of the jeep. It didn't make sense, the jeep was barely dented. How could Roy have died in such a small accident? He went back to examine his friend more closely. What was this strange bruising around his neck? It didn't look natural. Mitch knew this wasn't an accident, and suspected Clift was thinking the same thing.

He noticed the bruising on Roy's right hand and thought he saw what looked to be two finger indentations, same there at the bruises on Roy's jaw. He saw the blood dripping out of the side of Roy's mouth, and the stunned look on his face. Mitch reached down and closed those eyes. Nothing about any of this was making sense. Roy's neck was severely bruised all the way around. And, what little evidence there was of what happened there was long gone.

Mitch looked around, he couldn't find any skid marks, no attempt to stop. There were footprints all over, and car tracks everywhere. The coroner's car was pulled up alongside, pretty much messing up the tracks. Mitch couldn't stop shaking his head, he didn't want to accept any of this.

"I don't like it Clift, how could Roy die in such a minor accident?" Mitch shook his head sadly.

Clift just kept looking at the scene, now shaking his head in unison with Mitch.

"I want an autopsy."

Clift looked at Mitch and sucked on his teeth long and hard before he spoke. "I dunno Mitch, someone drove by and dis is what he found. No one knows what happened here." Clift motioned with his hands to the other man. "Get da yellow sheet, mon."

The man came back with the official yellow tarp and laid it across Mitch's best friend, Roy.

Mitch bowed his head and said a prayer to himself.

Mitch remembered that he had the license plate number, the one of the car Roy was following, sitting there on his desk at home. Roy had given him the information he would need now. Something real bad was up, nothing about this was right. And right in the middle of it all was Terri. *Of all people! And with a daughter, too.*

Mitch felt so responsible. He had opened his door and taken Kendra in. Somehow this girl had turned out to be Terri's daughter. And now look, just as had happened before, one thing was leading to another, and again, someone was dead. This time it was Roy. Mitch decided it was best to tell Clift what he knew.

"Clift, Roy was following someone for me, I had asked him to."

"Who?"

"I don't know who did this, but I have the license plate number. Will you run it for me? Please?"

"Look Mitch, meet me at my office and we'll talk dis afternoon, let's see what da coroner says, OK?"

Mitch looked around at the scene one more time as they zipped the body bag shut and lifted Roy's body onto the coroner's stretcher. They shoved it deep into the wagon's cavernous interior.

"I'm coming with you," Mitch didn't want to leave his buddy's side. "I'll meet you there so I can get his personal belongings. He's like my brother. I'm going to get to the heart of this."

<u>31</u>

Rick, Joe, and Peg were brought back to Sir's large house on the water. Bannister ordered them out of the back seat and taped their hands together with silver duct tape. They stood in the large garage, Joe pleading for Bannister to let him be able to blow his nose, it was dripping. His plea echoed through the concrete garage. Instead, Bannister sealed his mouth with a strip of duct tape.

Peg, who was continually trying to connect with Bannister in any feminine way, showed Bannister her support while Joe tried wiping his nose on his shoulder, which he could barely reach.

"That ought to stop your whining," she scolded her gagged husband, snapping away at her gum, then looking at Bannister for his approval. "I'm so sick of you blowing that red nose."

Bannister tore off another piece of tape and sealed her mouth tight, leaving her wad of gum stuck in her mouth.

Rick was silent, as he had been for quite a while now. But his face said so much about what he was feeling. The look on his face was distraught and worn, haggard. And now he knew what was coming. Bannister tore off another piece of tape. Rick took a large breath from his mouth before Bannister sealed it shut.

******

Next they were led into a back room and ordered to sit down. Bannister used the duct tape again, this time to tape their legs together so they couldn't move. They all turned and faced the doorway as the boss appeared. His wide body was silhouetted by the backlight shining behind him, adding to the mystery.

"You may call me Sir," the pudgy man said.

The three watched as he waddled into the room, slowly inspecting his three captives. His clothes were unwrinkled, his long sleeved shirt and matching slacks were clean, fresh, with the unusual scent of baby powder.

The moisture of the tropical summer air continually disagreed with Sir's delicate skin and temperament. He obsessively washed and powdered himself at least ten times a day. And when in the tropics, he regularly changed many times a day into clean, freshly ironed clothes. He simply couldn't tolerate the feeling of being dirty or perspiring even a little.

King Sir dreaded the visits to the tropics where sometimes his presence was required for business. Life was easier for him in the weather up in Canada. He couldn't wait to get home.

"Here we are." He walked up and stood in front of the three, examining them closer. "Which one of you three is the brains behind this mess you have created?" He looked at Rick first.

Rick watched as Sir's large wraparound sunglasses swung in toward his face for a closer look. Rick saw his own worried reflection being mirrored back and shook his head in slow motion suggesting no, it wasn't he who was the brains behind anything.

Sir snorted in disgust. He continued to Joe who was next to Rick.

Clear snot was running out of Joe's reddened nose, running like a river, racing down the silver duct tape. His shoulders were wet from trying to wipe the stream.

Sir shouted for his assistant. "Bannister! I can't tolerate the look of this man's face, Bannister, it repels me!"

The look on Joe's face turned to horror. *What does* that *mean?*

"Yes Sir." Bannister left the room and came back with a wet towel. He stepped up and ripped the duct tape without warning off Joe's mouth. Joe screamed in pain as the tape pulled a layer of skin off his right cheek. Bannister wiped Joe's face off with the wet towel, quite roughly. Then he wiped the hair away and off Joe's face, leaving a shiny red surface. Joe sniffed and took long deep breaths from his mouth.

"I couldn't breathe man, I couldn't breathe." Joe started to hyperventilate, trying to catch his breath.

"Where is my money?" Sir demanded of him.

"I don't have it, Sir," Joe gasped as he tried to catch his breath. "We have that plan though. Please give me a chance to breathe."

"Yes, your plan. The medallion, we will soon see about the medallion." The man paced the length of the three strapped to their chairs, then stopped in front of Rick again. "Your plan has proven to be quite feisty, I can see where Kendra gets her spirit." Rick looked at the man, his eyes widened.

"You must be the daddy. Yes. Daddy. Bad daddy. Bad, bad daddy." He began to circle Rick with a look of disgust.

"Fortunately for you, I find your daughter's natural beauty quite inviting. She will need some taming of course, some grooming." He looked at Bannister as he said this. Rick could feel the pudgy Sir winking at him behind those dark sunglasses. "But she won't be harmed."

Rick tried to stand up, but couldn't stand all the way. His face was bright red with anger as he yelled through the duct tape. Bannister walked over and shoved Rick hard, stuffing Rick back down in his seat.

Joe kept his mouth shut and focused on his breathing.

"I wish I could say the same for her mother." King Sir looked at his polished nails, catching them in the light. "I have had to extend my stay longer than I wished to be here. It was supposed to be a quick visit, a signature and some minor paperwork to get my ex-wife and everything about her, including this house, out of my life forever. You three have made this quite difficult." He let go of a heavy sigh to underline his point.

Now Sir stepped over to the window and looked out. "I should have taken care of this house matter before my wife disappeared." He was doing his best to keep his cool and the perspiration nagging him at bay. "I must have been too emotional about her disappearance," he said as he let out a snort, emphasizing the word, "disappearance," with sarcasm, "and so I missed a detail...so unlike me." He looked himself over, every inch an attended to detail, from his cufflinks to the evenness of his pant legs, neatly pressed, to the hem of each pant leg, stopping just as it rested on the top of each of his shoes. Even his belt appeared to land at a level dividing his round frame precisely in two.

"Bannister!" Sir practically yelled his name out even though Bannister was standing right there in the room. "Get me those papers! Now!"

Bannister left the room. The boss, Sir, was an inch away from losing his patience at the untidy sight of his three guests.

"Pa...papers?" Joe dared to ask a question.

Bannister walked back into the room with a small stack of typed papers in his hands. He walked over and ripped the duct tape off of Peg's face without warning. She screamed out in pain.

A layer of makeup foundation stuck to the tape. Now her skin showed a long narrow stretch of red across her face. She wiped her face at her shoulders looking back at herself in the reflection of Bannister's sunglasses.

"You hurt me," she said coyly to him, delusional about her feminine prowess. He snorted.

"We're going to call part of this mess you created even, as soon as you two sign these papers I had my attorney write up."

The three looked at him with a glimmer of hope.

"Thank you, Sir, we are so sorry about all the problems we've caused," Peg offered, trying to smooth things over with another apology. *If only I can play this one right.* Perspiration had long since beaded into sweat on her face. Her red hair straggled down into her eyes, catching on her long fake eye lashes. She let out a small nervous smile as they all stared at her. Then she started chewing at the wad of gum she had stored in her mouth. It snapped out loud.

The noise made King Sir cringe, and he looked directly at her. "That noise you are making, it must stop."

Peg stopped chewing and looked back in disbelief that she was doing anything wrong.

Joe looked at her and sniffed. Then Joe snorted, sniffed again, wheezed, then sniffed and snorted.

Sir turned his attention to Joe and looked at him coldly. "I'll have Bannister cut that nose off if you don't stop that annoying noise immediately!"

Rick put his head down, avoiding all eye contact.

Sir pulled out a handkerchief and patted his brow. He was beginning to perspire, feeling so much disdain for the three filthy creatures in front of him. "You will sign the papers and all of the properties, your company will be mine now."

"What?" Peg couldn't believe it. "But—"

Sir glanced at Bannister.

Right then, as if Bannister had read the boss' mind, Bannister's open hand came down across her face.

"Did I ask you to talk? Or make a noise?"

She looked up at Sir, holding her duct taped hands up to her face. She was speechless.

Joe sat up in his seat at the sight but didn't utter a word for fear he'd be next.

Bannister put the papers on Joe's lap, pointing to each sheet, where to sign.

Joe didn't argue now, and wouldn't, not if this was going to get him his freedom. He compulsively sniffed, lifting his shoulder to wipe.

Sir cringed at him.

"How can this be legal?" Peg dared such a naive question as Bannister laid the stack of papers on her lap next.

"Don't concern yourself with questions, sign where asked and my attorneys will take care of all the rest."

"Then we can go, right?" Joe wiggled his nose trying not to sniff. Bannister re-taped Joe's mouth now.

"Bannister will be leaving shortly to pick up the ladies."

Rick looked up.

"After Terri brings me the medallion, which you promised she would have, Bannister will take you three away by boat."

Joe and Peg sat back in their seats, relieved to hear the news. *Certainly Terri will have the medallion to save her daughter*, Peg said to herself.

Rick shook his head, knowing nothing was going to be that easy. If they did have Terri, there was no guarantee anyone was going to get out alive.

"I must freshen," Sir announced to the room. "Bannister? Is the doll case complete?"

"Yes sir."

"It's time to go get the women, bring them here."

"Yes, Sir."

Sir and Bannister left the room while Rick, Peg, and Joe sat and squirmed.

Joe had a careful balance of air he could bring in one nostril at a time, feeling he was going to pass out from lack of oxygen. Peg had to pee and was a cough away from wetting her pants. Rick grew more and more uncomfortable, more nervous now: they were bringing Terri to the house.

PART FOUR

TORTURE, GREED, AND GOLD

VOLUME THREE: RAPTIS TRILOGY

****

32

The women were still in the back seat of the car. Terri was searching the landscape for an escape route they could run to, if the chance to escape arrived.

"This place must have a wall surrounding it." Terri squinted, trying to see what was past the vegetation on the hill.

"No, there's not," Kendra informed her. "Mom, I've been here before."

Both Terri and Kendra saw the boat coming toward the dock at the same time. They were silent as they watched it come closer.

Bannister was behind the wheel, all alone. Kendra was relieved to see that Sir wasn't with him. She let out a sigh. The thirty-two foot fishing vessel was the perfect size for Bannister's large frame.

Terri couldn't help but gasp as she saw Bannister climb out and walk up the dock. The floating wooden planks rocked with each heavy step. His bare legs were thick, dark brown, and muscular, like tree trunks.

Kendra looked away, not wanting to make eye contact. Her hair was down and the skin on her face was peeling, she was wearing baggy men's clothing, she was half hoping Bannister wouldn't recognize her. Then, there he was, standing at the passenger door on her side. She looked up. "Bannister, I'm sorry. I wanted to go home...." She broke down and started to cry.

VOLUME THREE: RAPTIS TRILOGY

****

Terri looked at her, trying to understand, and then realizing this was Kendra's captor. He opened the door and lifted her out by her arms. He then lifted his large hand up, looking at her, suggesting he was going to bring it down across her face, and oh, he wanted to. But he stopped short. The complete look of terror in Kendra and her mother's eyes was at least some of the satisfaction he needed.

Terri screamed, scrambling out of the car, jumping at the man's large frame, holding on to his mammoth arm and trying to pull it away from her daughter's face. He looked at her as if she were a gnat and threw her away. She fell backward onto her butt and hands. Her left ankle was lightly sprained.

"Mom!" Kendra rushed over to her.

Bannister took one large step and reached down, pulling Kendra off her mother.

"Get up!" he demanded of Terri.

Terri did what he said.

The other two men were standing in the background watching, neither one talking or doing anything.

Bannister walked over to them, handed them an envelope, and then said, "Thank you for your work. Remove the license plates and give them to me before you leave. Then take the car to the east end landing strip and leave it with the keys in it, unlocked. Your plane will be waiting to take you home. Good job." Bannister was cold and businesslike, there was no shaking of the hands, and there were no smiles or small talk between the men, just business.

Terri was looking to Kendra while Bannister was talking to the two men. Terri wanted to run, escape. Kendra was too scared to move, she stood still with a hollow look on her face, shaking her head no at her mother's facial gestures.

The men began removing both license plates as they were asked to do. Immediately Bannister was back with Terri and Kendra, giving them his undivided attention. He grabbed each of them by the arm and began leading them down to the dock, to the boat. Kendra obeyed, doing whatever he asked, but Bannister had to pull Terri along. As he did, Terri was kicking and yelling at the "brute" as she was calling him. He instructed Kendra and Terri to climb into the back of the boat.

Terri wouldn't budge. With her hands on her hips, she stared at Bannister. She wanted to know what they had done to her daughter.

Kendra was becoming blank, submissive, so unlike herself in the presence of this man. Terri wanted to fight back, resist, but Kendra wouldn't. After a strange silence, Kendra began pleading with Terri to stop resisting, to do as he was saying to do. Kendra had noticed Bannister's growing impatience and was afraid of what he would eventually do to her mother.

One of the men interrupted Bannister as Bannister began to pull on Terri's arm. "Excuse me, señor." He handed Bannister the two plates.

Bannister grunted back, tossing the license plates into the boat while still gripping Terri's arm. Then Bannister grabbed Terri with both his hands, picking her up easily while her hands were flailing as she beat on his back with her fists in protest.

He dropped Terri down into the back of the boat. She used her arms to catch her fall, rolling out of it although she hit her head hard. She tried her best not to get hurt again. Her left ankle was starting to swell from the sprain.

Bannister didn't care which way she landed.

He was more delicate with Kendra who had grown even more compliant. But Terri could feel the tension between the two, his anger, her fear. It was obvious he hated Kendra and had to force himself to be delicate with her. Clearly, he had been told by someone not to hurt Kendra, not in any way. And Kendra was terrified of Bannister; he'd trusted her and she had fled, and she knew he would never trust her again. So now Kendra complied, afraid of the punishment she knew he wanted to inflict.

With a turn of the key, the engines turned over and Bannister was quickly down to business, pushing the hull away from the dock. The engines gained speed and the boat skipped over the small swell, effortlessly racing toward Grand Key.

****

Terri recognized the small island as they approached. She and Mitch had passed by it numerous times, but they had never had a reason to spend time out that way. *Private property, rocky shores, strong currents*, that was all she remembered about the place. There were no notable dive spots, nothing to visit.

Now it appeared they were headed right for it. She could make out a house in the distance, and saw that it had a small dock. She looked around, taking mental notes on her surroundings. She looked down at the water, always planning for an escape route. But she would never escape without Kendra, she would never leave without Kendra.

Kendra was looking forward, nervously wringing her hands together as they approached. Bannister kept his speed coming into the passage, making a dramatic entrance. He slowed down suddenly, fishtailing the stern end around as he drifted up to the small pier. This was Bannister's personal fishing boat, a gift from his boss, Sir the King.

"Is that Rick's house?" Terri leaned over to Kendra's ear and whispered in a low voice.

"I thought it was," Kendra replied in a low monotone whisper of a voice. She didn't want Bannister to hear. Kendra bit her lip, trying not to cry. Her life was turning into a b-rated horror movie, the kind she and Derek would stay up late and watch. *Derek. Derek.*

Kendra started to imagine what was next. There was no telling what her mom was going to do if she saw Rick. She didn't know what to be more afraid of, her mom's reaction to Rick, or the Sir who she knew would be waiting inside.

Bannister motioned them both out of the boat. Terri was the first to oblige; she couldn't wait to get off. Her stomach was churning. It had been everything she could do to keep from getting seasick in that short amount of time. She was trying her best to appear strong for Kendra, but her inner ears could never tolerate a stopped, rocking boat.

Terri could see the silhouette of a strange, short, very round man standing at a large plate glass window, looking out. Kendra saw him too and cringed at the sight, but didn't say a word. Bannister led them up the groomed walkway and into the house. The short man turned to the two ladies and smiled.

"Twice the fun, how nice is that." He walked over to Kendra. "And you my dear, tsk, tsk, tsk, you really shouldn't have run away." He walked over to Terri but only addressed Kendra, examining the mother head to toe while she glared back. "There was only one way off the island, my dear, one way for you to go home, and we were waiting. I didn't expect to pick your mother up in the same trip. What a bonus for me."

He was looking up at Terri's face. She wasn't that much taller than this pudgy creep of a man, but tall enough that he had to look up into her eyes.

Terri ignored her reflection, trying to see past the lenses of his dark glasses. "Who are you?" she asked.

He let out a light chuckle. "That, my dear, is no concern of yours. What you need to be concerned with is handing me the medallion."

"I don't have any medallion." Terri played dumb.

"Well, someone I know says otherwise." He reached up and stroked his chin. "I had heard the rumor for years, about the two medallions being found, kept in a private collection." He walked back and forth between the two women.

Terri reached into her front pocket.

King Sir stopped short and smiled.

"Let me see it." He leaned up into her face.

"I don't have it. "

He looked at her and smirked.

"Of course you don't, dear." He slapped her cheek, hard.

"Bannister, tie her hands behind her back."

Before she could make a move, Bannister had her in a hold.

Kendra kept quiet until her mom grabbed Bannister's arm and he threw her down. Terri crumbled to the floor. Kendra could hear the wind get knocked out of her. Bannister picked her up and pulled her hands back, wrapping the silver duct tape around her wrists.

REDEMPTION

****

"Remove her shorts then tie her feet!"

Terri looked at Sir and started to run, limping because of the ankle sprain. She was slower getting away than she had expected to be.

Sir was able to push Terri backward onto the grass as Bannister grabbed her and then held her ankles together as she struggled. Then Bannister tore at the snap and zipper on her shorts and quickly pulled them off, while Terri clutched at her underwear from the back where her hands were tied, keeping them on against his strong pull. She was left in her underwear and t-shirt.

Kendra tried to move toward her mother, but Sir raised his hand up, and Kendra stopped in her tracks.

"You are becoming trained, dear." He looked at her.

Bannister wrapped the thick silver tape around Terri's ankles. The tightness of the tape felt good on her sprained ankle but she hurt all over.

Terri couldn't fight back anymore, she was unable to catch her breath. She was humiliated, stripped to her underwear, and didn't want her daughter to see her like this. It was torture.

Bannister brought her shorts over to the boss.

"Take those dirty shorts into the house and search them," Sir ordered and motioned for Bannister to move them away from his person. "I must get clean," he said as he was beginning to perspire. "Take my little doll here to the doll case, so we know she will stand and be the pretty girl she is." He half pinched one of Kendra's cheeks in a show of affection. "I won't have to worry about you running anywhere while you are in your case." He winked at Kendra and smiled.

"Hey! No! No! No!" Terri shouted as Sir reached for Kendra's hand.

Sir held Kendra's hand for a moment, then looked at Terri as he kissed Kendra's hand. Then he very gently put Kendra's hand back down by her side. His demeanor then changed as he turned to Bannister. "Strip her of this hideous costume, watch her while she bathes." He pointed to Terri and added, "This one won't go anywhere."

"Wait a minute! Wait a minute!" Terri screamed out, "Take me, take me instead! Leave Kendra alone!"

Bannister ripped off a piece of the silver tape. Then he leaned over and held Terri's mouth shut as she tried to scream with rage for her daughter. Once taped, only muffled sounds came out of Terri's mouth. Her shirt soaked through with sweat as she struggled.

Bannister led Kendra inside with Sir following. Terri could see Kendra holding the tears back as she walked away. She glanced back at her mother and put her finger up to her mouth, shushing her. Terri struggled to stand up but couldn't, she could only watch as they walked in and the door shut behind them.

******

Left out there, sitting on the grass in the direct sunlight, the heat bore down on Terri. She couldn't stand up with her hands behind her back, but quickly found she could scoot short distances on her butt. She scooted over and looked into the house. Maybe she could see or hear something.

Her back end started to itch badly, she was so allergic to the grass. She could feel the welts beginning to grow on her butt. But it was hard to scratch with her hands taped behind her. She tried to calm herself by looking out at the water and focusing on finding an escape route. She thought of the boat ride over. Where would they go if they did get away? Could Kendra do this with her? What would Kendra need to be able to do this?

Terri looked out to the passage and watched the waters for the flow of the currents. Tears streamed down her cheeks as she gathered strength and tried not to think of that horrible squat pudgy man, Sir, looking at her daughter, and of his cruel and huge servant, Bannister.

VOLUME THREE: RAPTIS TRILOGY

****

33

Hours later, Clift had called Mitch to come down. Now Mitch was in Clift's office, pacing. Clift had informed Mitch by phone that he had some information, important information about Roy's death.

Clift walked into the room and shook Mitch's hand. He was being so formal for a friend, Mitch sensed something was up.

"Mitch, we are gonna declare dis an accident. I'm sorry, but we couldn't find any other evidence suggesting otherwise." Clift watched as Mitch stood up, throwing his hands in the air.

"Not you Clift, come on, not you!" Mitch had his hands on the desk across from Clift who he now stared in the eye. He knew Clift knew something and was hiding it from him. Somebody was covering something up. "Come on Clift, what was it? Money? Did they pay you off to say this?" Mitch was clearly frustrated and angry and putting it right out there. "One more corrupt St. Todos official, money over matter, over truth." Mitch was relentless.

"Mitch! Sit down!" Clift motioned to the chair. "Look, dis is the way it is mon, I don't know what happened, OK?" He tapped his fingers together looking straight into Mitch's eyes. "I have a family, a big family, I love me family. We found a car, no plates, abandoned wid da keys in it, next to da airstrip. Who evah did this, they hid dis. Mon, dese men dangerous, dey will kill ma family to keep this secret!"

Mitch was sitting up in his chair, listening. "What does that mean?"

"Dis look like a hit Mitch, I tink dese men came in, from nowhere, did something bad, and somehow Roy got involved. Dey snapped his neck…."

Mitch cringed at the thought of his friend dying that way. His stomach began to turn and he put his head between his legs.

"I suggest you let dis go, Mitch, or you could be next." Clift shook a stack of papers at Mitch.

"I have the license plate number."

"I'm telling you, let it go, mon." Clift was nervous, he didn't want to be involved in any way.

"Please Clift, for me." Mitch pleaded. "Just run the plates, you don't have to do anything but please, run the license number for me." Mitch was relentless.

"Mon…you gonna get me in trouble."

"Here." Mitch put the paper with the license plate number written on it in front of him.

Clift sighed, then picked up the phone and called his secretary in. Handing the paper over, he asked her for a quick readout of anything associated with that plate number. He opened the drawer on his desk and pulled out a bottle of Jack Daniels and a small glass. "You like a short one while we wait?" Clift tipped the bottle toward Mitch, suggesting he pour Mitch one.

In an unusual move, Mitch took him up on it. He didn't like the way all this was going.

Clift pulled out a second small glass and poured. The two men raised their glasses. "To Roy." Each of them took a big drink, thinking of the morning's events, one trying to remember everything, the other trying to forget it all.

The secretary walked in and handed Clift a sheet of paper. Then she left. Clift stared at the paper, then looked up at Mitch. "You don wanna touch dis wid a ten foot pole. Mitch, don go dere, I won' let you."

Mitch stared at him, not wanting to hear any of this. "Ugh. No. Are you sure?"

"Dis car is associated wid a man who is untouchable, a man so powerful, no one—I mean no one—would tink of crossing him." Clift looked back into Mitch's eyes, and he looked hard. "And I am on dat list, Mitch. I can na touch him. I told you, I love me family too much."

Mitch knew Clift was dead serious, there was nothing he was going to do. *Call it an accident and let it go, he says. But how can I? I can't. ...* Mitch drove home and went straight to his computer. Whoever these dangerous people were, they had Terri and Kendra. Now that they had killed his best friend, Roy, it was even more personal. Terri and Kendra were in real danger.

****

Mitch thought back to any details Kendra might have told him about her dad, Rick. Could that man he detested so much, that idiot who had stolen Terri, really be involved with such a deadly circle of people? How?

Mitch then remembered that Kendra had used his computer during her stay. Maybe he could find something out there. He figured out how to access Kendra's email account. He decided he had to look back through her messages, even messages before her stay with him.

He read the email blast she had sent out quite recently saying that she was kidnapped, and then a newer email just yesterday, a quick note to her friends saying she was OK and coming home. "Don't tell my mom anything," the first email had said, as had the second one. Mitch tried to figure this out: *Kidnapped? Really? She was kidnapped? So Kendra was hiding from kidnappers while she stayed here with me? She didn't tell me, how could I know, how could I help? So she felt safe flying home, and not thinking they would be looking for her at the airport? Damn it, I should have gone in with her, made sure she was OK.*

Mitch now took all this immensely seriously. Kendra was in trouble, dangerous trouble, he could sense it. He read through the emails about being kidnapped again. In the first email. Kendra had written the name of an exclusive property management company on a private island. He had been by that island but had never had any reason to visit it.

He hurriedly picked up the phone and called the number of this management company. It rang four times on his end before an answering machine picked up, requesting he leave a name and number so someone could call him back. He hung up.

But Mitch had discovered enough. He made a few phone calls to business associates and found the agency was run by an ex-felon and his wife. Their connections were few and sketchy, and he couldn't find anyone who trusted them or knew anyone who had worked with their agency. That only left the most unscrupulous of characters for their clients. What Kendra had half told him was beginning to make sense. And Mitch was blaming himself now. *Poor girl! How could I have let her leave? How could I have not taken Terri's message, whatever it was, seriously, how could I have failed to put two and two together?*

He pulled out his chart of the islands and looked at the configuration of the small Grand Key, trying to remember what Kendra had told him about Rick's house there on the water. She had talked briefly about what it looked like with the small private dock, no other houses for miles, a passage that appeared swimmable but had dangerous currents. He found one area likely fit that description and circled it.

Rick wanted the medallion, Kendra had said so. Would Terri be that naïve? Was she trying to exchange this medallion for Kendra on her own? Mitch tapped his pen on his desk as he thought. He knew the answer. *Yes.* She would. *Of course Terri would. Terri. She would be that daring, yes, and that damn crazy.*

Now the question was: how was he going to do this, and just what was he going to do? Drive up in his boat to the dock and just pick the girls up? *No.* And where was that bastard, Rick, in all this? This was going to be bad, he had to thoroughly prepare for any trouble he would run into. He needed an escape plan, a plan for himself yes, and for Kendra, and yes, for Terri of course. *Terri.*

He walked into his office and removed the oil painting from the wall, revealing the sliding wall plank, then his safe. He unlocked the safe, reached in, then pulled out the medallion. As he held it in his hand, all the emotions came back. His grief, his anger, the joy of being independently wealthy, all mixed together. Kendra wasn't watching him now, so he didn't hold those feelings back. He didn't have to hide his feelings about what Terri had done to him years ago now that he was alone.

But the secret, the secret that had been protected for so long, the truth that he and Terri had found the medallions, two of them, this was out now. And if somehow this was not out, or if somehow his part was not out, well, there was no telling what Terri would say to save Kendra now. *Terri.* He had avoided thinking about Terri, because every time he did think about Terri he got quite upset and depressed. But now he knew he had to try to think about Kendra and treat Terri like an idea, or maybe a bad dream, or a fool. But Kendra needed his help and, yes, Terri did too. *Helping Terri again? Only to help this poor kid,*

Kendra, who is not at fault here in any way. What a strong pull I feel to help this kid, a strong pull. Like she was my own.

Damn it, Terri. Mitch knew he had to psych himself for up for a big fight with people he did not know and might not even recognize before they came at him. He told himself he had to, and that was that. He slipped the medallion into his front pocket and reached for the phone.

He called down to his marina. By now everyone knew their boss, Roy, was dead. It was time for payback.

Mitch was going to find Roy's killer, and Kendra and her mother, that was that. He left the house and rushed down to the marina. He had a plan but needed some help from his friends. He had a good idea where to start looking for Kendra. He dialed the coordinates of his destination on his boat's mapping device.

34

After several hours, Bannister returned to the garage where he had left Rick, Peg, and Joe gagged and tied. He walked over and harshly pulled the tapes off their mouths, one by one. Each let out a scream of pain followed by a gasping for breath. Joe was on the verge of passing out.

They were exhausted from fear and weak from hunger. The stagnant heat and now the smell of the garage were relentless.

Bannister removed his knife from its sheath and cut at the duct tape surrounding their ankles. He led them out the side door like animals and walked them around to the back. Terri sat in total humiliation, bound and gagged in her underwear on the grass.

"Terri! Are you all right?" She looked up at Rick and tried to scream at him, waving her arms behind her back wildly and stomping her bound feet.

Bannister walked over and ripped the tape off her mouth. She let out a scream. Inflicting the physical pain made him smile.

"You mother fucker, Rick! What have you done! Where is Kendra!" Terri screamed.

Bannister leveled the playing field and reached down and cut the tape off of Terri's feet. Full of adrenaline, she quickly bounced up to her feet and rushed over to Rick, banging her body into him, pounding her head on his chest, screaming.

"What have they done with Kendra?" She started to kick at his legs, they were the only part of him she could reach. He tried to dodge her feet unsuccessfully, taking one kick square in the shin.

Bannister smiled at the games.

The door opened and Sir stepped out.

Everybody stopped what they were doing and watched as Kendra stepped out behind him. She was dressed head to toe in flowing linen and long sleeves.

She held her head down, afraid to make eye contact with her mother. Her shame was becoming more than she could bear. It was obvious Sir had changed his clothes, they were totally different. He walked out, acting as if he was talking to everyone like they were at a backyard garden party.

"Let's tape them back up now, Bannister, before someone gets hurt!"

Bannister taped together one of each of their legs to one of another of their legs, so they were stuck together, leg to leg, like a chain of people.

"I've tried everything, and nothing seems to work. I talk, I listen, you promise me a medallion and what do you give me? A hoax."

"It's not like that," Rick interrupted.

Terri was enjoying watching Rick interrogated.

"Excuse me!" King Sir yelled back, extremely angry. "You dare to interrupt me?"

"I...I—"

The man reached up, grabbing Rick's jaw, and squeezed. "I don't want to hear it." He tossed Rick's head to the side as he released his grip.

"Bannister," he commanded.

The large man stepped over. "I think it's time to show them I am done with words. Action speaks much louder than words, don't you agree?" He looked over at Bannister who nodded his head in agreement. Scanning his captive audience, he looked to see if any others were agreeing.

"I'm waiting patiently for this medallion...." He looked at Terri.

"I told you, I don't have it." Terri was calm.

The man walked over to her and smiled.

"Clearly it was not in your shorts." He looked her up and down. "And while I'm waiting for the medallion to appear, I'm going to entertain myself. It's time for some action." He looked out to his audience, all on their knees in front of him.

"Fishing is a favorite past time of Bannister's, you might have noticed his beautiful boat." He pointed to it at the dock and looked out to each one of them, nodding at Bannister.

Bannister walked over to the boat, reached in and came back with a bat. He stood there proudly with his bat in his hand, a short stubby bat with a leather leash used for extinguishing the life out of a big game fish.

"In fact he considers himself a big game fish expert of some sort. He loves the large marlin out here." King Sir pointed out to the sea.

His audience looked over at the large brawn of a man five to six times the size of Sir.

"First we dangle the bait," Sir said.

He and Bannister walked past them, their captives lined up on their knees. Terri and Kendra looked at each other as Rick looked away. Peg looked up into the fat man's face, searching for his eyes behind his dark sunglasses, pleading for her life with her wet, red runny eyes as he walked by her.

Her husband Joe, a coward at heart, wouldn't shut up as he plead with his captor. His nose ran, dripping to the ground below him. "You've got our business, it's worth millions! You've got Terri, and Kendra! I know Terri has the medallion. I thought you were going to let us go!" Joe pleaded and shook with fear like a scared child. Sir ignored Joe's whining, he had already heard way too much.

Bannister stopped and turned to Peg, she smiled back. He looked at his boss and then back at Peg. The club came down without warning, breaking her skull wide open. Her husband screamed out, as he watched the look on her face in horror.

"Noo!" Joe leaned forward, vomiting as he watched her face, stunned, blood dripping down between her eyes and dripping off her nose.

With her eyes crossed, she fell forward, face down onto the concrete sidewalk in front of them. She had died instantly from the blow, her skull wide open with the flattened brain matter exposed. Her hair became drenched in bright thick red blood as it pooled around her head.

Kendra gasped and held her hands up to her mouth, her eyes were larger than saucers. She tried not to scream, fearing her mom would be next.

Sir turned to Kendra, using the moment to reinforce a lesson of obedience. "Yes, my delightful doll, that is the unfortunate side of misbehaving."

It was all she could do to keep from fainting at the sight.

He turned back to his audience. "As I was saying…after you catch your fish, you must first kill the big game you catch with a single blow." He looked at Peg's body without emotion. "Otherwise they may ruin your deck, or hurt someone." He looked over at Joe's sobbing face.

Terri tried reaching out to touch Kendra's hand with her head in an attempt to console her, make eye contact. Kendra backed away, out of immediate reach, shaking her head no.

"I have no use for such an animal, you may dispose of her." Sir motioned with his hands as if to shoo away the dead body.

Bannister smiled the largest grin yet, he loved this part.

With one ankle taped to her husband, the other to Rick, Bannister had to cut Peg loose now, so he took his knife out of his sheath. The men flinched back as he approached and cut the tape, releasing the body that had been attached to them. They rubbed their ankles. He pulled her forward out of the way then grabbed the duct tape, taping the two men's ankles together.

Bannister picked up Peg's dead, limp body by the scruff of her neck and began walking toward the pier. One of her hands and the tops of her feet drug on the concrete as he drug her over to the boat. He lifted her up with both hands like a barbell, dumping her over the edge into the back. She rolled across the back of the deck, leaving a small trail of blood from her head and mouth.

He went to the corner of the house and came back with a hose, washing away the blood pooled on the concrete. Rick and Terri welcomed the relief of the mist spraying from the hose, cooling them off. Joe cried as he watched the remnants of his wife being washed away. Bannister knew his boss would not be able to tolerate the bloody mess. Sir stood back toward the house in the shade with Kendra, being careful not to get splashed.

Bannister walked to the shed in the backyard and pulled out a large fiberglass tray, approximately four feet long. It was used for gutting and cleaning large fish. He clamped it tight onto one side of his boat. He went into the house and came out with a long canvas pouch tucked under his arm. It was filled with his fish filleting tools. This included his large fillet knife, a cleaver, and a rubber mallet to work through the cartilage in the joints. Terri could imagine the Neanderthal whistling while he worked.

"I will see you back here when you are done filleting and disposing of your catch."

Bannister headed toward the boat.

King Sir was beginning to perspire through his clothes with the excitement of watching. He felt a tingle, the urge to join in. Grabbing Rick's jaw and pushing was a tease. He didn't want to chance getting fluids splashed on him.

He missed the killing, the feeling you get inside when your knife moves through a person's flesh. He was quite good at it in his much younger years, but his obsessive compulsion for cleanliness took over and he could no longer tolerate the mess.

He walked back onto the neatly cleaned concrete and eyed the remaining three kneeling on the grass. They were wet with pink splatters on their clothes, stained from Peg's diluted blood. Each one looked back at Sir in fear of his brutality. Kendra stood away from him.

"You three will sit out here now and find that medallion, that's all I ask." He waddled over and stroked Kendra's cheek. "And you my precious doll, I'm sorry but I must put you in your doll case as I freshen, come with me dear."

Bannister had constructed a simple wooden box out of plywood. It was square with walls six feet tall, with a simple top and a bottom. The box was rudimentary, not quite fitting his boss's taste. But with the limited resources Bannister had been given to work with, he was proud of the simple case. The front panel closed with hinges and a lock. She could stand with little room to maneuver.

King Sir looked at Bannister.

"You may go now," he ordered Bannister who then turned and walked away, following orders.

"Get your hands off her!" Terri shouted, trying unsuccessfully to stand up.

"I do more and more see a resemblance." He stopped in front of Terri. "I do know how to make that unpleasant noise stop."

"Mom! Please!"

Terri looked at Kendra, surprised at her tone.

Sir smiled, Kendra was catching on, she could be trainable.

Rick and Joe both began pleading for everyone's life now that Bannister, the punisher, was gone.

"For God's sake, Sir. Please, my wife...."

But Sir was not impressed. He stroked Kendra's hair as he listened. He grunted back at Joe. Sir was becoming more irritable as perspiration began to penetrate his neatly pressed clean clothes, he had to bathe soon. He looked back to Terri. "The medallion, I'm waiting for it."

Terri swallowed hard, trying to clear her dry throat as she looked up at him. "I don't have it." She stared back at him with a blank poker face.

"Mmph, if you insist. Until Bannister gets back, you may look forward to our next fishing trip."

Terri couldn't help but notice his polished nails glimmering in the sunshine as he wiped the perspiration off his brow with a hankie. His voice grew more impatient, he was more and more uncomfortable.

"I'm going inside, you won't go far."

They couldn't go far, their ankles were bound together as if they were in a gunny sack race.

"You my little doll, follow me."

"Kendra! No!" Terri screamed out.

Kendra was emotionless and walked away with him, moving obediently on into the house.

Terri turned to Rick and started pounding on him with her forehead. With her hands taped behind her back, it was her only weapon. Rick stood there on his knees, numb, taking it. He felt he deserved it.

Joe broke down. "Oh my God, we're next, were next. I'm comin Peg, I'm comin!" was all Joe could babble over and over in his grief.

Peg had been the brains of any operation she and Joe had been involved in. They had been together since high school. Joe, the scrawny allergic kid everyone loved to make fun of, loved Peg.

Joe had hung out with the older tough kids, doing their dirty work for any approval he could muster. And he was always ready to do anything to impress Peg.

Peg, the red head siren, was so fashion forward most couldn't relate. With a blended style of the fifties meets disco, she was always dressed over the top. Joe loved her with everything he had. He would do anything for her including spending time in prison twice, taking the fall for her. He always did whatever Peg asked of him.

"Terri, the medallion, "Rick started, "these guys are barbarians, they will stop at nothing to get what they want, they'll get the medallion anyway, whether you are alive or dead. They will kill us all."

Terri let it fall on deaf ears. She knew what was going to happen next. The question was, who was next? She shut her eyes and tried to block out Rick's pleas for his own ridiculous life, she hated him. Right now, that sweaty creature in crisp designer clothes had her daughter under his control. That was all Terri could think about.

****

Kendra had obediently followed the man into the house. She knew what was coming. She was mentally worn down, willing to do anything to make the madness of her living nightmare stop. Upon seeing Bannister crack Peg's head open, Kendra detached. She had to. So she played the visual of that horror back in her head as if it was just a violent movie on television, one she'd seen a hundred times before.

Sir escorted her to the doll house Bannister had constructed for her. King Sir closed the front door so she couldn't see out and locked it. Then he went and took a leisurely shower, then changed his clothes. After he was dressed in clean clothes, she was forced to bathe while he watched, for her safety of course, he always said. Afterwards, he combed her long hair obsessively. He would carefully divide it into three equal parts with a comb and then braid it.

She never said a word the whole time. She kept thinking back to her life as it had been just weeks ago. She had been young without a real care in the world. Now in the short amount of time since she had left home and had been on this island, she had been forced to think only of her survival. Survival, whatever that would mean after all this.

******

No other boats passed as the three sat on the groomed tropical grass, their ankles taped together, waiting. Rick was talking to Joe and Terri about making a run, or a hop for it, together. Swim out into the channel.

"What could be worse?" he wondered aloud. *Who was going to be next?*

"You idiot, we'll all drown, a much slower painful death. Look at you, your ankles tied, your hands tied behind your back. You're so fuckin out of shape, that paunch." Terri rolled her eyes at Rick in disgust as if she were in such great shape.

Terri wasn't about to hide any feeling about her ex. Especially not now, and she let him have it. "You greedy fuck, thinking you're so smart. First you want half and more of my money, now my medallion. You don't deserve to live." She spit at his face, but she was so dehydrated that the spittle she could manage to toss stuck to his nose and cheek like snowflakes. He took the humiliation. He knew it, he didn't deserve to live. But he just wanted to live. He lifted his shoulder up and tried to wipe his face off.

Rick went silent and looked down. He didn't argue back, he knew he was going to die that day in one of three ways. It was either death by clubbing, death by drowning, or death by humiliation. The three turned their heads toward the passage, they could hear the boat coming toward them out there in the background. It was quickly approaching.

The boat returned to the dock, with Bannister's job out there done. He had cut up and disposed of Peg's body at sea. He had attached a hose to the water pump on the back of the boat and used the ocean water to rinse the blood away before he headed back. The red water had swirled around Bannister's feet. He had been in his twisted heaven on Earth.

Rick began pleading with Terri as soon as the boat docked, as Bannister turned the engine off and climbed out onto the dock. "Terri, the medallion, if you have it, now's the time, someone will be next!"

"Fuck you, Rick."

"Terri, you did bring the medallion, right?" Rick lowered his voice as he dared to ask again.

It all fell on deaf ears as Terri turned her attention away and watched the doors to the house. She was waiting to see if Kendra was going to be OK.

VOLUME THREE: RAPTIS TRILOGY

****

<u>35</u>

Sir appeared, coming out of the house, Kendra at his side. He was in a complete change of clothes as well as was Kendra. Her hair freshly combed and braided, she had a hollow look in her eyes as she followed her new master in fear of what was next.

As soon as Terri saw her, she couldn't help but cry out to her. Kendra showed no emotion as she stood next to Sir. She just looked out and beyond, refusing to make eye contact.

"Are you ready to tell me where the medallion is, Terri?"

"No. I can't. I don't even know what you're talking about. What do you mean, medallion?"

Bannister walked up to Terri. She tried to spit on Bannister's feet attached to the large tree trunks of legs standing in front of her, but was too dehydrated. Bannister looked down at Terri. He was seething inside as she pushed his patience to the brink. He wanted to kill her. It took all his self discipline to not kick Terri in front of his boss. He nevertheless lifted the back of his hand, suggesting he was going to bring it down across her. But Terri didn't flinch.

Terri simply stared at Sir's sunglasses, daring him. She held the key, and knew it. She took the chance he wouldn't harm her too much, at least not yet. Terri figured Sir thought she had something he wanted, had it somewhere, knew where it was. The medallion.

Bannister walked down to the boat to retrieve his club and returned to the three captives there on their knees. He let out an unconscious grunt as he stopped his large frame in front of them. He patted his bat into the palm of his left hand, examining each of them.

"Hmmph, you say you don't know about or have the medallion, do you? Well, if you insist. Let's go fishing, Bannister." Sir took a step closer to Terri, his overreaching gut close to Terri's face as she stood on her knees.

It was everything Terri could do to keep from cramming her head into the soft pillow of a man. She so much wanted to hit him, bite him, hurt him so bad.

The two men looked at each other, then down at their potential catch, smiling at their game, building the suspense of who was next.

"Come on Terri, I know you have it, I've seen it with my own eyes. Where is the medallion for God's sake!" Rick's body was shaking as he pleaded.

The two men watched in amusement, waiting for Terri to break under the pressure. Terri shook her head no, looking at Kendra, hoping to lock eyes with her.

Kendra wouldn't look back.

Bannister looked down at the three and walked back and forth between them, a pensive look on his face as he looked each in the eye. He stopped in front of Joe. Joe looked up, sniffling, his face dripping red from sobbing and the relentless heat of the sun. He could see his miserable reflection in Bannister's sunglasses. He leaned his face over to his shoulder to clean it off, wiping it on his sleeve. He looked back at the large man, searching, hoping for an ounce of humanity.

"Did you know that marlin mate for life?" Sir asked Joe.

Joe turned his head toward Sir and acknowledged the tidbit of information, then turned back at the executioner. Bannister was looking down at him, smiling as he swung his wooden bat with his powerful forearm down onto Joe's forehead, landing right between his eyes. Joe's eyes crossed on impact and his skull easily split open. He didn't drop as quickly as Peg. He looked at Rick and tried to speak, gibberish coming out of his mouth.

The bat came down again, this time on the back of Joe's head. The gibberish stopped and he quickly fell forward, his head landing face down between Bannister's large feet. Without a word, Bannister took his knife out of its sheath and cut away at the tape attaching Joe's leg to Rick's.

Rick and Terri were both completely silent. Rick was unable to pull his sight away from Joe lying dead in front of him.

Terri closed her eyes and prayed for a plan, *a chance, some kind of miracle.*

Kendra had turned and faced the house, refusing to watch. Sir was beaming as he watched Joe's eyes cross and fall. The blood and splatters from the kill quickly became too much for him though. His compulsive anxiety began to rise at the sight of uncontained mess, he had to escape the unsightliness. His brow began to bead and drip with perspiration as he watched.

"Come with me, Kendra, while Bannister cleans this mess." King Sir was tapping his side with his hand as he tried to work through the anxiety of seeing the mess. He had to remove himself quickly from the area. A part of him, his heart, yearned to go out on the boat with Bannister and dismember the body piece by piece. His mental side could no longer take it for reasons beyond his control. He now spent much of his life controlling his anxiety. He was in a hurry, taking Kendra's arm, walking her away to the house.

"Kendra, I'm sorry," Terri let out, tears formed in her eyes. She tried to blink them back as she watched her daughter turn and walk away without looking at her.

Bannister picked up Joe just as he had Peg, half dragging Joe down the concrete, Joe's limbs dangling, dragging, leaving a trail of blood down to the dock. Bannister picked him up and tossed him onto the back of the boat like a sack of potatoes which then rolled to a stop.

He came back to the side of the house and brought the hose out, then meticulously washed the concrete off again, using a bristle broom to clean the cracks. The bloody mist gave much needed relief, cooling down Rick and Terri, each silent as the man finished his chore.

After a thorough cleaning he wrapped the hose up and left the two kneeling on the grass. He walked down to the boat and started it up.

The hot sun overhead quickly evaporated the wet from the concrete around the remaining captives on their knees. The door to the house opened and Sir stepped out. He had on another change of clothes. Kendra was beside him.

"I've decided to bring the happy family together to discuss this morning's events." He looked back at Kendra, giving her an animated frown, suggesting he was sorry that he had to do this. "During this time, you might want to talk some sense into your mother, dear. Explain to her just how much you mean to me…." He ran his index finger down the side of her arm as he was speaking to her. Kendra was not bound or tied. She just stood there.

36

Bannister travelled far out into the open sea, out into the deeper waters. All alone with his kill, he was in his element. He stopped, put the engines in neutral not bothering to toss an anchor. He reattached the long cleaning tray and lifted Joe's limp body up onto it.

Bleeding Joe out, Bannister began to chum the waters. It didn't take long for the slime to disperse through the salt water, carrying the scent through the waters below. He began to toss parts of Joe over the side. The fish swam up and began picking at the feast as the pieces fell into the sea.

****

Sir left Kendra outside with Rick and Terri as he walked back up to the house. Kendra stood and stared at the door as he walked in.

Rick started to quietly sob. Kendra and Terri did not notice or respond to this.

"Kendra! Kendra! Snap out of it," Terri urged.

But Kendra stood there paralyzed with fear as she watched her master, Sir, walk into the house.

Terri knew Sir pudgy was not close enough to hear what she was saying to Kendra, but that there wasn't much time to get through to Kendra. "Kendra. Look at me. Listen. We're going to get out of this. Listen, quick, untie me before he gets back, we need to start swimming now, now Kendra," Terri urged, even commanded.

Kendra just looked at her. She had tried that escape route already. Kendra whispered, "I've tried it, Mom, I've already tried it. The current took me away." Kendra resisted pointing in the direction she went.

Her mom looked out to the passage again.

Kendra pointed with her eyes to her left, hoping her mom would get the clue, she didn't want Sir to notice.

"You've tried it? Really? Wow!" It's not that Terri didn't believe Kendra, she was impressed. *Kendra!!* Yet Terri knew that swimming across that passage was going to be their only hope, the only way. It had to be worth trying again, together they could do it. And if they didn't, Terri would face certain death and her daughter's fate would be worse than that. They had to try something.

 Rick looked down in shame, apologizing to Kendra. "I'm sorry, Cupcake, I'm sorry. All this, it's my fault, I'm sorry." Rick wanted to pleaded for forgiveness. "We can do this together, come on Cupcake, untie us! We'll have a chance!"

Terri rolled her eyes when Rick tried to join in.

Sickened by hearing Rick call her Cupcake, Kendra repressed a retort to this. Instead she focused on Terri. "Mom," Kendra spoke numbly, "did you bring the medallion? Sir just wants the medallion and it will all be over."

Terri was silent looking back at Kendra while Kendra and Rick both looked at Terri for the answer.

"Remember Kendra, remember what I was trying to tell you? Remember?" Terri whispered.

"Where is it, Terri?" Rick asked longingly.

Just the sound of Rick asking one more time was enough to send Terri over the edge. She lunged her body at him, toppling him over to his surprise. She pounded her forehead on his chest until she was out of breath. "You mother fucker! You fucker! I never want to hear your voice again! I will never! Never! Never save you!" She rolled off him to the side, her arms twisted behind her back. She was clearly stuck and in pain.

Kendra rushed over to her as Rick lay on his side. His unconditioned body was out of breath. "Mom! Mom!" Kendra began to cry.

"Help me, Kendra, just loosen the tape somehow, I'll do the rest, just get it loosened so I can break free when I need to."

Kendra did her best. Tugging at the tape, it stretched in the heat. She pretended to fawn over her mother and help her up, trying not to let Sir grow suspicious if he was watching from a distance.

"Trust me, Kendra, we can get out of this."

Kendra looked into her mother's eyes for the first time since they had been taken captive together. Kendra's shame was too much to bear, she knew what major trouble she had caused, how many people's lives she had endangered. She felt she deserved the punishment. But now she looked deep into her mother's eyes and felt not just the anger, but the love, the hope. Now she didn't want to look away. She needed to see this love and hope. "I trust you, mom," Kendra whispered, afraid Sir would overhear somehow.

Rick lay out on the grass, looking up at the blue cloudless sky. He was silent as he watched the dock. Watching and listening, he knew who was next.

All three turned their heads toward the passage as they heard the faint sound of a boat approaching or at least coming by. Kendra began to tense up. But Terri was hopeful as she watched. She could tell that this was a different engine sound, that this was not the sound of Bannister's larger fishing vessel. This sounded like an outboard, maybe two outboards. Terri faced the passage squinting, watching for boat traffic. There it was, the first sign of other life out there she had seen!

She watched as a smaller vessel came through the passage staying close to the small island across the way. *Hope*, Terri thought, *there is some hope out there*. That was all she needed. Then she watched as that boat appeared to slow down at one point, only to pick up speed and go away. Her small glimmer of hope was dashed as the small boat sped away.

The sound of the smaller boat leaving was replaced by the sound of Bannister's fishing boat approaching rapidly.

Terri locked eyes with Kendra's once more. "Play along and trust me." She looked over at Rick and gave him the evil eye. "When Bannister leaves again, you get out here, we'll make our move. That fat man won't, he can't chase us."

"Mom, how?"

"Trust me, Kendra, please. I'll make it happen, but you have to trust me." Terri pleaded quietly with Kendra to follow her lead, now was not the time to be a rebellious teenager.

The boat pulled up to the dock with Bannister smiling. His life was filled with so many mundane chores these days. He thoroughly enjoyed his time out at sea.

He missed the heat, the sun, it made him feel alive along with his fancy knife work. He wasn't fond of the cooler climate up north in Canada, but they would soon be headed back after all this mess was taken care of.

Bannister walked up the concrete path and noticed Rick laying on the grass. He yanked him up to his knees.

Terri was standing on her knees near Kendra. The door to the house swung open and Sir stepped out. His clothes were crisp clean, obviously changed again. Kendra stood still like a child in trouble as he approached.

Sir reached out and stroked Kendra's arm as he came to a stop in front of the mother daughter duo on the grass. "Bannister? Did you enjoy yourself?"

"Yes boss," Bannister grinned as he looked at his easy prey kneeling on the grass.

"Has my doll here been able to persuade her mother to hand over the medallion?"

Terri shook her head no, firmly looking at him. She could see the fear in Kendra starting to rise as Kendra took a cautious step backward.

Kendra's eyes drifted off, she was detaching from the situation again.

Terri could see the hold this man had on her daughter, like a fist clenching on Kendra's psyche. One minute earlier, Kendra was strong. And now, as Kendra stepped back behind Sir, Terri saw Kendra's strength put out like a light. *Why?*

The answer struck Terri like a lightning bolt as she reran the last minute in her head. Kendra was more afraid of what her mom was going to do than of this man. *That made sense.*

Terri began to grow light headed. She started daydreaming right then and there, replaying old memories, realizing how her own messy behavior had affected her daughter. Her daughter had watched her mother being careless, aggressive. And the more careless and aggressive Terri had been, the more Kendra had pulled away from her.

Now Terri looked at Kendra with different eyes. Kendra was no longer a child. Terri's eyes rolled slightly back in her head as stars started shooting out against the dark and blurry background. Her electrolytes were becoming dangerously imbalanced as the heat exhausted and dehydrated her.

She thought of Kendra swimming that channel alone and tried to focus her eyesight on her. Kendra was strong. Voices echoed in the background as Terri closed her eyes and fainted sideways into Rick. King Sir watched, shaking his head.

"Wake her up, Bannister, I don't want her to miss a minute of fun."

Rick moved Terri off of himself. He too was weakened from dehydration. She fell sideways in front of Rick, with her eyes half opened. Part of Terri wanted to close her eyes and go to sleep, the other half wanted to open them and fight.

Kendra resisted the urge to run to her mom's side. Kendra wasn't completely convinced that her mother was faking it. Maybe her mother was really passing out. Meanwhile, Kendra had to keep King Sir convinced she was being obedient, trying to regain his trust.

Bannister walked to the shed and brought out a machete. On the far edge of the neatly groomed property were coconut trees with the young green nuts. There were numerous large clusters of the green fruit hanging low.

With one carefully placed whack of the machete, a large cluster of the nuts dropped to the ground. He skillfully used the long sharp knife to remove one from the cluster. He opened up the end, forming a drinking vessel.

He walked back to Terri and laid her back, opening her mouth, pouring the sweet nutritious clear milk into her. She sprung forward, gagging awake. She coughed it out as the milk dripped down her esophagus. When her eyes began to focus, she could identify the round green globe and opened her mouth. He poured, she chugged down all of the remaining milk. Gulping, trying not to miss a drop, it carelessly dripped down her cheeks, overflowing as he tipped it upside down. She stuck her tongue out trying to bite at the soft young meat around the edges. He let her taste it, chew at it like an animal.

Sir was repulsed. He had just changed his clothes and was comfortable. Without saying a word he pulled on Kendra's arm, leading her back up to the house before he perspired through his shirt again. Terri watched from the corner of her eye, too tired to scream, there was nothing more she could say.

"I need another, please," Terri's said in a scratchy voice as she began to wake up to her reality. Bannister grunted and walked back to the cluster. Terri's head began to feel relief from the small amount of nourishment the coconut had provided, and he was bringing her more. He poured the milk quickly down her mouth as she opened it like a young bird. She held her head back, gulping as much as she could. This would provide much needed fuel for her body if she was going to swim anywhere.

Rick licked his lips and looked over longingly as the milk flowed down Terri's face. Dehydration was beginning to take its toll on him. His face was bright red and his gray hair was matted down with sweat. "Please? May I have a drink? Just a taste?"

Bannister scowled back at him, the look on his face shouting no. In a show of strength, Bannister took the empty large green globe in one hand and threw it, hard. It flew out into the passage, hitting the water with a splash out in the middle. Bannister's strength appeared superhuman as they watched.

Both Rick and Terri were physically and mentally exhausted.

Terri watched, her head in a daze, as the coconut floated, drifting out on the water. She looked over to the tree where Bannister had cut down some clusters. There were still some on the ground. She couldn't make out how many, but enough to provide some flotation. The coconuts would still be attached to each other with their sinewy cord-like branches.

Terri looked down at her feet. A small patch of blue veins had sprung up from the depths of her ankle along with some yellow and green bruising. Not a bad sprain, but enough to slow her down. That small cluster of coconuts on the ground could be a life saver. Or life extender, she thought as she looked around at any other prospects.

Their options were dim, there was nowhere else to go. They would have to swim like hell. Her goal would be to try and drift around the point of the small island on the other side where there could be more boat traffic. But it would only be a matter of time before Bannister would be on his way back and then out looking for them. Terri heaved a heavy sigh out loud, unconsciously, as she thought out the details in her head. She prayed for another random passing boat, fisherman, sightseer. *Anyone!*

Bannister took a few minutes to tidy the area up for his boss. There wasn't much he could do with Terri's face, the hair dangling down into her eyes and the coconut milk drying on her chin. She looked up at him, wondering what next.

Rick sat next to her, obediently looking down.

Bannister walked down to his boat and came back with a terry cloth towel. He wiped it across Terri's face in an attempt to make her face look clean. His boss was having an increasingly hard time with messes. Sir needed a lot cleanliness, and he also needed straightness, even rows. Terri's bangs were wet from her sweat and dangled crossways, stuck here and there. A mess. That sloppiness with those crooked lines would repulse Sir further.

VOLUME THREE: RAPTIS TRILOGY

****

37

The back door to the porch opened and Sir stepped out, Kendra one step behind him. Bannister was standing in front of his prey. Sir walked up to him. "Thank you Bannister, it's time to go fishing. What do you think we'll catch? A liar?" Sir's face turned to Terri. He stared at her a minute, then turned his head and looked at Rick. Bannister walked over and picked up his fishing bat sitting on the grass and quickly walked back and stopped in front of Rick. He glanced at the boss, who was smiling.

As much as Kendra disliked Rick, and didn't want to even just *think* of him as her father anymore, she also now knew he was pretty stupid, in fact a total idiot as her mother had told her. Kendra realized that he had played her for a fool, had lied about everything, had brought her down there into serious danger to get money from her mother. And he had humiliated her. She despised all this about him, she hated him for it, but she didn't want to see him dead. After all, as he had told her, he was her father.

Now Kendra tried to keep her poker face, hiding behind the oversized round figure of her master, Sir. Kendra was peeking over at her mom, trying to make her mom hear her thoughts: *Please Mom, give up the medallion!*

Terri looked at Kendra at just the right moment. She saw the pain in Kendra's eyes, the pain she was trying to convey to her mother.

Bannister lifted his arm back, and Rick shut his eyes. The bat came down with a long exaggerated back swing.

In the middle of the swing Terri's voice rang out. Surprising them all, herself most of all—

"OK! I have the medallion!"

Bannister turned his head slightly as Terri's shrill voice broke the momentum, his swing dropped a foot as he tried to stop it. The sound of Rick's arm snapping into a compound fracture pierced the air with a loud crack. The broken jagged white bone was sticking out of his upper arm as Rick was grabbing at it and screaming. Kendra put her hands up to her mouth, holding back her screams. She turned and looked the other way.

Sir's and Bannister's attentions were on Terri.

Rick couldn't stop crying out in pain as his arm dangled, useless.

Sir looked at Bannister and nodded.

"Wounded prey, such a miserable sight," the boss commented as Rick writhed in pain, trying to hold onto his arm above the open wound to stop the bleeding. Blinded by the pain in his arm, he never noticed the swinging bat coming down on his head. Bannister was quick to step back as blood began to trickle out of Rick's smashed head. Rick fell forward.

Sir felt his insides tingle as he watched the life drain out of Rick, only to then be taken over with the same old feeling of anxiety creeping in. He licked his lips, watching the blood pool for as long as he could bear the mess, then turned his attention to Terri. "The medallion, where is it?"

"You didn't have to kill him!"

"Oh yes, I did. He was useless, a coward."

Terri looked down at his dead body. She feared for her daughter's mental health, with Rick being killed in front of her. Kendra was still looking the other way toward the house. She knew what had just happened, she had cringed at Rick's screams of agony, but had refused to look. Once the screaming stopped, she didn't want to witness the mess.

Her mother had finally admitted to having the medallion. It was a showstopper but it wasn't enough to save her dad. Sir couldn't get himself to come any closer to Terri. Her appearance, her smell, he couldn't take it. Bannister walked over to the side of the house without prompting and came back with the hose.

"Where is it?" King Sir demanded of Terri.

Bannister was slowly cleaning up Rick's mess. Terri noticed the beads of perspiration forming on the fat man's brow. It would be a short matter of time before he would need to go in, take a shower. Terri could sense his anxiety, she had her own.

"It's slightly complicated. I do have a request." She looked at King Sir's face as he scowled.

"What kind of request?"

She put it out there. "I need a shower."

Everyone was silent at such an unusual request. This was not what anyone had expected to hear. Even Kendra had to wonder why her mom would suddenly be concerned about her hygiene.

Bannister picked Rick's body up with two hands. Rick was larger than the others and it had been a long day. Bannister dragged him down to the small pier and tossed him onto the boat as Sir spoke with Terri.

"A shower, an unusual request. Time consuming." The man tapped his fingers together, contemplating his answer.

"Yes Sir, an unusual request. If you can grant this one wish for me, I will produce the medallion for you." She was steely eyed, and unwavering as she spoke to him.

He was intrigued with her game of cat and mouse. *What harm could it do?*

"Bannister."

Bannister stopped what he was doing and looked to his boss.

"We are all going inside, I need you to first put our doll here in her case." Sir looked at Kendra with an animated look of sorrow. "And please, don't touch her."

"I trust you will behave while your mother showers?"

"Yes sir." Kendra was relieved to leave the grisly crime scene, she wanted to sit but was going to have to settle for standing all alone in a box, the "case." In the hours she had already passed in the case, she had found a crouching position that was halfway comfortable if she leaned to the left just the right way. She had to trust her mother now.

Bannister grunted as he stood in front of her, his large frame overshadowing her petite figure. She looked up at him and then walked toward the house without any words being exchanged.

Sir focused on Terri's eyes instead of the mess surrounding her.

"You will have your shower. Cleanliness, a virtue I didn't see in you." He glanced at her and then put his hand out, examining his polished nails. He determined it was time for a manicure, one fingernail appeared slightly longer than the others. This would bother him until it was fixed. Many things were bothering him more and more these days.

Combing his doll's hair soothed him, as did concentrating for hours on the evenness of her braids. Taking a shower worked well for him. He always followed his ritual, sometimes quickly, mostly slowly, and it always relaxed him. After his shower, he would take his time dressing, meticulously making sure there were no wrinkles in his clothing to begin.

Bannister returned to his boss' side, and looked at Terri. She was a sight, still kneeling in her underwear.

"After you're done cleaning this, please go and secure the bathroom. Only take her up after the bathroom is secure. I don't want there to be any way for her to escape or hurt herself."

"Yes boss."

Terri closed her eyes and thought of how great that fresh water hitting her skin was going to feel. She decided that she would take a calculated risk and drink some of the shower water to hydrate further for her planned escape with Kendra.

Bannister left for the house to complete his boss's wishes, leaving Sir and Terri all alone.

"If I give you this medallion...."

Upon hearing the word "if," Sir raised his eyebrows, his forehead wrinkled.

"... you will let Kendra and me go, right?" Terri wasn't sure what was going to happen but she needed time to retrieve the medallion, gather strength, and then have Bannister go away. She was counting on Bannister standing guard while she showered.

Sir studied Terri silently, wondering just what her intentions were. *What harm would it be, one last request.* His new doll would see he was not the ogre everyone made him out to be. "Yes dear, go get cleaned up. Find my medallion, obviously it was not hidden in the hem of your shorts."

Sir looked at Bannister who was feeling impatient now. He had Rick's body lying out in the back of his boat. It was already attracting flies and insects. "I could have Bannister here use his knife and fetch it for me if, as you might say, it could be faster...."

"I'll hurry so Bannister can be on his way." She made her way to the bathroom six steps away, not accepting any other scenarios. She shut and locked the door behind her. The men could still hear her from the other side. "I'm hurrying!"

Bannister stood next to the door, listening for any wrong moves.

She immediately stripped her clothes off and sat down on the cool porcelain toilet. Her ankle was beginning to throb and she wondered if she felt feverish. She washed her hands and face off in the cold water in the sink. This felt like paradise as she tried to dismiss any symptoms of not feeling well.

She looked in the mirror, her face was red from the sun but underneath it she looked pale, exhausted. She sat back on the toilet. Reaching into herself with her index and middle finger she grimaced in pain. She felt the edge of the medallion and pulled it out slowly. This was painful and felt as if it was tearing her on the way out. Her stomach cramped.

Looking at the large golden piece in her hand, she wanted to sit back and reward herself with a moment's rest. Yet she kept moving, she needed to keep Bannister happy and get him out on his way. She turned the shower on and stepped in, letting the water run down her body, cooling her off completely.

Opening her mouth, she let the water run through it, swishing it through her teeth. She couldn't resist taking a sip and swallowing, knowing it would most likely complicate matters later…. Bad water always did make her sick. She couldn't remember the last time a shower felt so good.

She let the water run down her body. Grabbing the soap and lathering head to toe, she rinsed off, still clutching the medallion tight in her hand. She scrubbed her underwear in the running water, then hung it on the top to drip. She braced herself against the wall of the shower and rested, her body felt weak. She noticed she was finding it harder and harder to move her limbs.

She climbed out and dried herself off. She pulled on her wet underwear and dirty clothes with no other options. Running her fingers through her hair like a comb, gaping at herself while looking in the mirror, she did her best to look somewhat presentable. Hopefully, she looked better than she felt on the inside. She looked at herself, beaten up and slouching over. She stood up straight to gain confidence, and avoided looking in the mirror to keep it.

Terri closed her eyes and put her game face on. She was as ready as she would ever be. She opened the bathroom door and walked past Bannister as if she owned the place. She walked into the living room where Sir was standing at the large plate glass window, looking out to the sea.

Terri announced herself. "How can I trust you?"

"You're just going to have to," the man replied as he turned to her.

She walked up to him and held her fist out.

He reached his hand out toward her, smiling.

She opened her fingers slowly and dropped the medallion into Sir's palm. Bannister walked over and looked as Sir held the piece up and admired it.

Terri stood there.

"Bannister, take her back outside. Be sure to tape her ankles and wrists."

"Is that necessary? I thought maybe you would trust me now."

Sir smirked at Terri's suggestion without taking his eyes off his golden prize, the medallion.

"Yes, I'm afraid it is." He never took his eyes off the golden piece as he spoke.

Bannister grabbed her arm and pulled.

"Hey! Where's Kendra!"

Bannister opened the backdoor and pulled her to the outside again. Her body ached and she found it hard to resist his strength. She tried to keep up with him without stumbling down. He took her to the grass and held her arms together with one of his large hands while he tore off a long piece of duct tape with the other. He wrapped it around both of her wrists in front of her.

He tore off another long piece and pushed her backward. She fell back onto her butt. She was too weak to soften the blow to her body. She tried to roll out of it. Her head ached in her temples, she felt feverish. Bannister reached down and wrapped the tape around her ankles. Her body welcomed the moment to lay down and rest, she closed her eyes for a minute.

Bannister left her laying on the grass and went back inside, waiting for orders. Should he do away with Terri now?

Sir wanted Bannister to hold off on Terri for now. "These rumors I heard, these stories of the lost medallions found, they were all true." Sir stood in the front room, tossing the medallion up from his palm into the air and catching it, over and over, smiling like the cat who just ate the mouse. "If I am right, and I think I am, she knows where or at least who has the second medallion. I heard they were found by a young couple. This would be many years ago. She and some man around the islands." He was putting the pieces to the puzzle together. "That Rick, her ex-husband, he never had one, she found that medallion with someone else." Sir knew he was onto something, as he rambled on and on, muttering to himself, playing detective.

****

Kendra stood in her box quietly. She could hear most everything that was going on. She heard her mom come out and give the medallion up. She thought she noticed a weaker tone in her mom's voice, just when she thought her mother would sound more refreshed after a cool shower. She heard Bannister leave, taking her mom with him, probably taping her up outside. And now she heard that Bannister was back. She listened for next moves and prayed hard that her mom would be spared.

Kendra heard Sir talk about the second medallion. The second medallion, no! Kendra knew who had it. *Not Mitch, please don't bring Mitch into this!* Kendra shut her eyes and prayed hard to her God to please keep her mom and Mitch safe. She could clearly make out the words "kill that bitch" and knew King Sir and Bannister were talking about her mom. She tried not to panic. She put her ear up to the wall to hear every word more clearly.

"Or just kill Terri, make it look accidental or something. Then we will put her picture in the paper with a story about her death. That should draw out her old friends, eventually, the friend with the medallion."

Bannister nodded in agreement, a man of few words.

"I will think for a while, think about what is the best way to get the second medallion. First, go and dispose of that ridiculous Rick's body before we attract any more flies."

They looked out the window, past Terri laying on the grass, to the boat as it bobbed up and down on the ripples of the water's surface. "I know you'll enjoy that, I wish I could join you...."

Bannister agreed with a grunt and walked outside.

Sir followed a few steps behind, but then turned around to avoid the flies.

****

Terri opened her eyes to see Sir standing over her. The boat's engines had started with a roar in the background. She knew Bannister was on his way to dispose of Rick's body, that the clock was officially ticking now, that she had just a little while to get Kendra and herself off this island and as far away as fast as possible. Her head ached as she talked. "Can I see my daughter, please?"

Sir smiled back at her.

"Thank you for the medallion. I do say, you are quite clever! Now. Who has the other medallion?"

Terri was caught off guard with this question. *How did he know about the other medallion?* No one knew. She had never told Rick about it. She wasn't even sure she had told Rick about hers, the first medallion. She thought hard. *Did I really at some point slip? Wouldn't I know if I had slipped?*

At that moment, Terri realized that Rick had known about at least the first medallion all along, that he maybe had been waiting for a chance to get his hands on it. Somehow he had found out about the other one. Rick had figured out how to get her and the first medallion with her, or better yet, get rid of her and then get both medallions eventually. So Terri saw now that Rick had planned to find Terri in the bar that fateful night so long ago, where she thought they had met by accident.

Sir asked again. "Who has the other medallion?" He looked around uncomfortably as the unevenness of the hardscape drying in some places more rapidly than in others caught his anxious attention. He couldn't look away from the mess, he wanted to correct it, and he couldn't. Bannister had left. He tried to focus on Terri. The wet pools of water scattered around him sat there, insisting on reflecting back at him.

"Sir, I don't feel well, please, let me see Kendra and then I'll think back."

He sensed Terri's weakened physical state. He had to keep her alive to get what he wanted from her.

"You're good at this game of cat and mouse. You did honor your word last time."

He walked into the house, giving the landscape more time to dry, his anxiety level rising because of the appearance of the grounds. Then he unlocked the doll house and led Kendra outside to her mother. The sight of Kendra actually calmed his nerves a small amount, he loved the color of her eyes and the color of her hair. But now he needed another shower.

"I'm going to leave you to talk some sense into your mother, my dear." He stroked Kendra's arm as he spoke. "I believe she knows who has the other medallion. Do you think she will tell you?"

Kendra looked down at her mom just lying there, looking awful. She hoped her mother was faking it, she didn't look well.

"It could save her life," King Sir suggested to Kendra.

Kendra was silent a moment, then said, "I will try, Sir." She stood there trying to figure out what to say next.

The puddles kept taunting Sir's anxious compulsivity, forcing him back inside. He left the two women alone.

"Mom. Mom." Kendra got down on her hands and knees next to her mother.

"Loosen the tape on my wrists, hurry," Terri murmured. "Block the view from the house with your body so he doesn't see, just in case."

Kendra followed her mother's directions, although knowing the compulsive Sir would be in the shower and not see them for a while. Still, Kendra moved to block the view. And then she yanked hard at the tape around her mother's wrists. The tape was warm from the tropical heat and stretched without too much effort. She freed her mother's hands.

Terri reached down to her ankles and unwrapped them quickly, trying to preserve the long twisted piece of tape.

"Go Kendra, grab the roll of duct tape, there. And grab the cluster of coconuts he cut down, drag them to the beach for me! Go! I'm right behind you! Get into the channel and swim! Now!" Terri whisper-shouted under her breath and Kendra felt the urgency.

Kendra didn't have a moment to protest as she hurried doing exactly what her mother told her to do.

She didn't think about King Sir or Bannister. She thought about saving her life and her mother's life. They had to go right then, had to go any way they could, whatever it took. The adrenaline pumped through her veins as she moved faster and blocked out her fear. She saw her mom struggle to get up, she was limping on her hurt ankle. Kendra had gotten the coconuts to the water's edge and started back to help her mom. The roll of duct tape was pushed up her arm like a sleeve.

"Go Kendra, turn around, don't hesitate, swim! I'm right behind you!"

"But Mom! Your ankle, let me help!"

"Go! Damn it, I said go *now*!"

Kendra saw the look of fear in her mother's eyes, turned around and started running for the water.

Terri was right behind her, she moved as fast as she could. Her body was heavy, her ankle hurt, and her head was pounding with a fever. She could hear the door to the patio open behind her. In front of her, Kendra dove into the water and started to swim. Terri was almost there.

VOLUME THREE: RAPTIS TRILOGY

****

38

Mitch was armed with a small makeshift armada, a fleet of different sorts of boats, all out to avenge Roy's death and to save Terri and her daughter. He had cleverly devised this plan with his friends and they were anxious to participate. Two of them were to bring their respective jeeps, both with front end hitches, and meet Mitch at the far east end landing strip. This was a little known strip that was once used regularly, but now used privately by those in the know. This was the same strip where the vehicle had been found.

The tall wooden antenna painted with red and white stripes was an ill conceived and uncompleted project on that east tip of the island. No one had accounted for the hellacious winds and storms that pass through on the tip of the windward side. Well, there had been the few who had objected, pointing out the obvious, but no one had listened. It hadn't taken long for the poorly set antennae to come down, along with wires and cables and the like. The next time more cables were put in, they were sturdier ones, only to be blown down again. People had done this rebuilding again and again until they finally had given up. So what was left now was a large selection of long thick cables and cords.

One of the larger heavier cables was attached to the rocks below. That end of the connection still held firm. The other end of this heavy cable was stretched out long and was loose. It was a boating hazard in the shallow sandy cove that was marked with a "private" buoy.

Now two men working with Mitch dove down to the sandy bottom of the cove. There they retrieved the end of the long thick cable that had been buried deeper and deeper in the sand over time. Then the men heaved and pulled on the cable like a tug of war across the cove. A zodiac boat hovered above with three men on it helping pull the heavy cable upward. Slowly the cable moved like a slithering snake across the silty bottom.

Pulling it forward and up onto land, the men attached the loose end of the cable to the hitch on the front end of one of their jeeps. The jeep slowly backed up in a circle around the base of a mature coconut tree near the water's edge. The cable tightened across the cove to the level just below the water's surface. Anyone coming by wouldn't be able to see the cable lurking beneath the surface, especially not from a boat.

All this was a lot of work. When this was done, when Mitch was satisfied everything was set according to plan, he left to find Kendra and Terri. The men spread out and hid in their support positions, staying there waiting to hear from Mitch.

<u>39</u>

Terri heard the door open behind her but didn't take the time or the energy to turn and look. That sound could only mean one thing. That horrible Sir was coming after them.

"Come back here!" Sir shouted, he was angry. "There is nowhere to go!" He saw Kendra already swimming offshore. Terri managed her way to the cluster of coconuts near the shore and picked them up, running, jumping on top of them into the water.

It was silent behind her. Terri couldn't hear, her heart was beating and the sound filled her ears. She was desperate to catch up with Kendra who was, thankfully, ahead of her. Terri hooked her arm around the coconut cluster's sinewy cords and let the cluster hold her up as she kicked and pulled at the water with her hands. Her head ached, but the coolness of the water felt soothing on her skin. She was already breathing hard, she gave it all she had and tried to kick harder.

Kendra stopped, treading water, looking back for her mom. She could see the green globes bobbing in the distance and her mom struggling, attached to them. The current was beginning to whisk Kendra away toward the center of the passage. Just as Kendra realized this was happening, she saw she couldn't fight it. She again remembered what her mom had said. *Swim diagonally, don't fight against it.* Kendra waited for her mom to catch up and watched as Sir went into the house, then returned to the backyard.

A shot rang out and then another. Kendra turned and watched her mom in fear. The third shot rang out and she heard her mom cry out in pain, "Owwww, damn it!"

Kendra had stopped swimming as she was watching, and was now seeing her mom caught in the same current and rushing toward her faster. Another shot rang out.

"Mom!" Kendra shouted out. "Over here!"

Terri was silent.

Kendra treaded water, waiting for her mom.

Terri finally floated up to where Kendra could swim over and grab hold of the cluster to which Terri was clinging. A stream of blood rose to the surface from Terri's leg. Terri had been shot on the inside of her calf.

Kendra held on to the cluster and together the two floated with the current.

Terri's eyes were half open as she tried to rest. She was so exhausted. "My leg, I need help."

Kendra could see down through the water. She could see the hole in her mom's leg.

"Oh my God, you're shot." Kendra looked around for her bearings.

"Tape my leg, Kendra, the duct tape. Tape my leg tight to stop the bleeding." Terri was holding on, floating, focusing on keeping her mouth above water and taking long slow breaths. Terri didn't want her daughter to panic. They had floated far enough away quickly enough that they could no longer see the large white house they had escaped from.

REDEMPTION

****

Kendra picked off an edge of the tape with her nail, then pulled off a long strip. Terri shut her eyes and tried to smile as Kendra reached down and wrapped the tape around her leg. Kendra tore off another piece, the stickiness wasn't holding well when wet. She tugged at the center and pulled down, making two strips on one side. She wrapped the leg again and then tied the two strips together in a knot to hold it together.

"Oh my God, great work Kendra, great work." Terri was relieved, the pressure helped take some of the pain away.

Kendra began to kick again, keeping them at a diagonal angle to the current, hoping to get to the other side of the ripping current in the center of the passage at some point, and before they both drowned. Her mom promised the current would stop if they could just drift to that other point, and they were more than halfway there.

Terri did her best to help, she didn't want to be dead weight. She moved her legs up and down the best she could against Kendra's wishes. A chill went through Terri's body.

****

Mitch had heard the shots ring out, one after the other. He was out on the east tip of the small key, sitting on his boat. He had watched as someone he couldn't identify, someone who seemed to be an extremely large man, was driving further away in his fishing vessel, still heading out to sea. What was this guy up to? Mitch had no time to guess.

Now Mitch turned the engines on and pulled up the anchor. He swung the boat around and headed around the windward side of the small island across the passage. In the late afternoon hours, he watched the surface carefully to see what he could see, as there was glare from the sun on the ocean.

He stayed tight to the shore as he passed the tip end and entered the passage. He slowed down and lifted his binoculars up to his eyes, while, with his other hand he put the boat in neutral. He could make out a fat man pacing across the distant lawn. The fat man appeared to have a gun in his hand. *That must explain the gunfire.* There was no sight of the girls....

****

Kendra struggled as she swam hard, pulling her mom, encouraging her to hold on. Terri kept dunking her face in the water to cool her face down. She could feel herself burning up with fever and didn't want to scare Kendra. The temperature of the water was some eighty-three degrees, fifteen degrees (or more since she had a fever) cooler than her body temperature. The water helped keep the core of her body cooled off.

They both heard the boat in the background. Terri was positive it sounded like the same boat they had seen before. A stroke of luck for them, Terri hoped and let herself feel a tinge of relief knowing someone was there. But they were still in trouble.

They bobbed on the surface of the water, their bodies hidden behind the small choppy swell caused by the current.

Mitch scanned the water for any signs of anything unusual, but couldn't see any.

Both Terri and Kendra had heard the boat engine come close, then stop, and then head away. But they couldn't see past the chop above their heads to get a visual of any boat.

But Kendra could see the small island and knew they were slowly getting closer. The tidal exchange was in their favor. She hoped they would make land right at the tip.

REDEMPTION

****

<u>40</u>

Sir paced between the house and the water's edge while looking out into the passage with his binoculars. The late afternoon breeze and late sun made it difficult for him to see anything on the water's surface as it glared back at him. The last he saw they were halfway out in the channel, making their way to the point on the far side. He didn't want to waste any more shots without a clear visual. Too many shots could call someone's attention, unwanted attention. *But there aren't any people out here*, Sir assured himself.

He looked again and was startled to see a boat come around the far point across the way and stop. He strained to see more. Looking through his binoculars, he could make out one man behind the wheel.

"What's this?!" *A coincidence? Is he looking for something or someone? What? Who is he looking for?"*

He could feel the stranger looking back and observing him. He resisted using the radio to inform Bannister he was needed. There would be others out there to pick up the radio transmission, he couldn't risk anyone hearing his voice. He was forced to wait for Bannister's return.

"This could be my big break! Is that someone over there concerned with Kendra and Terri? Who else would know them down here? Who had helped Kendra on St. Todos? The person with the other half of the medallion?" Sir was mumbling to himself, his body tingling all over at the thought of such luck. His life had always been that way, he was blessed. Alone, he talked away to himself—asking questions and answering them, back and forth.

Born albino in a dark skinned, Latin world, he was considered oddly lucky, even God sent. People had showered his parents with gifts of food and material things just for the chance to touch or speak to the fat albino baby.

Already at an early age, Sir had had an ability to kill while looking his victim in the eye, and while feeling no empathy whatsoever. He hadn't cared what anyone thought of him. Young friends, older peers, it didn't matter when they looked at him sideways. Rumors of his viciousness grew bigger and bigger as he grew and his actions became unstoppable. Young men followed him, his army grew. Soon he was king of his world and he had all he wanted and more. He simply did away with what displeased him. He became the leader of his own drug cartel. Human trafficking was his personal hobby. He had a long running doll collection of his own to add Kendra to.

From adolescence, he'd had a sexual dysfunction that left him vulnerable to women, unable to ever completely function. He pleasured himself and showed complete control by choosing and taking whoever he wanted. He brainwashed the women with touch, denial, and torture so he could add them to his personal collection. Kendra was impulsive, unplanned, but beautiful and a challenge like no other.

But now, all this had started to feel as if it was slipping out of control, as if everything was unraveling, and he was trying not to panic. His only support, Bannister, was out at sea. But Bannister would soon be back, thank goodness. Sir reassured himself that he knew the vicinity of Kendra and her mother. They could be tracked. And this other boat out there would be no match for Bannister's.

****

Bannister was far out at sea, beginning his task of dismembering Rick. The sharp crackled sounds he heard in the distant background resonated like gunfire. His instincts could sense trouble. He felt the pressure to hurry his job and head back right away.

He pounded harder with his mallet, the cleaver cut through the bones with a loud crack. He tossed the shorter pieces overboard. The larger fish began to appear from the depths, smelling the dinner served in front. He tossed each serving, one after another, making sure it found a diner before floating off from sight. The next stop with these currents would be in the South Americas, no one would figure anything out that far away.

Aware of the time and the potential danger of any unknowns, he wasn't sure if that was his boss firing the gunshots. Bannister didn't waste time enjoying himself. He hurried as he connected the hose to the back pump and washed the back of the deck off, spraying away all evidence of left over skin or blood. Lastly he scrubbed his hands and sprayed off his legs, cleaning the blood splatter and debris off them as well.

****

"Mom, the boat, we can make it!" Kendra had a renewed sense of strength, a light at the end of the long tunnel.

"Kendra, I can't make it. I'm slowing you down. Go." Terri was doing her best to move an arm, kick, do anything to help, but her body was becoming more and more sapped of strength as her fever set in. Her weight was taking them both with the current. She had to get Kendra to move on.

"No mom." Kendra rose her body up above the water and waved her hand, hoping the person in the boat would see her soon, before Bannister got back.

"No! Get down! That creep might see us too!"

Kendra dropped back down immediately. "Sorry, Mom."

"Don't yell either."

"OK."

Terri was sick and holding her daughter back from safety. Terri knew what she had to do.

"Kendra, you have to swim to the boat alone. Go. You can make it, look, it's right there." On the crest of each swell, Terri could see the boat within reach. At one point she thought someone was looking over, scanning the area.

"Go Kendra, you can make it, then come back and get me. I'll be right here. You'll know how to find me."

Kendra gulped, she knew her mom was right. If she didn't take the chance now, they would drift out of view and then it would be too far to swim.

"Go Kendra, don't waste any more energy, swim."

"I love you Mom, I'll be right back to get you, I promise." Kendra pulled off a piece of the silver duct tape and wrapped it around her mom's wrists to tape them to the floating cluster, as these would keep her mom's head up.

Kendra was real scared to leave her mother alone out there. She didn't look good at all. Kendra could see the tape around her mom's calf. The bleeding had stopped. Kendra looked at the waters around them and then kissed her mom on the forehead.

Terri's sight was on the boat, now out on the point.

"I'll be right back for you, Mom, I promise." Kendra started to swim like an Olympic racer toward the boat on the point.

Terri could hear the sound in the distance of another boat on the other side of the passage. She knew the chances of Kendra finding her again would be slim and that soon Bannister would be on the hunt. But Terri was grateful that Kendra was going to get away, she prayed that Kendra would get fully away.

Terri saw that the currents were changing ahead. As soon as she would drift into the changing currents, her direction would shift, her velocity would change. Yes, it would be difficult, like a needle in a hay stack, for anyone to find her if they didn't know the waters.

Kendra swam as hard as she could. She pushed the scary thoughts of sharks out of her head. She just held the thought of getting back to her mom very soon, and with help. She swam harder, pulling with everything she had at the water with each stroke. She could see the boat and someone in it. She put her head down to streamline and swam harder, determined to get within yelling distance.

****

Mitch scanned the water with his binoculars, he hadn't seen or heard anything. He watched as the other boat was approaching the private dock. The other man out there, the one with the gun, had just gone inside the house.

"Help!"

Mitch heard it faintly, very faintly. He looked out, it sounded like a voice.

He heard it again.

"Help!"

Looking out into the passage, less than a hundred feet away, someone was swimming toward his boat. He started up the engines and put the boat in gear.

He was to the swimmer within a minute, and couldn't believe it when he realized who he was looking down at. She lifted her head and watched him glide over.

"Mitch!" She shouted out to him.

"Kendra!" He put the boat in neutral as he drifted up. He put his hand out and caught her, maneuvering her to the back transom step up.

"Oh my God. Oh! My God, Mitch, I can't believe it's you! My mother!" Kendra pointed in the direction of Terri, who Kendra could not see out there.

Kendra was beginning to shiver from the exposure. Mitch reached into the cabin, pulled out a long sleeved denim shirt, and handed it to her. He had to figure out what to do. He had his binoculars in hand and quickly looked out toward the house. He could see the two men heading back toward the pier, soon they would be on their way.

"My mother, Mitch, my mother. Oh my God. WE HAVE TO HURRY!" Kendra's teeth were chattering as she tried to still herself. "Those guys want to kill her, they shot her, they killed Rick, they kidnapped me!"

Mitch was scanning the waters for Terri. *Terri!*

****

"I'm coming with you!" Sir was insistent.

Bannister felt he was unprepared, as Sir usually required a tranquilizer cocktail of some sort for such a ride.

"This is it, Bannister, I will have it all."

Bannister helped him climb into the boat.

Sir then looked around for something clean to hold on to. His frustration began to mount. "Damn it to hell, Bannister, your world is filthy." Sir stopped short, knowing that in Bannister there was a fine line between either being the tough man he was, or feeling terribly insecure about insults. And when Bannister felt insulted, he counteracted with deadly force.

Bannister could feel his boss's pain, his boss's desire to be in on the chase. He felt compassion for him. He reached into the cabin, pulled out a terry cloth towel, and meticulously wiped an area down for his boss to hold onto.

"I'm sorry boss, I didn't know you would like to join me."

"Let's go, Bannister, before we lose sight of them."

Bannister turned the key and the engines went on.

Sir held on and didn't move as Bannister untied both the bow and the stern line and drove them away from the pier. Sir's knuckles were white with exhilaration and the compulsive fears he faced. He let go momentarily with one hand as he pointed the way.

VOLUME THREE: RAPTIS TRILOGY

****

<u>41</u>

"There she is!" Kendra pointed. "There she is! Oh God!"

She saw her mom drifting facedown, still attached to the coconuts.

Mitch turned and they were over to Terri within seconds. He slowed the boat, then put the engine in neutral. He commanded Kendra to hold the wheel and Mitch dove in after Terri.

Terri's face was burning, she looked up from the water, her face was balanced just right between two coconuts, keeping her mouth above water.

"Mitch? Mitch is that you? Or am I dead?" Terri didn't know whether she was hallucinating, this was almost unbelievable and her head was pounding so much. She saw Mitch looking back at her. He felt her forehead.

"Terri, you're burning up, we've got to get you to a doctor." He was swimming her over to the back transom as he talked to her, trying to keep her lucid.

"Daughter, Kendra," she managed.

"I've got Kendra, she's OK."

Terri smiled as the sound of the other boat loomed in the background.

Mitch and Kendra looked at each other. Kendra was on the back and helped pull her mother in.

"Hurry! Hurry!" Kendra was trying not to panic. Her mom's leg came out of the water as they lifted her over the back. The duct tape was still wrapped tight around it. The bottom of Terri's leg was pale with the blood flow restricted to it. Mitch lifted her up and over. Terri weakly helped lower herself to the floor of the boat and laid there. Mitch climbed in behind her and stepped over toward the front. There wasn't a minute to lose.

"Watch over your mother." Mitch started giving directions as he started the boat. "Pull her up close on the right side here." Mitch put the boat in gear and took off. As the boat grew closer, he wanted to stay out of accurate gunshot distance. Mitch was pushing the throttle down and the boat lurched forward.

Terri let out a groan. "I'm going to get sick."

"Yes, Mom, you're sick." Kendra assured her, looking down at her and holding on. Kendra's concern was split between her mother and the boat approaching from behind.

****

"I think they just picked up Terri." Sir had watched through binoculars when some man dove in and pulled out a woman's body. Now they were closing the gap between them. "They know where the other medallion is. Let's go faster!"

Sir held on tight as Bannister's boat sliced through the troughs of the swells. Sir held it together, barely, as the salt water splashed on his face. He wanted to scream out in frustration of lack of control over his surroundings. But his desire for the second medallion was greater than his frustration.

This was a job so big that Sir couldn't trust Bannister alone. If Bannister were to fail at this mission, if Kendra and Terri, and whoever else that was, were to get away without handing over the second medallion, Sir would be forced to discipline Bannister. The only way to relieve that frustration would be Bannister's death. That would be difficult for both of them. Sir would miss Bannister.

******

"Take that towel, dip it in the ice chest water over there, and wrap it around your mom's head," Mitch directed Kendra as he drove and picked up speed. He constantly looked over his shoulder for the other bigger boat slowly catching up. "Let some blood flow into her leg right away. Some only."

Kendra did as she was told.

Terri let out a groan, her eyes were shut.

"Mom," Kendra, tried to reassure her, "We're on Mitch's boat, we're going to be OK." The boat hit a swell and lifted off the water then dropped for a half a second, landing with a thud. Terri bounced on the deck with it.

"She's sick, she wouldn't be laying there, taking this, if she weren't really sick."

Mitch looked at Terri over his shoulder. He was driving his boat toward the eastern end of St. Todos as the other boat was trying to close the gap.

"Mitch, Mitch I'm sorry, I'm so sorry." Terri was half delirious as she spoke. "I'm so sorry." She kept repeating herself over and over. "This is Kendra. I'm so glad you're here with her."

"With us, he's here with us, Mom." Kendra worried her mother thought she was dying. And Kendra worried her mother might actually be dying. Kendra reached down and adjusted the cold towel.

"I'm calling for help on the radio." Mitch grabbed the radio handle with his right hand and turned to channel twenty-six. "Tree Squirrel, Tree Squirrel, Blue Sea, over." Mitch turned a knob as he drove, looking back over his shoulder. "Tree Squirrel, Tree Squirrel, Blue Sea, over."

"Aren't we afraid of those guys behind us listening in?" Kendra could see them slowly closing the gap.

"That's a good concern, Kendra, but your mom," Mitch looked down at Terri bouncing on the deck as they skipped across the swells. "She's sick, real sick. We're this far, let's not risk losing her."

Kendra took a big gulp. She had never seen her mother this sick before, her mother was always so strong. She didn't like the tone in Mitch's voice. He was clearly very concerned about her mother.

"Blue Sea, Tree Squirrel, over." Mitch said. "Tree Squirrel, please have medic, emergency, over."

"Confirm medic, Blue Sea, over."

"Affirmative, medic, affirmative, over."

Kendra could see the larger island of St. Todos in the distance. Mitch put the radio handle down and reached for the throttle.

The surface of the water changed and Mitch drove the boat faster, the bow tilting as it went into a smooth plane. He was a comfortable distance from the other boat and was confident in his maneuvers. Something about Mitch, just being around him again, made Kendra feel safe. She had hope now. Did she feel a bit more like herself again? *Maybe*, she thought, *maybe. But my MOM!*

She looked over at Mitch and managed a smile through her fear. His face was focused forward, watching forward, then backward, his lips pursed with concentration. He winked at her, acknowledging her bravery.

****

Bannister and King Sir were listening through the channels and heard the transmission between Tree Squirrel and Blue Sea, Blue Sea who they assumed was the boat in front. They heard the word "medic" and knew someone was hurt.

"I shot her, I'm sure I shot her. I don't miss," Sir insisted. "They must be headed for shore," he surmised.

They had several shots left and didn't want to risk wasting them at this distance. They clearly weren't prepared for this scenario. "We will follow them to shore, catch up with them. I want the person driving that boat! Be careful, damn it. Don't hurt him or the girl! I need that medallion!" Sir tried not to panic now as he couldn't control his world or even the environment right around him. His anxiety level sent his fight or flight to new levels, he had to win under any circumstances.

Their boat skipped and jumped across the swells as Bannister headed for the other boat across the passage. Salt water sprayed to Sir's left side, he ducked inward to the right, trying to avoid having it touch him. He took a deep breath and closed his eyes momentarily, trying to center himself, a technique they had tried to teach him over and over to help him cope with his uncontrollable level of frustration—frustration which now was mounting inside.

When he made it to the changing currents, Bannister pushed the throttle forward to go faster. Then the seas flattened out some. Again, they had the advantage. Their boat was slowly closing the gap between themselves and the second medallion.

"When you get close enough, I will shoot the driver in the arm, just the arm, that will slow them down." Sir patted the handgun housed in its holster, clipped on his belt. He noticed the spot of saltwater sitting on the leather case. Seeing this began to unpeel another level of anxiety in Sir. And right at that moment he fixated on that spot. The blemish, he had to remove it from his sight. Now.

He removed the gun from the holster and checked the safety. He slipped the gun into his front pocket, then pulled upward on the holster, removing it off of his belt. He flung the holster into the sea, out of his sight. The gun weighed his pants down unevenly in front, one side lower than the other. He struggled for a level of comfort so he could concentrate.

Bannister saw the holster fly away in the wind, but was focused on one thing: catch up to the boat ahead. He could see two people in the boat, one of them Kendra. This would be a piece of cake.

42

"Kendra, I know your mom is not going to like this, but we have to keep her safe."

Kendra was holding on with both hands, trying to keep herself on the boat, it was moving and bouncing so rapidly and wildly. Her arms and legs were rubbery, she was so exhausted from pushing so hard on the swim.

Mitch was on a mission. He pushed the throttle forward just enough to keep the other boat far enough away. He had to be careful, the coral reefs in this area lay just below the water's surface. They weren't visible at certain times of the day because of the sun's glare. Fortunately, Mitch new these waters well, very well. But even the most seasoned sailor must never take his eyes off or turn his back on the sea. Mitch knew this too. "Kendra, lay your mom up against the side of the boat there, up against the corner."

Kendra bent down and struggled as her mom wanted to resist being moved. Terri's body ached all over and she was about to get sick to her stomach. The movement of the boat was complicating the pain in her head. Terri felt so awful she wanted to die.

"Mom, Mom, I know this hurts, but you have to deal with it. Please. We have to get you to a safe place, and get you medical help." Kendra pushed then pulled on her groaning mother until she lay halfway against the side of the boat.

The boat hit a swell, Mitch turned slightly and Kendra grabbed for the console, trying to keep herself from being ejected.

Mitch could see the point he was trying to reach as he rounded the corner. The swells began to rise on the windward side as he maneuvered sideways, the best he could, into the swells without slowing down.

"Now take that rope, and the bungee cord, secure your mother to the boat in case of any sudden moves, we don't want her to fly away or slam into anything."

Kendra quickly unwound the two ropes and looped them around her mom's torso, tightening them up to the cleat on the side, just snugly enough to hold her in. She did the same with the other rope, then looped the bungee around her mom's legs for good measure.

Kendra took a moment and wiped the bile from her mom's mouth. Now her mom's face was white as a ghost and her eyes were shut. Kendra went into the cabin and found a small clean towel, dipped it into the remaining ice water, sopping it up.

"Kendra, Kendra, I'm dying...." Terri tried to speak. "I don't want you to be alone, you won't be alone. ... You have Mitch now."

"It's OK Mom, you're going to be OK." Kendra tried not to cry as she wiped her mother's forehead with the ice water one more time. Her mom looked so sick, so weak. Kendra knew she had to be strong for her mother, to try to save her life.

"Mitch, Mitch, he's ... he's...." Terri's eyes rolled back in her head and she passed out, unable to finish her thought about Mitch.

Mitch had just heard his name in the background. Terri had said something about him, but he couldn't look away from the water's surface. It was time to make a move.

"Hold on real tight, Kendra!"

The boat jolted and the back of Kendra's head hit the opening of the cabin. The boat behind them had a deeper hull and was gaining speed. Kendra was hurt and her grimace showed it. Kendra rubbed the growing knot hard to help relieve the pain, then got right back to her mom.

Kendra reached down and grabbed the wet towel she had dropped, wrapping it around the upper part of her head like a turban. A shot rang out as she stood up, narrowly missing her, piercing a hole through the windshield. She looked to Mitch to see if he was OK.

Mitch could see the small plane he had asked to have ready, there at the end of the strip. Mitch had been so thorough in his planning. Now the small plane became his beacon to hone onto as he headed straight for it. He had finally made his way to the sandy cove next to the airstrip, they were almost there.

****

"Faster, Bannister! Faster!" King Sir screamed into the wind as the exhilaration of the chase began to set in. Now they were gaining ground on Terri, Kendra, and their friend. Sir was upset he had missed his shot and blamed it on Bannister's driving skills, there could be no other reason for a miss. He would not miss his next shot.

He held his gun out, aiming at the back of Mitch's head. Kendra looked back and saw him aiming.

"Look out Mitch, he's got his gun!" Mitch ducked his body down and zigzagged the boat slightly. A shot rang out. Another hole was pierced though the windshield.

"Damn it, Bannister, you made me miss again! I can't tolerate this!" Sir screamed.

Bannister pursed his lips, he so wanted to snap back, he so wanted to crush the boss. Bannister knew it wasn't his driving that had caused Sir to miss. And to waste bullets. Bannister pushed the throttle further forward, going faster. The boat skipped off beat at the tops of the swells, causing the deep hull to slam into and push through the deep troughs, up and over out of rhythm.

This caused the boat more sudden pounding. Sir was not aware of what happened, and suddenly his face was intensely stern as he held on for dear life. Bannister's strong legs, slightly bent at the knee, knew just when to go up and down to keep his body steady. They could see the point Mitch was heading to.

"The plane at the end of the strip. They must be planning to get away by plane," Sir said. Salt water sprayed off both sides of the boat as it plowed through another trough between swells. "Faster!" he yelled.

Bannister pushed the throttle forward. White smoke came out of the back as the boat lurched forward even faster, now bordering on unsafe conditions given their speed with their angle to the swells. Bannister held onto the wheel with both hands, determined to catch up to the side of the other boat.

Bannister set his eyes on the other boat and didn't take them off for a minute as they began to catch up. He pushed the throttle even further.

Mitch looked behind and saw them gaining. The cove was up ahead, he had to reach the cove. But they were coming in at too much of an angle.

Mitch turned the wheel slightly to the right and the boat turned against the swell out to the sea. A blast of salt water spray soaked his side.

This move confused Bannister on the boat behind, so Bannister followed suit.

Kendra held on tight without question through the sharp turn Mitch had taken. Her mom lay against the side, bouncing uncontrollably as the boat sped over the swells. Kendra saw that her mom now had her arms up, wrapped around her head, protecting it the best she could, trying to be in a fetal position.

Mitch needed a sharp ninety-degree angle approach to the sandy cove's entrance. He also needed a bit more distance for maximum speed going in.

"Duck Kendra, hold on and duck down!" Mitch shouted to his copilot.

Kendra held onto the railing and crouched down as far as she could. She looked up to Mitch, he winked back to let her know she was doing a good job.

Bannister fishtailed his boat right up behind Mitch. Now Sir was once again with gun pointed at Mitch, determined not to miss this time.

Kendra screamed out as she saw the gun pointed.

"Mitch! Mitch! The gun!" Mitch's eyes were forward, intensely focused on his mission.

******

Bannister's focus was on the steady distance between his boat and Mitch's. He didn't want his boss who was now taking aim at Mitch, to miss and blame it on him.

Sir aimed his eye down the barrel, lining up the groove to the bead on the end at Mitch's head. They were right behind them. He took aim and fired, a shot rang out.

Mitch had instinctively begun to crouch down, pushing the throttle forward for more speed and turning the steering wheel hard to the left, that ninety degree angle. They took off full speed toward the entrance to the cove. The bullet cracked the windshield, but not before grazing the side of right side of Mitch's head.

It tore across the flesh on the side of his head, the top half inch of his ear was gone. It quickly began to pool blood and bleed down the side of his face, dripping down on Kendra. She looked up with shock on her face but didn't scream, she didn't want to scare him when he was driving. It stung painfully numb, he knew he was hit, but didn't know how badly. He had to focus on the water's surface and his markers or they would all die.

The plan was risky at best, but it was all they had, and Mitch had one chance to get it right. The boat headed straight in for the entrance. He stood up to see his markings clearly, he had the throttle full forward, gaining speed rapidly. Bannister was right behind him and gaining speed.

"Get him! They're headed for the beach! Don't let them get on that plane!" The boss was convinced they were headed for a shore landing to make a run for the plane. "Come up to their side, now!"

Bannister pushed the throttle forward and they went faster against his intuition, the water was growing shallow, his hull was deeper than the other boat's. At this speed, they could ram a coral head and that would be disaster if they weren't careful.

Sir yelled into the wind in frustration. The water had sprayed in his face, his world was out of control. His intentions to catch the other boat and his desire to kill them overtook his common sense. He was unable to hold it in. "Get him! Faster!" Sir, convinced Bannister wasn't being aggressive enough in the chase, took his manicured hands and pushed forward on Bannister's large hand wrapped around the throttle. The boat lurched forward still faster. They charged up to the side of Mitch's boat.

Mitch's eyes were intensely focused forward, he didn't flinch.

The man held up his gun again, Mitch could feel them to the side of him. *Almost there.*

"Mitch!" Kendra cried out again.

Mitch turned the wheel with both hands and made an immediate u-turn. The other boat was too close, going too fast to respond in time. Bannister's boat continued forward into the cable Mitch had set. A fishing net had also been set there and dangled below it to stop the boat if all else failed, but it wasn't necessary.

****

Bannister felt the resistance, but it was too late, his boat moved forward. The cable sliced through the fiberglass hull horizontally at full throttle, slicing Bannister's boat like a sharp cheese slicer.

The cable reached Bannister's legs before he could react, his hand was on the throttle pushing forward while trying to slow down when the momentum threw him backward, pulling him forward instead. So his boat lurched forward at full speed. The cable worked through his thick tree trunk legs, right below the knee cap, snapping through the bones and ligaments like a butcher's boning knife, his legs were sliced in two. He fell to his stumps with a painful thud.

The boat continued forward as it cut through Sir's upper thighs. It sliced quick and easy through the fat, a slight hesitation as it hit the bone, and then cracked as it sliced through the resistance of the calcium. Sir screamed in shock. Bannister's hand was frozen to the throttle as he was standing on his bloody stumps in shock, the throttle pulled back. So his boat continued forward.

Sir held on to the railing, holding up the weight of his remaining body as his legs fell away. He looked at Bannister, his eyes half open in shock, blood dripped from his mouth as he tried to form a word, a thought. Still holding onto the throttle, the boat sped forward through the resistance and the front bottom was pushed down. The cable hit the gas tank causing a spark, the whole boat exploded.

Bannister was bent over on his hands and large stumps. His arms and stumps were on fire. He grabbed the side of the boat and hurdled his large frame into the salt water, with the movements of an ape. He waved both of his arms violently as he hit the water, trying to extinguish the oil fire on his body, fighting as if he were going to win.

He never howled, he never screamed, he never asked for help, he finally stopped, laying in the water face down. They watched him take his last shallow breath face down, his back slowly raised then quickly dropped. His body gyrated and convulsed one time, stopping with a hard jerk. The unusual giant of a man was dead.

The top half of Sir's burnt body was ejected in the explosion, he flew in the air like a round tractor tire on fire and landed floating face down, his synthetic clothing burnt to his skin. The boat quickly sank, the tip of the bow resting on the bottom with the propeller shaft bent and wound around the cable. It began to twist in the propeller as the boat exploded. The transom held up the cable at the water's surface.

****

REDEMPTION

****

On the beach a jeep was pulled forward with the torque of the pull on the cable. It tightened around the soft flesh of the coconut tree, squeezing the life out of it as it toppled. The jeep with its emergency brake on was pulled forward and toward the water, stopping when the boat exploded and stopped.

Everyone ran to the beach's edge and stared at the boat. A large plume of black smoke was rising from the last of the stern being held up above the water line. It was a job well done. They released the cable from the jeep, rolling it out from the hitch in front, then allowing the weight of the cable to settle back to the bottom of the cove.

VOLUME THREE: RAPTIS TRILOGY

****

43

"Blue Sea, Blue Sea, Tree Squirrel, over," they called out to Mitch on the radio to let him know the channel was open.

He wasn't far away. "Tree Squirrel, this is Blue Sea, we need medic, over."

"Blue Sea, come on in to the starboard side of wreck, we cleared a channel, over."

Mitch came forward and watched his friends as they maneuvered him through the tight channel. He came up to the sandy beach and turned the engines off. His friends had gathered around and each had their hands on the bow of the boat, steadying it.

The ambulance was parked up at the road. They carried a stretcher down to the water's edge as Mitch carefully unstrapped Terri. Kendra was quiet, standing back, so grateful to have Mitch's help.

"My medallion...." Terri whispered, groaning, eyes closed.

Mitch made a serious grin at her. "Don't worry about your medallion."

He turned to Kendra, it was time to lift Terri out of there.

"Take your mom's legs, Kendra."

Kendra bent down and grabbed both of Terri's legs. Mitch reached under Terri's torso and picked her up, she was barely conscious. Her pulse was low and her forehead was burning with fever.

"On the count of three. One, two, three."

The crew from the ambulance took over. They lifted her up. Terri let out another groan, she ached all over. Kendra touched Terri's head and looked at Mitch, still more grateful for all his help with her mother. Mitch looked back at her, winking again, it was his subtle acknowledgement of her gratitude.

"Mitch, you're bleeding, show them."

"They see, don't worry about me." Mitch kept noticing something familiar in Kendra as he tried not to stare at her smile, the way she moved her head. It was like he had seen it before, on his mother. He looked at her again, her profile, as she looked away and back at Terri.

Terri was secured on the stretcher. The ambulance team had an IV ready and began to attach it to her arm. Terri tried to open her eyes. She was smiling inside through the pain. Mitch was always so safety conscious and he worked so well with Kendra.

"You're going to be OK." The man in the white coat looked down at her.

"Please, get my medallion, Mitch," Terri didn't know exactly what all had happened or for sure who she was talking to. *Is this really Mitch?*

"I want to go with her! Can I please go with her?"

"Yes, ma'am, come on!" Kendra looked at Mitch. He needed help too.

But Mitch waved her away, "Go! Go! I'll see you soon."

Kendra waved goodbye and hurried up to the ambulance. They were taking Terri's blood pressure, attaching her to a machine. Kendra climbed in next to her mom. The engine was on and the driver put the van in gear. With a flip of the switch, the bright red and blue lights twirled on and the siren howled as they rolled away.

****

Mitch was left behind with the mess and his own injury. He didn't intend to clean up too much, only to make all this look like an unfortunate mishap, running into the cable and all. That cable was a danger known to the locals but not marked on any nautical map. They pulled the jeep out from the sand and off the beach, raking its tracks with dried palm fronds. No one would ever guess what had happened that day.

Three men swam out to the bodies, turning them over and checking their pockets for any identification, cash or jewelry, a perk for helping. They turned the pudgy man over, the plastic frames on the sunglass were melted to his face, the lenses melted out. His eyes were stuck wide open with fear frozen on his face, both irises red like a white rabbit's.

They found the medallion in the pudgy man's front pocket. It was the only piece Mitch requested if they found it. The rest of the wreckage was for his men to lay salvage rights on, they could have what was left. He knew no one would go near this or even think of calling it a crime scene. It would be called one more unfortunate accident. Mitch was satisfied in his vengeance for Roy.

Now it was time to go to Terri. She hadn't looked at all good and had lost a lot of blood with the gunshot in her calf. *And Kendra, how on Earth is she going to handle all this? What kid can handle all this? What adult can?*

VOLUME THREE: RAPTIS TRILOGY

****

<u>44</u>

Terri lay in the ICU, sedated because she still thought she needed to escape from Sir and Bannister. She was still fighting for her life, and in and out of feverish delirium. She was being pumped full of IV solutions including antibiotics to help kill the bacterial infection which had exploded in her body. Her fever had gotten dangerously high. Fortunately, the long time she had spent drifting in the ocean had helped keep her core temperature down. The bullet wound and loss of blood were complicating matters, making Terri's situation far worse.

The ice Kendra was helping keep on Terri's head was probably also helping save her life. Kendra was at her side every moment, and there was nothing much more she could do but wait. The wait itself was almost killing Kendra. The guilt weighed so heavily on Kendra as she sat and stared at her mom's fragile existence. Kendra was realizing how much she had taken life for granted—and realized she'd been spoiled. With her mother's idea of living, they had been everywhere and had had what seemed like everything.

Kendra was realizing now how much she had rebelled when life stopped being handed to her, when there was not as much money. And she had blamed this on her mom and her mother's inability to cope. Now Kendra thought about how angry she had been with her mother when the fancy lifestyle had stopped, and how she had been embarrassed because her mom wasn't the average soccer mom like all her friends' mothers were.

And now Kendra knew that she actually had the most amazing mother. *Please make Mom live. Mom, please live.* Kendra realized now that she had the best mom ever, one who would give her life for her, and that her mother actually had been giving her life to save her daughter from these horrible criminals.

Kendra had grown up so much these past few weeks. She couldn't wait to show this to her mom. Kendra had seen the strength and perseverance in her mom and knew that this is what taught her, the daughter of this amazing woman, to be strong, to know that she could survive this mess these fast few weeks. She reached out and clasped her mom's hand.

Mitch walked in. "How is she?" He rubbed Terri's toe and gently pulled on it. *Terri always used to like that, maybe it will bring her around,* Mitch thought to himself hopefully.

"Still the same." Kendra said nervously. She didn't take her eyes off her mom.

"You can come and stay at my house tonight, we can get you back and forth."

"I don't want to leave her, but thank you so much."

Terri moaned.

They both looked at Terri and right then saw the corner of her mouth lift just a tiny bit. It seemed that Terri had just half attempted a smile. Mitch and Kendra looked at each other, relieved, hopeful, smiling. Terri was OK, she was going to be alright, that tiny smile was a great sign of life.

Then Terri managed to get her eyes open just enough to see Mitch and Kendra beside her. Terri tried to talk to them. "I... I... wanted... to see... if you... were... talking shit... about me...." Terri had managed to put a sentence together! Then her eyes shut. She fell back asleep as quickly as she had woken up.

But for Kendra and Mitch this attempt to communicate was a great thing. They laughed as they could tell Terri was going to be OK. And that personality had made it through.

****

The following day Mitch drove Kendra around and showed her different spots where her mom used to work, some of her mother's favorite dive spots.

"You really loved my mom, didn't you, Mitch?" Kendra looked over at him as he drove her back to the hospital. They had called and heard that Terri was awake and feeling better, which made them both very happy.

Mitch smiled. "Your mom was probably one of the best things in my life, and one of the worst...." He bit his bottom lip. "I don't know what your mother told you."

"She always talked about you like you were some kind of god, a hero. I can see why, you saved our lives," Kendra said gratefully and sincerely. She admired Mitch, she had never met such a brave man before. "I sure see why my mom was so impressed. She told me she never felt good enough for you, could never live up to you."

Mitch was a modest guy, so it was hard for him to take compliments. He nodded in acknowledgment and smiled. He did say something about, "Not sure why she would say something like that. She was the heroine out there." He pulled into the hospital parking lot. He was actually anxious to talk with Terri about some important things, things he wanted to get clear, but wanted to wait until she felt better.

"Tomorrow I think, well they say they might let her out tomorrow, if she stays alright now. She ate food today, the fever is down, she's stable. They say she is going to be OK,"

Kendra said with tears in her eyes. She was so excited about her mom's recovery, as she had been preparing herself to perhaps lose her.

"I'll tell you what. Tomorrow when she is discharged, I'll send a taxi. He'll take you to a hotel room for you and your mom, not far from town. I'll take care of it. You two can spend a couple days relaxing and being near doctors here if needed before you head home."

Kendra looked at him and nodded yes to his plans. She had enjoyed spending time at his house with him. "Mitch, thank you, I don't know how to thank you. I don't know what I would be doing without your help here."

"Really Kendra, it's fine with me. I'm glad to help and to see you both will be alright." Mitch thought to himself how he had enjoyed having Kendra spend time with him, even though he wished it had been under other circumstances. He had found Kendra familiar in so many ways, and so easy to have around. They had like idiosyncrasies and both shared a love of books. They had whiled away the hours, looking over his collections in his library. He would miss Kendra, he sure would. He would talk to Terri about Kendra before she and Kendra went home. He had to talk to Terri, Mitch told himself, had to, darn it. *Terri! Kendra???*

REDEMPTION

****

<u>45</u>

"When were you going to tell me, Terri? Ever?"

Terri looked at Mitch, stunned. "What are you talking about?" Terri looked down and played with her napkin, trying to avoid eye contact with Mitch.

"Did you know when you left? I've been doing the math and the likelihood is at least fifty-fifty." Mitch glared at Terri while trying to soften his tone. He was angry to say the least but still, Terri had just barely survived. He told himself he should have waited.

Terri was silent a while, her shoulders and head dropped down. "What?"

"Her hair, her eyes, that smile? Just like my mom's!"

Terri couldn't help but smile, she knew he was right. She had always known. She had been more and more sure as Kendra grew up.

A smile? Why? What? Now Mitch tried to read Terri, tried to understand this, tried not to get more angry. *What on earth is there to smile about? Well, other than the fact that Terri and Kendra have survived, thank God. But this is too big to let go. Kendra!*

"I know, can you believe it?" Terri looked Mitch in the eye. After all these years, here she was, here was her chance to come clean to Mitch. He used to be her closest friend in the whole world. "Mitch, I ran because I was a coward, not because I was pregnant, I didn't know I was when I left. I was a foolish coward because I couldn't tell you I loved you so very much, but was not ready to get married yet. I had to feel better about myself first. And I felt so undeserving of you. You had the education, and the right life style, and you were so together. I was anything but all that. ... I know I was wrong for running, very wrong." Tears rolled down Terri's cheeks. She looked at Mitch's clenched hands.

Mitch looked back at her, staring fiercely as she went on. He was truly furious with Terri and at the same time more than immensely grateful she was alive. But she had broken his heart *and then gone off for years with a secret like this?*

Then Mitch reminded himself of all the hundreds of calls Terri had made to him, calls he never answered and never returned. He had made it clear he wanted nothing to do with her. He had played some part in this mess.

Terri started to ramble, trying desperately to explain things, but feeling she couldn't. "I didn't realize I was pregnant until I was out to sea, at least a month. Then I felt trapped and was sure you hated my guts. I did try and try to call you, whenever I could. You were obviously cutting me out of your life. You had a right. So, I felt I deserved to have to handle all this alone. ... I chose to live with my choices, so to speak. As bad as they were for you, Mitch, for all these years, my choices were also very hard for me. ... I'm so sorry. Sorry really doesn't say all I feel about doing this. ... Later, after I got off Rick's boat, I did try more times to reach you, but you still would never take my calls. Never. ... I wanted to tell you, but I couldn't get through to you, couldn't just leave a message about something this major. And after a while, after trying and trying, I figured rightly that you rightly never wanted to hear my voice again. ... So I figured there I was, alone with my child, my beautiful child. This was my fate and I would have to deal with this alone."

Terri stopped talking.

They were both silent for several minutes.

Mitch didn't know what to feel. Terri was right. He had refused to take her calls. He had never wanted to hear her voice again. He had made it impossible for her to reach him. And he had been furious. Now he wished he had handled it all differently, but that was how he had handled being abandoned at the altar.

Even now, knowing she had tried to tell him by phone, and at least once in person, and had never had the chance to, he nevertheless wanted to be angry, he told himself he should be angry. But suddenly now he just couldn't be angry knowing she had tried many times, and for sure he couldn't be angry right now when Terri was back from the edge of death. He wanted her to recover in full.

Mitch swallowed hard and made a decision right then and there not to be angry any more, to simply be grateful Kendra and Terri were alive. "Terri, OK, OK, well, that is what it is, the pain has gone on so many years, we have to be done with that pain, and grateful we three are all alive. ... So hey, it's gonna be OK. Don't try to explain any further. I could have answered at least one call in all those years. And if you had left such a message about all this, well, frankly I wouldn't have believed you, not at all. ... I even remember burning letters from you without reading them. ... I was too much in pain to want to think about you. ... So, hey, darn it, maybe we have to just forgive all around."

More silence.

Terri had tears in her eyes.

Mitch couldn't stand to see Terri cry. Mitch reached out and wrapped his hand around Terri's. "I appreciate your honesty

Terri, very late honesty, but still appreciated, it helps me trust you now. And I know I made myself impossible to reach. I never wanted to hear from you again. But I feel different now, different and over all that. Grateful you and Kendra are alive. Kendra, my daughter!!!, is alive! And so are you! And so am I! That is what counts now."

Terri looked at Mitch. "Thank you Mitch, thank you. I was never sure what to do. I even brought Kendra down here to meet you years ago, but you wouldn't see us. She remembers that, but she doesn't know why, not all of why anyway. It was hard, real hard for me. I still loved you. What's even more important, I brought Kendra to you to introduce you two, and then no you. That was so painful and I know I cannot blame you for that. ... I've had a hard time living with myself, with the way I treated you. This whole situation has been so hard on all of us, you too, I am sure."

Mitch patted her arm. "I've been OK Terri, just fine." He smiled at her, "How are we going to tell Kendra?"

Terri didn't know what to say to this, so she went to the other pressing matter. "The medallion Mitch, I lost the medallion. I gave it up for Kendra, did she tell you?"

"All about it, Terri." He reached into his pocket and pulled it out, showing it off to her. "Here it is, someone was nice enough to retrieve it for me from that horrible man's pocket." He was still smiling as he handed it over to Terri.

"Oh God, thank you Mitch, amazing!"

"But Terri, that was not a bright move, doing all that, coming to saving Kendra all by yourself. Not bright at all."

"You didn't pick up your phone, Mitch. Still mad at me or just wanting to forget all about me."

****

"Would you have picked the phone up if you were me?"

"Touché. No, I never would have talked to you again." Terri knew he was right, she wouldn't have ever picked up her call if she were Mitch.

"You must really think I'm stupid, this medallion thing must be off the chart valuable." She quickly looked at it, then put it in her front pocket.

"It is, Terri, extremely valuable, and worth even more side by side with the other one, mine, because the two together prove there are two, at least two. Together. Which is exactly where they are." Mitch knew it was time for even more truth now. He swallowed hard. He had to tell Terri now.

Terri cocked her head. She was confused. She had just put her medallion, the one he had just handed her, in her pocket.

"I'm sorry, Terri, but I never had a chance to tell you. And I'm sorry I didn't feel you were responsible enough to have this information. That and, at the time, you already had so much wealth from your split of the other treasure we discovered, you didn't need to be concerned. You left so fast…not telling you was, I guess, my way of getting back at you. And I sure didn't trust that Rick guy, showing up and getting at you and your wealth. I think he already knew about your money and medallion, *about the money we had divided between us and maybe even about both our medallions,* when he approached you. He'd been stalking you, waiting to reel you in. I'm sure he got a lot of your treasure wealth. … Thank goodness you didn't really have your medallion…."

"What on earth are you talking about, Mitch? You just handed me my medallion. … And Rick, well he's dead now, so I will never know how long he was after whatever it was he thought I had of whatever value he thought it was. Forget about Rick.

… But I am still trying to understand what you were just trying to say about the medallion I have here."

"A *copy* of the medallion, you have a copy of the medallion." Mitch stared Terri in the eye. How would she take this now?

"What are you talking about, Mitch? You know I have one of the medallions, I always have had it." Terri was still confused here.

"Not exactly, Terri."

"What? What are you saying?" Terri sat up real straight now.

Mitch gulped. *Time to really tell her.* "A copy, Terri, you have a copy."

"What!?!?!"

"Settle down, Terri, you need to take it easy still. I am just trying to give you some information I was going to give you someday." Mitch held up his medallion. "Look, I have a copy of the medallion, too."

"Wait, you mean we don't have the medallions after all?"

"No, we do."

"You aren't making any sense."

"Yes, I am. I made them, I made the copies of these medallions a long time ago. You just don't remember when I borrowed yours. I borrowed it to get it cast along with mine. But I never told you I was getting copies made."

"I don't know what this means. I am still real tired. Either that or you are not making any sense here. Why would you do this, and why would you never tell me?"

"Terri, the real ones are so incredibly valuable that I put them in a safe deposit box in Switzerland. I did it already back before our wedding, I mean before the wedding we were supposed to have. … Anyway, these are 18 karat gold copies we have in our possession. I made exact copies of both of our medallions." Mitch held his up, looking at it. "But beautiful copies. A nice investment in gold, solid gold copies!"

Terri wasn't sure what to think. Mitch had taken her medallion and made a copy and put her real medallion far away to protect it? Terri pulled the medallion, the copy of it, out of her pocket and examined it. She had never before questioned the newness look of it. But now she realized this medallion looked far too new. She twirled her medallion in the light, looking at it.

As she was admiring it, she realized that the original was something she would have just kept in that shoe box in her closet. That was not very smart, it was very careless. So Mitch was probably right making copies and never telling her the originals were far away and safe. "Hmmh. OK, probably best I didn't have the real one." She held her medallion, her copy, up as she told him, "I never sold it though and never tried to. I remember telling Melvin I would never sell it."

"I miss Melvin…."

"I do too. I didn't come down when he died because I knew you wouldn't want to see me there."

"I wasn't there either. I couldn't bear to see you and thought you'd be there."

"Oh, wow, how sad. Maybe we can have our own ceremony for Melvin someday."

Mitch took Terri's hand, "Sure. And Terri, I was going to tell you about the medallions someday, but I figured you would not need to know unless you wanted to sell yours. And if you did, you would find out you had a copy and would call me. And if I didn't answer you would indeed leave a message."

"Message maybe. Who knows. But you would never take my call."

"I would've someday."

"I'm not going to try to figure all this out, Mitch, but wow you protected this valuable thing, this medallion, from me actually. From my stupidity."

"You are definitely not stupid, Terri, just a bit wild."

"Wild?"

"Yes...."

"Anyway, about Melvin, I bet you miss him, Mitch. I miss him badly, but he was your closest friend." Now it was Terri's turn to reach out and put her hand on Mitch's. She felt she was going to get her friend back. She had missed him and had mourned the death of their friendship so much.

"Yes, I miss Melvin, a lot. He was a good man, and a good friend, the best. ... Melvin loved us both so much. ... And Terri, I'm sorry about Rick, sorry he was killed, sorry he hurt you, sorry he did all this to Kendra, and sorry he paid for it the way he did. I mean I have to say he did at least something right. Kendra told me he saved her life." But then Mitch looked down and shook his head, he didn't really want to think about Rick. He had tried every day to keep the anger as well as the deep feeling of loss at bay, it had hurt so badly when Rick had stolen Terri from him.

Terri didn't know what else to say, she patted his arm in comfort. "As much as I hated him for luring Kendra down here, and for all he had taken from me over the years, you have no idea the years of spousal support I was ordered to pay him, and as much as I wanted to hit him so hard for this, and mostly for getting Kendra down here like this, I would not have wished him dead, or that horrible death, as awful a person as he was."

Mitch wanted to stay strong here, not show his hurt and anger. He thought of Kendra, how Kendra had been thinking of Rick as her long lost father...it must have been a hard loss for Kendra, too, and a shocking thing to see. The whole experience was so traumatic for Kendra, it was a wonder she was over there sitting at the bar, talking with Mitch's friends, enjoying desert before dinner, managing all this.

Mitch had asked Kendra for some time alone with her mom first, before they ate dinner together. Kendra was happy to comply. Now Mitch looked over to the bar, waving to get Kendra's attention, calling her over.

"Let me do the talking, please!" Terri half whispered to Mitch as Kendra stood up and walked over. She sat down, smiling at the sight of the two sitting at a table together.

VOLUME THREE: RAPTIS TRILOGY

****

REDEMPTION

****

<u>46</u>

Terri began to look everywhere, all of the sudden she felt on stage, having to think of how to explain so much of her life. There was nowhere to escape to, no place to run and hide from the emotions she was feeling. Terri knew it was time for the truth. She rubbed the palms of her hands together and looked at Kendra. "Your dad...."

Kendra rolled her eyes, she didn't want to talk about Rick, not tonight.

"The dad you *thought* was your dad." Terri rephrased it and got Kendra's attention as Kendra sipped on the piña colada she'd had delivered to the table, thanks to the cute bartender. Soon she would have to go back to California, a land where civilized rules such as drinking ages apply. *Ugh, after all this adventure and freedom? How will I survive back home? I will survive, that's for sure, and that's what counts after all this. ... But wait, what did mom just say?*

"I don't understand, mom. What *are* you saying?"

"The dad you thought was your dad...."

"Are you trying to say that Rick wasn't really my dad? What? ... Who was he then?"

"He thought he was your dad. But I always wondered if he suspected. On the other hand, he never tried to figure it out, and never asked, so probably not."

"Suspected what, Mom?"

Terri was silent for a while.

"Mom, suspected what? Rick never suspected what? Never tried to figure what out?"

Terri took a deep breath. She owed it to both of them to tell Kendra. "That Mitch is your father, Kendra." She'd blurted it right out.

Kendra gasped as she tried to hear what her mother had just said. She didn't know what to think. She looked at Mitch. She wasn't sure what to feel. "Did you know this?"

"No, I never knew, Kendra. Not until recently here, after a short time of getting to know you, when I started to wonder about you, who you were, who you were related to. You reminded me so much of my mother in so many ways. Then I suspected something." He was looking at her, smiling, hoping this shock would be OK for Kendra, especially after all she'd just been through. But then this had to be the time to tell her, waiting would hurt more later.

A range of emotions crossed Kendra's confused and shocked face. There was some anger, some sadness, tears almost, then what might have been a tiny chuckle. Finally, Kendra broke into a huge smile. Seriously, after being so hugely disappointed in Rick, horrified that man who said he was her father would do such a thing to her, this was a major relief. Wow, Mitch was the dream dad she wanted and he was actually her dad now, her real father! She finally grinned from ear to ear, and held one hand out to each of them. She held their hands so the three connected in a circle.

"Honey," Terri looked at Kendra as she spoke, "I'm glad this is out now, I am. I had tried to figure out how to tell you, and after all that went on between me and Mitch, I had to tell him, and could not, so I waited and eventually it got to be too late, I thought." Terri had tears in her eyes. "And now look, I am back down here? In the islands again? Sitting here with Mitch and you. I would never had believed this could happen, and all because of Rick of all people."

Kendra was crying. Mitch had tears in his eyes. Terri almost broke down sobbing but stopped herself. This man had saved her beloved daughter's life, HIS daughter's life. Terry looked at Mitch. "Wow! I never thought I'd be back here with you let alone back here again!" Terri kept looking at Mitch, grinning, shaking her head back and forth. "Thank you for saving our lives, Kendra's and mine too. That whole thing got bad, real bad. We were so lucky you were out there. We wouldn't be alive if it weren't for you."

Terri then looked at Kendra. "So long as he will have this, Mitch and I will be the best of friends. And we are your mother and father. And isn't it great Mitch and I have you to share!"

Mitch squeezed Terri's hand in agreement. He didn't know what would happen between himself and Terri, he couldn't guess, but reconnecting for Kendra was already fabulous.

"Whatever happens, Mom, no problem. I am so glad you lived and came here to get me out of this big horrible mess I caused. I am so so sorry." Then Kendra switched to her best island accent, "And now I hav ma motha, and my fatha too! And myself!!!"

Mitch and Terri laughed. Terri turned to Mitch with her next big idea and a quick way to change the subject away from all this emotional stuff, at least for the moment.

"Hey, Mitch, I have an idea. We should make several copies of our medallions, put them for sale on the internet, sell them as gold copies, just what they are! Come on, Mitch! We'll make millions!"

Mitch looked at her and smiled. So good to have this Terri back. And this time with this Kendra. Ultimately a great gift no matter how the three of them got there.

Such redemption.

THE END

Basic Scuba Diver Gear Diagram

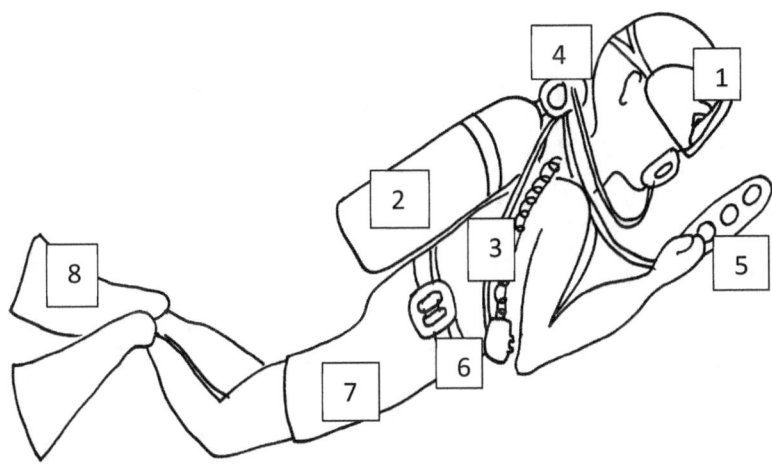

DIVERS:

(1) Our **DIVE MASK** provides a space of air to see through.

(2) Our **TANK** of air is attached to our backs.

(3) Our **BOUYANCY COMPENSATOR** is worn like a vest. It fills with   air from our tank.

(4) The **REGULATOR** comes in two STAGES. The 1st STAGE attaches to the tank's valve and breaks down the immediate pressure from the tank. You also attach all your gauges to the 1st STAGE as well. The 2nd STAGE goes in your mouth: you inhale and exhale through the 2nd STAGE.

(5) Our **PRESSURE GAUGE** is attached to the 1st STAGE of the regulator. It tells us in PSI, pounds per square inch, how much air we have.

(6) Our **WEIGHT BELT** offsets the buoyancy of our body fat and wetsuit.

(7) We lose body heat in even the warmest of oceans. The layer of water between us and our **WETSUIT** keeps us warm.

(8) Our **FINS** propel us through the water.

See the following pages for other
Diving and Boating Terms
used in this book...

Scuba Diving and Boating Terms
Used in This Book

ANCHOR LINE: The ANCHOR is attached to the bow of the boat with a long nautical rope, the ANCHOR LINE. Dropped down into the water, it sinks to the bottom and holds the boat in place.

BANG STICK: This is a long cylindrical "stick" with a handle on one end. The other end holds a bullet. When the stick is pushed into an object, the bullet is triggered and released into that object. Some divers use the bang stick for safety (for example, as a shark deterrent).

BOUY: This is a round bright marker floating on the ocean's surface, usually left to mark an area for certain use (such as an underwater fish or lobster trap, or a place a boat can tie up to).

BOUYANCY COMPENSATOR: This is a vest the diver wears, attaching it to the TANK. This COMPENSATOR VEST controls the diver's BUOYANCY on/above and below the water's surface. A hose is attached to the 1ˢᵗ STAGE of the REGULATOR to fill the vest with air from the tank or with air by mouth (when simply blowing the air in). As the diver descends deeper into the water, compressing and becoming heavier, adding air to the vest helps achieve a NEUTRAL BOUYANCY, a suspended floating.

BOW: The front of the boat.

CLEAT: This is attached to the top side of a boat, used to fashion rope around to hold it, or to attach different objects.

CONTROLLED BREATHING: Because the diver is breathing air that is compressed, and is further compressing when DESCENDing, the diver must be aware of breathing at all times. The diver CONTROLs breathing to conserve air. The diver also CONTROLs breathing when ASCENDing. While ASCENDing, the COMPRESSED AIR in the diver's lungs expands so the diver must consciously exhale slowly.

DINGHY: A small boat used to maneuver to shallower areas larger vessels cannot reach.

HOOKAH RIG: Instead of wearing a TANK, the diver can have another air source, an AIR COMPRESSOR, floating on the surface. To this compressor, long hoses are attached and on the other end is the diver's mouth. A single AIR COMPRESSOR on the surface can serve more than one diver at a time.

PORT: Looking forward toward the BOW, the PORT side of the vessel is to the LEFT.

PRESSURE GAUGE: This gauge is attached to the 1ˢᵗ STAGE of the REGULATOR. This gauge informs the diver of the amount of air in the tank, by PSI.

PSI: POUNDS per SQUARE INCH is the pressure of the air the diver puts into the tank. Tanks are designed to hold between 2250 PSI to 3000 PSI of air.

REGULATOR: The 1ˢᵗ STAGE of the REGULATOR attaches to the tank's VALVE and controls the air pressure in the tank. The 2ᴺᴰ STAGE of the REGULATOR is attached with a low pressure hose to the 1ˢᵗ STAGE. The diver puts the 2ᴺᴰ STAGE in the mouth to inhale air.

SAFE BOTTOM TIME: Because the diver is breathing compressed air, there is only so much time the diver can stay underwater without having a NITROGEN build up in the diver's body. The NAVY SUBMARINERS developed tables for divers that tell them the safe time limits for remaining down at certain depths. Too much NITROGEN will make the diver sick.

SCUBA: This is the general acronym for SELF-CONTAINED UNDERWATER BREATHING APPARATUS.

STARBORD: Looking forward toward the BOW, the STARBOARD side of the vessel is to the RIGHT.

TANK: The diver brings air down underwater compressed into a tank which is worn on the back. On top of the tank is a VALVE with a handle. When the diver attaches the REGULATOR, then the VALVE can be turned on to release the air to the 1ˢᵗ STAGE of the REGULATOR.

TRANSOM: This is the rear outside of the boat. A platform with a ladder can be attached to the TRANSOM for divers to use to climb up onto the boat.

VISIBILITY: This is how far the diver can see underwater. Mud, silt, and sand in the currents all effect visibility. In ZERO VISIBILITY, the diver sees only 6 inches in front of the mask.

WEIGHT BELT: The diver wears a belt with lead in it to help offset the POSITIVE BUOYANCY of the body fat and of the wetsuit if wearing one. This belt has a quick release to ditch the lead in an emergency.

WETSUIT: Even the warmest ocean waters are below the diver's body temperature and eventually the diver gets cold. The diver uses different thicknesses of neoprene, worn as different WETSUITS. It is the layer of water there between the suit and the body that helps keep the diver warm.

RAPTIS TRILOGY
Volume One: DIVE TOUR • Volume Two: TREASURE HUNT • Volume Three: REDEMPTION

Raptis Trilogy
Afterword

This keen, sharp, edgy sense, this suspended from real life sensation, this journey into a terribly thrilling, frightening, disturbing, even evil situation, this is the thriller reader's experience. A great thriller writer is an artist. And we turn to this art to not only distract us from life, but to let us live out our worst fears in the world of fiction, to allow our imaginations to do this in fiction and then when done, simply close the book. We love the suspense, we even crave it. We may hate the fear, but we can't turn away. Instead we turn the page for more.

So what is a thriller? Well, if you've been on the edge of your seat, or at least feeling on edge while reading these books by Tracee Raptis, you know the thriller reader experience. And indeed, Tracee Raptis knows how to bring out in we readers a strange suspended curiosity, a sort of must-know what next, almost a temporary addiction or at least compulsion to read on and on, to want to know what the bad guys are doing, to want to know whether and how our heroines and heroes survive, to want someone to survive.

Suspense, fear, hate, love, perseverance, twisted brilliance, the odd, the strange, the evil, the good, the hero and anti-hero, are all involved. (Of course here in these Raptis Trilogy tales, our greatest hero is a heroine named Terri who may, we hope, survive all three of these Raptis Trilogy tales.) Author Tracee Raptis knows these emotions, she knows how to bring these out in readers, even in her characters. Her wisdom screams into our minds that this story is, or at least could be, real real real, really real and this is all the more unnerving. Fasten your seat belts, readers. Something's lurking in the shadows....

Dr. Angela Browne-Miller
Editor-in-Chief, Metaterra® Publications
www.Metaterra.com

VOLUME THREE: RAPTIS TRILOGY

****

TRACEE RAPTIS

THRILLERS

I'd like to thank my editor, Dr. Angela Browne-Miller, for believing in me and showing me the way. And a special thank you to my family and friends for their encouragement and support.

About the Author
Tracee Raptis

Adventurer, painter, sculptor, diver, author Tracee Raptis was born and raised in the Coachella Valley, in Indio, California. She fell in love with the ocean as a child and spent as much time as possible with her family in the Corona Del Mar coastal area, in Orange County, California. Tracee became a certified scuba diver at the age of fifteen. At the age of 19, she followed her dreams, left her life in the U.S., and headed off to the Caribbean islands where she taught scuba diving and led scuba tours for many years. There her life was filled with adventure, romance, and a great love of the underwater world. One of Tracee's most exciting adventures in the Caribbean was working with an underwater archeological expedition company, discovering how much mysterious and intriguing history is down there under water, and searching for treasures lost in time. "There is a whole wild and mysterious world down there, one that reveals its beauty, secrets, and dangers as it wishes to. You have to really live in it, be with that world for a long time, to start to see what it is all about," Tracee says. Tracee now lives in California where she is writing several books and book series.

About the pre-quels…

YOU HAVE JUST COMPLETED

Raptis Trilogy, Volume Three:
REDEMPTION

NOW YOU CAN READ THE
THE PRE-QUELS TO
REDEMPTION:

Raptis Trilogy, Volume One:
DIVE TOUR

AND

Raptis Trilogy, Volume Two:
TREASURE HUNT

***

Brought to you by
Metaterra® Publications

Stay tuned for more from
Author Tracee Raptis….

Find these and other books by
Tracee Raptis on
Amazon.com

Watch for announcements on

TraceeRaptis.com
and
Metaterra.com

www.ingramcontent.com/pod-product-compliance
Lightning Source LLC
Chambersburg PA
CBHW070213260626
47160CB00002B/540